Readers love

The Impetuous Afflictions of Jonathan Wolfe

"The drama that occurs when you really love someone, not as a lover but as a friend, and they keep making stupid decisions that you have to confront…it's powerful in this story."

—MM Good Book Reviews

"I loved this book in a squishy-hearted, grinny-faced kind of way. Sometimes when you read something that touches you in an otherwise inexplicable way, ya just gotta make up words when it comes to saying how you feel…."

—The Novel Approach

"I really am just enthralled with this series. Cochet really is the master of historicals in this time period and she captures the details and setting just so well and so naturally."

—Joyfully Jay

The Heart of Frost

"It is a story about the power of hate and, more importantly, the power of love."

—Prism Book Alliance

"I think I can recommend this series based on this book alone as there is a certain feel I get with seasonal romance such as this, and it is enchanting as much as it is humor filled."

—Rainbow Book Reviews

"This is a must buy. It's not necessary to read the first book in the series to enjoy this one. Get it now and use it to warm your heart on a cold winter's day."

—Hearts on Fire

By CHARLIE COCHET

AUSPICIOUS TROUBLES OF LOVE
The Auspicious Troubles of Chance
The Impetuous Afflictions of Jonathan Wolfe

NORTH POLE CITY TALES
Mending Noel
The Heart of Frost

THIRDS
Hell & High Water
Blood & Thunder

Published by DREAMSPINNER PRESS
http://www.dreamspinnerpress.com

BLOOD & THUNDER

CHARLIE COCHET

Published by
DREAMSPINNER PRESS

5032 Capital Circle SW, Suite 2, PMB# 279, Tallahassee, FL 32305-7886 USA
http://www.dreamspinnerpress.com/

This is a work of fiction. Names, characters, places, and incidents either are the product of author imagination or are used fictitiously, and any resemblance to actual persons, living or dead, business establishments, events, or locales is entirely coincidental.

Blood & Thunder
© 2014 Charlie Cochet.

Cover Art
© 2014 L.C. Chase.
www.lcchase.com
Cover content is for illustrative purposes only and any person depicted on the cover is a model.

All rights reserved. This book is licensed to the original purchaser only. Duplication or distribution via any means is illegal and a violation of international copyright law, subject to criminal prosecution and upon conviction, fines, and/or imprisonment. Any eBook format cannot be legally loaned or given to others. No part of this book may be reproduced or transmitted in any form or by any means, electronic or mechanical, including photocopying, recording, or by any information storage and retrieval system, without the written permission of the Publisher, except where permitted by law. To request permission and all other inquiries, contact Dreamspinner Press, 5032 Capital Circle SW, Suite 2, PMB# 279, Tallahassee, FL 32305-7886, USA, or http://www.dreamspinnerpress.com/.

ISBN: 978-1-63216-177-2
Digital ISBN: 978-1-63216-178-9
Library of Congress Control Number: 2014943214
First Edition August 2014

Printed in the United States of America
∞
This paper meets the requirements of
ANSI/NISO Z39.48-1992 (Permanence of Paper).

ACKNOWLEDGMENTS

To Barb, Melanie, Nikyta, and Valerie, thank you for your continued support and enthusiasm. For your guidance, thoughts, and love for these fellas. Thank you to Dreamspinner Press for helping bring this series to life. To my amazing author friends who keep me sane and remind me to come up for air. A big thank you to my wonderful readers who continue to read my stories and ask for more. Your heartfelt messages and comments are always an inspiration. To my family for joining me on this crazy adventure. Thank you.

CHAPTER 1

"YOU SURE this is the place?"

Dex shifted his entry weapon to one side and stepped up behind his brother at the surveillance console while the rest of the team double-checked their equipment at the other end of the BearCat. Cael tapped away at the keyboard, bringing up a grid of the area, satellite mapping, and a host of surveillance feeds from local businesses he'd undoubtedly "borrowed."

"College Point, Queens, near the Canada Dry bottling plant. That's what our source tells us."

"Reliable?" Dex asked, receiving a curt nod.

"Hasn't let us down yet."

Hopefully this wouldn't be the first. The last thing they needed was to waste more time with another dead end. Four months of reconnaissance and intel gathering from Unit Alpha's Intel and Recon agents, and Defense agents finally had something useful to go on regarding the whereabouts of The Order of Adrasteia, though they still didn't know how big the group was or how spread out they were.

Despite being Human perpetrators, which should have fallen to the jurisdiction of the Human Police Force, the threat was against Therian citizens, not to mention the Order had declared war against the THIRDS by executing a THIRDS agent. The online video of Agent Morelli's death had gone viral and ended up being broadcast on television two days before Christmas. Dex could still hear the bastard's voice in his head as if he'd watched the whole thing yesterday, the spiteful words dripping with venom.

In order to cure our city of its disease, we must dispose of its carriers, starting with the organization that promotes the sickness. We will unleash Hell upon these sinners, starting with the THIRDS.

Seconds later, the THIRDS organization went to Threat Level Red. They had to stop the Order before they had any more loss of life and before any more zealots jumped on the crazy train. Since then, the already tremulous relationship between Human and Therian citizens was growing more unstable by the day, which was exactly what the Order wanted.

The THIRDS had recruited volunteers to patrol the city, removing the Order's hateful propaganda, but it was a futile endeavor. With every poster spouting "Humans 4 Dominance" or sporting the Adrasteia goddess symbol the THIRDS took down, three or four took its place. So many flyers littered the streets, they resembled the aftermath of a ticker tape parade. Everywhere Dex looked, the Order was leaving its bloodred mark, promising hellfire and chaos, refusing to give in unless they got their way, or the city burned, whichever came first. The media wasn't helping any either. Turning on the TV, one would think a presidential election was going on, what with all the ludicrous accusations and childish attempts to discredit the opposing side.

In the middle of it all were the THIRDS. Since the Order had surfaced, the organization had been accused of everything from sitting on the fence (too cowardly to pick a side), to being traitors to their species (depending on the agent being accused), to being the source of evil itself, to being the only thing keeping this city from crumbling. No matter what they did, someone accused them of something—not working hard enough or fast enough or not giving enough of a shit. It would have driven Dex out of his mind ages ago if he let it get to him, which was why he didn't. Most importantly, he wouldn't allow it to get to his team.

Sloane strode up to him, addressing Cael as he handed Dex his ballistic helmet. "What do we know about the area?" Dex snatched the helmet from his partner with a groan.

"I hate this thing."

"When a bullet hits your helmet instead of your skull, Rookie, you'll love it."

Damn. Can't argue with that.

Cael didn't bother hiding his amusement as he answered Sloane's question. "Mostly industrial estates and construction firms. Fifteenth Avenue ends at the East River, though there's a small dirt drive that heads into the sign and window factory's parking lot—if you can call it that." His expression sobered, his Therian pupils dilating in his silvery eyes. "But the immediate area surrounding it is residential, with Popps a couple of blocks away."

"What's Popps?" Dex asked. He wasn't all that familiar with the area, and after months of running around the city, the neighborhoods were all starting to blend together.

"The Poppenhusen Institute. It's a community center offering programs for kids and families."

Ash joined them with his usual cheerful growl. "Great. Bastards know what they're doing. The industrial sites offer plenty of cover, but the residential area makes it difficult to go in aggressive. Last thing we need is a stray bullet catching some poor kid."

Sloane nodded his agreement before motioning to the console's large flat screen. "Do we have an exact location?"

"Here." Cael pointed to a small area near the edge of the river at the end of Fifteenth Avenue. The property consisted of two small buildings on a small expanse of dirt with a chain link fence going around the front and the East River around the back. "It's listed as IGD Construction Supply Services, but it's a front. At least now it is. I conducted a search for businesses and individuals who've had contracts with them and turned up plenty of hits, but they were all jobs completed over a year ago, with nothing in the works since. I called from one of our secure lines back at Recon, pretending to be a client and the 'secretary' said the company was in the middle of a restructure and not taking on any new projects."

"Security?"

"A piss-poor security network, consumer-grade crap. There's a camera on the north side, another on the south, and one on this house here, which acts as the office. I can have the feed looped faster than Dex can sing the chorus to Alice Cooper's *Poison*."

Dex opened his mouth, and Sloane clamped a gloved hand over it. "No. Cael, don't encourage him. Ash, entry."

"I don't like this." Ash studied the screen, his beefy arms folded over his tac vest. "We're talking confined quarters. If they're in there, they've got to be prepared. The second structure is our primary target and where they'll most likely be. It has no windows, two small entrances on the side, and three vehicle entrances at the front. The good news, it's aluminum, so it'll be easy to blow that shit sky high." Ash's frown deepened.

"Either way, 110th Street is out of the question. They'll see us coming. I say we have three teams. Team one comes up Fifteenth Avenue, past the bottling plant, to there," he said, pointing to a medium-sized, tan brick house on the screen. "They can use that entryway. The wooden fence and the house will cover them. They go around the back, cut through the chain link fence, and end up in the back of IGD's yard. They can sneak up on them from behind, take out whoever's in this office, and then come in strong from the front, especially since the windows have burglar bars so our perps won't be able to get out that way. Anyone comes at the team, they can throw the bastards in the river, but that's just my opinion.

"Team two takes the same route, comes up behind the primary target, breaches the perimeter using this door here, giving you room to maneuver should the bastards come through the second and third entrance, or the side doors. And speaking of, if they do, we'll have the third team ready across the street having approached through the back of the sign and window factory. There's enough construction equipment and debris to conceal them."

With a curt nod, Sloane gave Ash a firm pat on the shoulder. "Good work. You heard him, team. Cael, you're our eyes. Keep us informed of all activity."

"Copy that." Cael turned back to the console while Sloane addressed the rest of the team.

"Letty, Rosa, you're team one. You take the office. Calvin, Hobbs, you're team two. Go around the back of the primary target, take out the door, and smoke 'em out."

Calvin gave him a curt nod and walked off with Hobbs close behind to prepare the necessary explosives and nonlethals.

"Ash, Dex, you're with me. We're coming in behind the sign and window factory." Sloane tapped his earpiece. "Agent Stone, Agent Taylor, this is Agent Brodie."

The Team Leaders' gruff voices came in over their earpieces. "Agent Stone, here. What are your orders, Agent Brodie?"

"Agent Taylor, here. Ditto."

Sloane rolled his eyes. "Agent Stone, I want you and your team situated at the corner of 110th Street and Fourteenth Road. Make sure no one comes in or out. Have Beta Pride on standby and keep an eye out for civilians."

"Copy that."

"Agent Taylor, you and your team take the corner of 112th Street and Fifteenth Avenue. You know the drill. Have Beta Ambush on standby and keep an eye out for civilians. Try not to scare any kids today."

There was a deep rumble of laughter from the other end. "And take away Keeler's fun? Perish the thought."

"Kiss my ass, Taylor."

"You just come on over here and bend over, Keeler. We'll have ourselves a gay ole time. Taylor out."

"Pussy," Ash muttered.

"That's kind of the opposite of why I'd kiss your ass," Agent Taylor said with a laugh.

Ash opened his mouth for a rebuttal—undoubtedly one laced with enough obscenity to make their ears bleed, but Sloane was too quick, tapping Ash's earpiece and jutting a finger at him. "You and Taylor can have your battle of wits some other time." Ignoring Ash's glare, Sloane turned his attention back to the team.

"All right, watch your backs, and let's show those sons of bitches what happens when they mess with our city. Letty, Rosa, give us a five-second lead."

"You got it." Rosa put on her ballistic helmet and lowered the visor; the rest of the team followed suit. Sloane's voice came in loud and clear.

"Let's move out."

Destructive Delta's BearCat was parked at the corner of 112th Street and Fifteenth Avenue, and they gave a small wave to Beta Ambush's truck as it pulled up to the sidewalk a few feet away from them. Everyone scrambled out, heading toward their respective starting points.

Dex fell into formation behind Sloane with Ash at his back, their rifles in their hands as they quickly jogged down the sidewalk and turned onto Fourteenth Road. They could see Beta Pride's BearCat parked near the corner, and they headed toward it, alert to everything around them as they passed all the two-story houses with their white picket fences. The sky was blue with some wispy clouds hovering over them, the weather in the mid-60s, and the neighborhood quiet at this time of day. No one would ever suspect anything was wrong, unless they looked out their windows and spotted the three heavily armed THIRDS agents dashing by.

Before they got to the truck, Sloane signaled for them to cross the road, where they stopped at the corner of 110th Street. Although they were a block away from IGD, Sloane wasn't taking any chances of their getting spotted. They turned the corner, and following his silent signal, they dashed behind the parked cars and waited. As soon as they received the okay, they darted across the street, down the side of one of the businesses, and around the back to its parking lot.

A man in a gray suit carrying a portfolio and armful of papers froze on the spot, eyes going wide. Dex motioned for him to go inside, but it took three tries before the guy snapped himself out of it. He made like the wind back toward the building's exit, nearly running into the glass door in his attempt to flee. Sloane motioned forward, and Dex readied himself, inhaling deeply and releasing it. Eight months on the team and at times he still couldn't believe he was a Defense agent for the THIRDS. His agency dog tags pressed against his skin under his uniform reminded him he was no longer a homicide detective, but a soldier. He'd been awarded his tags six months in, after passing his probation with flying colors.

Despite his initial reluctance to join the THIRDS after HPF bureaucrats had all but forced him into it, Dex had never felt more content than the moment his lieutenant placed those tags around his neck, with his dad and brother looking on nearly busting at the seams with pride. Those tags were a reminder of his new life, and everyone who now depended on him. Destructive Delta had taken him in, even if it had been a shaky start, but one thing he knew for certain, he had no intention of letting them down.

They reached the wooden fence separating them from the back of the sign and window building. Sloane stepped aside and gave Dex a nod. Rookie gets to breach. Let the fun begin. Dex turned, giving Sloane access to his backpack and the Hooligan kit inside. Seconds later, Sloane handed him a small crowbar, and Dex jammed the end between two of the wooden boards before giving the iron bar a fierce jerk. The wood creaked and splintered. He grabbed the looser board with a gloved hand and tore it off. Once the second board was off, it was easier to remove a third. He turned to give the crowbar to Sloane only to be met with a set of scowls.

"What?"

Ash motioned to the fence. "Your skinny Human ass might fit through there, Daley, but we'll be lucky if we can get a shoulder in."

Seriously? Dex turned back to the fence, grumbling under his breath as he stabbed the crowbar between two planks. It wasn't his fault his Therian teammates were built like brick shithouses. He was lucky he didn't end up having to remove half the fence. Not only was he still getting used to being on a tactical team, but on a Therian one. Being inconspicuous while armed to the gills took skill. Being inconspicuous while standing at nearly seven feet, weighing almost three hundred pounds, and armed to the gills took some kind of voodoo magic. He was still trying to figure out what manner of sorcery Hobbs had used to disappear behind a Scion iQ during their last assignment.

"Move your ass, Rookie," Ash growled.

"You'd like that wouldn't you?" Dex replied with a groan, tearing off one particularly stubborn board. "You really need to stop eyeballing it, man, or I'm gonna start getting ideas." He chuckled when Ash cursed him out under his breath. With the task complete, Dex handed the crowbar to Sloane, who quickly returned it to its place in Dex's backpack. He gave Dex a pat on the arm to signal he was done, and Dex stepped aside, falling into formation once again. He paused, arching an eyebrow at Ash.

"I'm not going to look at your ass, Daley. Not if you were the last fuckable thing on this planet."

Dex grinned widely. "So you're saying I'm fuckable?" God, he loved winding the guy up. It was so damn easy.

Ash gave him a shove through the fence. "I'm saying if you don't shut your trap, the next time I look at your ass will be while I'm taking aim to shoot it."

"The next time?" Dex laughed. "Oh shit. Keeler's been looking at my ass."

"Sloane," Ash grunted.

Sloane shook his head as they used the heavy machinery around the sign company's yard to conceal them. "Dex."

It wasn't quite a warning, more a friendly reminder to shut his pie hole. Regardless, Dex looked over his shoulder at Ash who was grinning smugly. Dex mouthed the word, "narc," causing Ash's grin to fall away to a glower. That was more like it.

They scurried along the side of the building, their sights on the target across the street. A small bulldozer was parked a few feet away from the building's back entrance, and they crouched down beside it in the dirt and patches of dry weeds. He heard Sloane's quiet words come through his earpiece.

"Letty, Rosa, what's your twenty?"

"We're coming up behind the office now."

"Copy that. Calvin?"

"We're about to fix the det cord to the door. Do you want us to—"

Calvin was cut short when a shot popped through the air.

"Calvin?" Sloane edged toward the front of the bulldozer. They could hear low groans coming through their earpieces, and Dex's heart was in his throat. Sloane's curses continued as he tried to get an answer from their teammate. "Goddammit, Calvin, talk to me. What the hell happened?"

"Shooter," Calvin wheezed, his breath ragged as he tried to talk. "I'm okay. Got hit in the vest. Fuck, shit hurts. We're under fire." Just as he said the words more shooting erupted. It was coming from somewhere close by.

Sloane peeked around the bulldozer looking to pinpoint the location of their shooters. "I've got a visual. There's a charter bus just ahead. All the windows are smashed to shit. It's been stripped. I make two shooters inside."

"Looks like someone wasn't happy with their service," Ash muttered.

"Cael, is the area clear?" Sloane asked.

"Aside from our shooters, affirmative. No civilians."

"Agent Stone, Agent Taylor?"

"This is Agent Stone. Area's secure."

"Agent Taylor here. Area's secure."

"Copy that. Destructive Delta, we're going in aggressive. Go, go, go!" Sloane darted out from behind the bulldozer with Dex and Ash on his heels to a chorus of gunfire, bangs, and shouting across three locations. They sprinted to the stripped black-and-gold charter bus, and Sloane pitched a couple of smoke bombs through one of the smashed windows before they breached the bus through the open driver's side.

"On the ground! Get on the ground now!" Sloane yelled. The two Human shooters threw their rifles to one side just as Ash grabbed them and roughly forced them onto the floor of the bus.

"Hands behind your backs," Ash spat out, taking zip ties from his utility belt and securing their wrists.

Calvin's warning came through their earpieces. "Fire in the hole!"

"Dex, side doors!" Sloane pushed Dex to the front of the bus. They ran across the street to the aluminum structure as the third vehicle door catapulted off the building in a burst of smoke, skidding across the dirt until it launched off the side into the river. Like there wasn't enough shit down there already.

Dex and Sloane positioned themselves to either side of the smaller entrances with their backs to the aluminum structure and waited. They didn't have to wait long. The doors swung open, a rifle poking through the doorway beside Dex. He snatched it with his right hand and thrust his left elbow into the gunman's face, snapping his head back and bloodying his nose. Dex tossed the gun to the grass beside him with one hand, and with the other, pointed his rifle at the emerging Humans coughing and gasping, their eyes bloodshot and tearful from the smoke.

"On the ground! Get on the ground now!" Dex ordered. "Hands where I can see them!" One of the gunmen tried to reach under his open plaid shirt, but Dex shoved a boot down against his back, pushing him harshly onto his stomach against the dirt. "I said hands where I can see them!" He unhooked a handful of zip ties from his belt, crouched down, and lifted the hem of the guy's shirt to find a revolver. He tossed it out of their reach, then looped a tie around the man's wrists and gave it an extra tug, enough to make the guy hiss. As soon as he'd checked all three for additional weapons and secured them, he stood and tapped his earpiece. "I've got three in custody."

Rosa's breathy voice came through, "We've got four in custody."

"We got five in custody," Calvin added roughly, yelling something at one of the perps. His teammate sounded grumpy, but then who wouldn't be after taking a bullet to the vest? Dex took a step back, watching in amusement as Ash dragged over the two gunmen from the bus, both practically dangling off the ground. Unit Alpha's Therian Defense agents were all made of Apex predators, large Felids, each Therian agent with the strength of two Human agents. When the teams faced Therian perpetrators, the score was pretty even, with a Therian agent's advantage depending on the shape they were in, their skill, and their smarts. When facing Humans, Therian Defense agents didn't even break a sweat. Dex liked those odds.

Sloane stepped up beside Dex and patted him on the back in approval as he gave his orders. "Beta Pride, Beta Ambush, move in. I want our perps lined up, asses to the floor. Agent Taylor, Agent Stone, see if you can get any information out of them."

As soon as their fellow agents from Beta Pride and Beta Ambush showed up, they left the perps to them, and Sloane motioned for Dex to follow. Along the way, they removed their ballistic helmets and handed them to one of the agents standing by. They headed into the main structure, which was still smoky from Calvin and Hobbs's entry.

"What have we got?" Sloane asked as they took in their surroundings. The aluminum structure was supposed to be a three-car garage, but instead had been set up as a base, with insulated walls, rows of metal shelving running down two of the walls, a third wall strewn with corkboards containing maps, newspaper articles, invoices, and a host of other random paperwork. In the center of the room were three large metal tables with supplies, boxes, burner phones, masonry tools, and weapons. Dex caught Hobbs's gaze and followed the silent agent's finger pointing to one of the large shelving units. Calvin joined his partner and called them over.

"Sulfuric acid, nitroglycerine, batteries, timers." Calvin picked up a box of heavy-duty nails. "From the looks of it, they weren't thinking about just taking out buildings."

Sick bastards. It was bad enough they wanted to plant bombs, but to build them with the specific purpose of killing and maiming innocent citizens? How deluded could they be to think they'd be doing good? Like crime in this city wasn't bad enough, now they had a whole new level of fucked up to deal with.

"Any explosive devices already constructed?" Sloane asked.

Calvin shook his head. "No, just the materials, though Hobbs says they'd need more than this. He thinks maybe they were in early stages, collecting supplies, getting ready to build the bombs." He cast Hobbs a glance, and his large Therian partner nodded somberly.

"Okay, thanks, guys." Sloane let out a sigh, and Dex knew what his partner was thinking. Unless one of those bastards out there spilled, they wouldn't have much to go on. Getting these assholes off the street was a win, but until they had Isaac Pearce, the danger was nowhere near over. Who knew how many more bases just like this one were out there. How many already had devices waiting to go off?

Dex stepped up to the corkboards, hoping to glean some information, anything that might give them a clue as to where to find the Order's leader. "Everything's so neat."

"What do you mean?"

Sloane joined him, and Dex waved a hand over one of the corkboards. "All the maps are brand new, like they'd just been bought, and they're not of any specific locale. There's a street map of Brooklyn, a subway map of New York City, a bike map of Manhattan, and I'm pretty sure that one there of this area is an Internet printout. The news articles are perfectly clipped and all from the last two months. They pinned up the invoices for Christ's sake. What bomber pins up their supply invoices? Are they planning on writing off the expenses?" He leaned in closer. "They're also all dated two months ago." Looking around the room, he strode back over to one of the shelves, where he ran a gloved finger over one of the timers. "There's a thin layer of dust on most of the supplies. Like they'd been placed on the shelves and not touched since. They could have been waiting for orders, or...."

"They could have been waiting for us," Sloane finished. He stroked his jaw. "Good job, Dex. You're right. This all seems too… easy. Let's see if anyone's cracked." He tapped his earpiece. "Cael?"

"Call in the CSA's?" Cael replied over their earpiece.

"Yeah. I want this place swept from corner to corner, and I want to be notified as soon as they get the detailed inventory attached to the case file."

"You got it."

Dex followed Sloane outside where fifteen perps were sitting on the ground in a neat row, hands secured behind their backs with nearly twice the number of heavily armed agents positioned around them in case someone got a stupid idea in their head. It was amazing what some criminals did when they were desperate. Just as the thought crossed his mind, one of the men jumped to his feet and started running.

Ash stared after the guy. "Where the fuck does he think he's going?"

With an agent drawing in from every angle, the guy came to a skidding halt then stunned them all by jumping into the East River where he proceeded to sputter, gasp, and in between drowning, call out for help.

"Seriously?" Dex had seen some pretty stupid shit in his time, but this one was right up there with the guy who tried to steal his patrol car with him in it back when he'd been an HPF rookie. Ash let out a snort of laughter. "What an ass hat."

After losing a round of Rock-paper-scissors, one of Beta Ambush's Therian agents started stripping, cursing up a storm the whole way. Down to his colorful boxers and flipping off his fellow teammates whistling and throwing catcalls at him, he dove into the river, popping back out a few breaths later and dragging the wheezing man with him. The dark haired agent pulled himself up with one hand and tossed the man up onto the dirt with the other.

The agent climbed out, snatched the towel from a teammate, and glared at their arrestees. "That's the last time I'm doing that. Someone else want to be a moron, you're going to drown. Shit, that water's cold." He gave a sniff. "Ugh, it reeks. Am I going to be quarantined? This shit smells toxic."

His teammates laughed until Sloane held up a hand, silencing everyone. He stepped up to the line of somber looking men, a couple looking no older than Cael. In fact, one in particular caught Dex's attention. The kid was sixteen, seventeen at most.

"Where's Isaac Pearce?" Sloane demanded. He paced slowly in front of them, his intense amber gaze studying their perps. Dex wasn't surprised to find fear creeping into some of their defiant gazes. None of them looked like hardened criminals. Standing over six and a half feet tall and weighing 240 pounds without the eighty pounds of equipment strapped to him, Sloane Brodie was imposing to most even when he wasn't in intimidation mode. Add the fact he was a Therian with the government tattoo on his thick neck marking him as a jaguar Therian and the twenty-odd years of field experience, and you'd have to be dumber than the guy who swan-dived into the river not to be scared shitless.

"Do you realize the severity of your situation? Do you think the THIRDS takes terrorism lightly? Your so-called leader murdered an officer of the law in front of the world. He's made threats against innocent civilians, against innocent children. He's looking at life in prison, if he's lucky. This is your chance to do the right thing, to save what's left of your future."

One beer-gutted idiot spat at Sloane's feet. "We'll never talk to you, Therian freak. Your kind is a mistake. The Human race is superior. You're nothing more than a glorified pet. Your kind should be locked away in zoos with the rest of the animals or put down. Humans for dominance!" The guy started chanting and Dex rolled his eyes. "Humans for dominance! Humans for—"

Sloane's boot against the guy's chest, knocking him over and onto his bound up arms, put a stop to the chanting. It wasn't even a kick. A tap from Sloane was enough to send the guy tipping over and flailing like a turtle on his shell trying to right himself. Dex put a gloved fist to his mouth to keep himself from laughing. "Anyone have something useful to say?" Sloane asked.

Dex studied the silent, glaring group, his gaze landing on the teenager again. The kid swallowed hard, his eyes not moving from the ground. An older man with a strong resemblance knelt beside him. Dex tapped his earpiece. "Sloane." His partner glanced at him, and without a word walked over, following Dex to one side.

"What's up?"

"I think we should try the Deceptive Dash."

Sloane arched an eyebrow at him. "You think it'll work?"

"That kid's ready to shit a brick. I'm thinking the guy next to him is his old man. Probably dragged him into this mess."

His partner rubbed his jaw then nodded. "Okay." Sloane turned and signaled Ash over.

"What's going on?" the surly agent asked, and Dex could tell Sloane was trying hard not to smile when he spoke.

"We're going with the Deceptive Dash."

As expected, Ash let out a low groan. "Fuck me." He glared at Sloane. "I can't believe you not only allowed him to make this a thing, but you let him name it."

Sloane shrugged, his eyes lit up with amusement. "You couldn't come up with anything better."

"Because I didn't agree with the stupid idea."

"Yeah, well, it's effective, so suck it up." Sloane gave him a hearty pat on the shoulder, chuckling at their teammate's pout.

"Who's the target?" Ash grumbled.

"The kid." Dex tapped his earpiece. "Cael, drive the BearCat up."

"Copy that."

Dex headed toward the approaching BearCat and hopped into the back when his brother opened the doors.

"What's up?"

"We're doing the Deceptive Dash." Dex positioned himself to one side of the truck, hearing Ash cursing and growling as he approached.

"I can't believe you convinced Sloane to adopt that as an official strategy," Cael said with a laugh, settling in behind the surveillance console. Guess his brother was going to stick around for the show. "Ash *hates* it."

Dex wriggled his brows. "I know." Though he knew Ash's disapproval of the maneuver stemmed from it being Dex's idea and that it worked. His teammate especially didn't approve of having his name married with Dex's to form "Dash." For all his bitching, Ash couldn't deny their clashing personalities had a way of providing results when it came to interrogations. Ash was the kind of guy who made babies cry just by looking at them. The maneuver was less "bad cop/good cop," and more "holy fuck get him away from me/I'll talk to you because you're not psychotic." The best part was, there was little acting involved.

"Get the fuck in there." Ash shoved the wide-eyed teen into the back of the BearCat so rough he stumbled. Dex caught him before he could run headfirst into something and knock himself out.

"Jesus, Keeler, take it easy." Dex ducked his head to look at the kid. "You okay?"

The kid pressed his lips together, his brows furrowed. Dex motioned to the long bench where the team usually sat.

"Why don't you take a seat, um…. What's your name?"

"You gonna sing him a lullaby too, Daley?" Ash snorted.

Dex ignored Ash, his focus on the kid who'd reluctantly taken a seat on the bench. "What's your name?"

He received no reply. Ash stormed over and grabbed a fistful of the kid's shirt, hauling him off his feet with a snarl. "He asked you a fucking question. Are you going to cooperate, or am I going to have to shift and pick my teeth with your scrawny ass bones?"

Dex schooled his expression, doing his best not to laugh at Ash's cheesy lines. The kid's eyes widened, a squeak escaping him when Ash dropped him roughly onto the seat and loomed over him. "You got five seconds to state your name before I get really pissed. Five."

"Keeler," Dex sighed. "That's not going to help."

Ash rounded on him, poking him in the vest. "That's your problem, Daley. Too busy making daisy chains and cracking jokes to get your hands dirty."

"What the hell's that supposed to mean?" Dex planted his hands on his hips. Ash stepped closer, his voice a low growl, but Dex wasn't intimidated.

"It means you don't got the balls to get in there and do what you gotta do, always trying to be the good guy."

"I *am* the good guy. We're all the good guys! Screw you, man. I know how to do my job, and just because I don't go around scaring old ladies or trying to make it rain vengeance and wrath, doesn't mean I'm afraid to get my hands dirty."

Nostrils flaring, Ash stormed over to the kid and lifted him off his seat again. "Now you listen to me, you little shit. Every minute you spend not talking, is another minute I gotta be in here with that gummy-bear-eating, Cheesy-Doodle-crunching, eighties-music-singing asshole, and that puts me in a bad mood. Do you want to put me in a bad mood?"

The kid shook his head fervently.

"Then answer his goddamn questions, or I swear on my momma's grave I'm gonna make you wish you were never born."

"Simon!" the kid burst out. "My name's S-Simon Russell."

Ash dropped the kid roughly onto his ass before turning to bark at Dex, "Get on with it, Daley."

Dex took a seat beside Simon who was looking rattled and miserable, his shoulders slumped, and his wary gaze going from Ash to Dex.

"I apologize for my teammate, Simon. He gets cranky when it's time for his sippy cup of OJ and a nap." Dex could have sworn he saw the end of Simon's lips twitch. "My name's Agent Daley, and despite what you might think, I'm here to help you."

Simon looked Dex over, assessing him. "Dad says all Human THIRDS agents are traitors to their race."

The words were low, but Dex could hear the uncertainty in them. Dex would bet his salary the kid never would have gotten involved in this kind of thing if his fuckwit of a father hadn't filled his head with hateful nonsense. "I'm not a traitor, Simon. I'm just a regular guy trying to do the right thing. It's my job to protect innocent citizens and help those who are feeling lost. I believe everyone has a chance to lead a safe, happy life, no matter their species. You know, I was an HPF officer before I became a THIRDS agent, just like my dad was."

Simon tilted his head and shifted slightly. Dex knew everything he needed to know about the young man in that instant, and he continued while he had Simon's attention.

"My dad was a homicide detective for the Sixth precinct. He and his best friend Tony were the best at what they did. I was so proud of him. My friends would get sick and tired of me telling them how great my dad was," he said with a chuckle, still feeling a squeeze to his heart when he thought of his father. A day didn't go by when he didn't miss his parents. "He was my hero."

"Was?" Simon asked with a frown.

"Yeah, he was killed during the riots, along with my mom." Dex let out a sigh and shook his head. "He'd gone off to deal with the riots on several occasions while on the job, and then he goes out to the movies one night with my mom, their date night"—he swallowed hard, his gaze on his gloved hands clasped in front of him—"and there was a shootout at the movie complex. My dad tried to get everyone out, including my mom. She… got hit in the crossfire. My dad got shot in the chest trying to save her."

"I'm sorry," Simon mumbled, looking even more deflated.

Dex gave a sniff and blinked back the sting in his eyes. Twenty-eight years and it still felt as though it were yesterday. "Yeah, I miss them, a lot. But, soon after, Tony adopted me, and a few months later, I got me a baby brother. I wouldn't trade him in for anything. You got any brothers or sisters?" He didn't know what possessed him to share what had happened to his parents with Simon, but as soon as he started, it came tumbling out. Simon was young. He had his whole future ahead of him, if he would only stand up for what he wanted, not what his father wanted for him.

Simon nodded. "An older brother. Matthew. He lives in Boston now."

At least Matthew had gotten away. "He a good big brother?" Dex asked, noting the way Simon's eyes lit up. Dex tried not to curse. The kid was younger than he'd anticipated. Fifteen at most.

"He's awesome. He always looked out for me, played video games with me. We got into fights, but brothers do. He never thought he was too cool to hang out with me, even when his friends teased him about it. What about you?"

Dex smiled widely. "Am I a good big brother? I don't know. Let's find out." He turned his head, grinning at Cael. "What do you say? Be gentle."

"Aside being really annoying sometimes," Cael replied, his smile reaching his eyes, "yeah, you're an awesome big brother."

Dex turned back to Simon whose jaw was all but hitting the floor. When he recuperated, he sputtered. "*He's* your brother? But… but he's a Therian!"

"Tell me something, Simon. If something happened and you ended up… different, would Matthew turn you away?"

Simon opened his mouth then seemed to think better of it. His shoulders slumped, and he shook his head. "No. He'd love me no matter what. I know he would."

"So why would I do that to my little brother? He's a regular guy, just like you." Dex shrugged. "Maybe his DNA's different, but I love him just like your big brother loves you. He's also the only guy who can kick my ass at video games. He's a total nerd."

"Pot meet kettle," Cael snorted.

Dex put his hand on Simon's shoulder. "Something tells me Matthew doesn't share your dad's views."

"No. They fought a lot. Dad had always told us Therians were wrong. Abominations from hell trying to corrupt God's children. Matthew believed it at first."

"But then?"

"He met Jenny."

"Ah," Dex smiled knowingly. "Your brother fell in love with a Therian."

"Yeah. I was so scared for him. When Dad found out, he went nuts. Threatened Matthew, but Matthew refused to leave Jenny, so Dad kicked him out of the house, said he was dead to him. Dad told me I no longer had a brother, but I couldn't do it. I couldn't act like Matt was dead. I wanted so bad to go with him, but Matt was only sixteen, and Dad threw him out without any money, didn't even give him a chance to get some clothes." Simon's frown deepened, his voice growing angry. "How could he do that? How could he kick Matt out like that? I wanted to hurt dad so bad, but I was small and scared. I hated him." He hung his head, tears in his eyes. "God, I'm such a pussy."

"Hey." Dex squeezed his shoulder. "Don't be so hard on yourself. There wasn't much you could do, and your dad's bad decisions are on him. It's okay to be scared, but you're not a kid anymore, Simon. You can make your own decisions. What your dad's involved in will put him away for a long time. He wants to hurt innocent Therians, Therians like Jenny, like my little brother." Simon's gaze shifted to Cael before guiltily darting away. "Is that what you want for yourself? Do you want to give up any chance of a future, at seeing Matt again, for your dad's mistakes?"

Simon bit down on his bottom lip, and after what seemed like an eternity, he shook his head. "No, I don't want to go to prison, not for that asshole. I never wanted to do this, but he told me if I was going to be a Therian fucker like my brother then I should leave, that I'd be better off dead." A tear rolled down his reddened cheek. He met Dex's gaze. "Can you really help me?"

Dex nodded. "I promise, Simon. I will do everything in my power to get you to Matt, but I need you to help me."

"Okay." Simon gave him a curt nod, his expression determined. "What do I need to do?"

"I need you to tell me everything you know about Isaac Pearce."

CHAPTER 2

"WHERE ARE we with those explosives?"

Isaac Pearce stepped up beside his disciple and placed a hand on the young man's shoulder. So loyal. His flock of sheep, ready to go wherever he led them, to do whatever he commanded. Finding his followers had been easy. All he had to do was find the right buttons and push.

"Nearly finished, sir. We're waiting on last of the C4."

"Excellent. Let me know when we're ready to move." With a smile and a pat on the back, Isaac continued his rounds of the small, once abandoned facility, checking that everyone was at their stations making the necessary preparations.

It had taken a few months to strengthen his flock, gather the necessary supplies, and put together his next course of action. He'd opened two new, fully operational branches, which housed the Order's latest recruits. By now, the THIRDS should be closing in on IGD. With the right information leaked in the right places, it was astonishing how easily he could have those circus animals jumping through his strategically located hoops. He'd lose a few disciples, but war was filled with necessary casualties. It was a sacrifice he and his following were willing to make for the greater good.

No doubt those THIRDS bastards believed he didn't have the balls to continue with what he'd started, but they'd soon come to realize he'd been biding his time. As a former HPF detective, he was well schooled in the art of patience. It had taken him months to meticulously plan the murder of those HumaniTherian cockroaches, followed by the kidnapping of Agent Brodie.

Isaac closed his eyes, remembering the brief moments of pleasure he'd had torturing that Therian filth. Brodie should have died in his hands, left a bloodied, carved, and burned mess. Instead, Isaac had been forced to use his contingency plan, detonating the strategically placed explosives under the metro line. He smiled widely at the memory. They'd believed him dead, thought they'd rid themselves of him, but like a phoenix rising from the ashes, he emerged as a humble servant of the great goddess Adrasteia, ready to fulfill his purpose. The Human race was in jeopardy, and he wasn't about to go down without one hell of a fight.

He'd spent countless hours deciding where—or more importantly *who,* he would strike next. If he and his species were going to have any chance at winning this war, he would have to destroy the THIRDS, and thanks to Agent Morelli, Isaac had a solid lead. The Therian filth had managed to be of some use before Isaac put him down like the mutt he was. The information wouldn't have seemed like much to anyone else, but he'd solved cases with less to go on.

Confident everything was running according to plan, he retreated to his office in the subbasement, not to be disturbed. Switching on his monitor, he let out a sigh, chastising himself for being such a sentimental jackass. How could he mourn the loss of a friend he'd had for such a short period of time? Of course, it felt as if he'd known the man longer. He'd been watching him, studying him for months. What an idiot he'd been, thinking he'd found someone who understood him, who might possibly join him at his side, a trusted partner, a position he had once hoped his brother Gabe would accept. Instead, Dexter J. Daley had chosen that diseased freak Sloane Brodie, just as Gabe had. Isaac clenched his fist on his desk as he stared into Dex's smiling blue eyes.

Dex would have made the ultimate disciple. He was fiercely loyal, smart, audacious, skilled, and when he set his mind to something, would move heaven and earth to make it so. Goddamn that Therian bastard. He'd corrupted Dex just like he'd corrupted Gabe. Isaac launched to his feet and started pacing. If Brodie hadn't gotten to Dex first, Isaac would have found a way to make Dex understand his worth, to show him where he truly belonged—here with him and his species, not with those animals. There was still time. Dex wasn't completely lost to him, though his window of opportunity was growing smaller by the day.

He stopped pacing and returned to his desk, pulling out the layout of their first target. If all went according to plan, he wouldn't have to worry about Sloane Brodie anymore. He finally had what he needed. Killing Brodie wouldn't be enough. Isaac wanted to destroy him, take everything from him, and leave nothing of him but the remnants of a shattered husk, and *then* he would kill him. But first, he would stand back and watch the THIRDS crumble to dust as the city fell to chaos. When nothing was left, when the disease had been cured, Isaac would approach Dex once again, and this time, if he refused, Dex would join Gabe in the afterlife.

IT WAS his lucky day.

Dex's target was finished. The guy just didn't know it.

He inched up to the doorframe, his weapon gripped tightly against his vest. One shot. That's all he needed. He could do this. Silently, he crouched down and angled his head, trying to get as much visibility as possible without exposing himself. With the coast clear, he made a dash for the blockade, slid in behind it, and pressed his back against the smooth surface.

Deep breath. It was now or never. By the end of this, one man would be left standing, and he had every intention of being that man. Popping out from behind the safety of the blockade, he aimed his weapon at the same moment as his enemy. Teeth gritted, Dex fired off a round, hitting his target straight in the heart. His enemy fell back with the impact of the blow before crumbling to the ground in a heap.

Dex waited. The only sound meeting his ears was that of his own ragged breath. Cautiously, he edged closer to the structure his enemy had fallen behind, making certain to keep his weapon at the ready just in case. He rounded the corner and grinned smugly, his gaze on his sprawled victim.

"'Oh, *you're* in charge? Well, I got news for you, Dwayne. From up here, it doesn't look like you're in charge of jack shit.'"

Sloane glared up at him. "Screw you."

With a dopey grin, Dex held his hand out, laughing when Sloane smacked it away and got to his feet without help. A deep pout came onto his partner's face when he looked down at the array of blinking red lights on his vest. Pressing the reset button, the lights flashed green before the sensor switched itself off.

"Have I mentioned how not fun it is playing laser tag with you? I never should've gotten you this stupid thing for Christmas," Sloane grumbled, removing his vest as he left the kitchen and made his way over to the living room. He tossed the sturdy equipment onto the floor by his feet and dropped down onto the couch.

After cheerfully skipping to Sloane, Dex plopped down beside him and gave the tip of his nose a gentle poke. "*Boop.* 'I killed you dead.'"

Sloane swatted his hand away. "And do you *have* to quote *Die Hard* every single time?"

"What's the point of playing laser tag if you don't pretend you're John McClane? Besides, you're the one always calling me that so you only have yourself to blame really."

Rolling his eyes, Sloane settled back against the cushions and put his feet up on the coffee table, which Dex swiftly proceeded to nudge off with his sock-covered foot. His partner knew better. Sloane's usual gripe about feet on the furniture was cut short by some sort of revelation.

"Wait, wasn't Dwayne a cop?"

"Deputy Police Chief," Dex replied, removing his laser tag equipment. He gently placed it on the floor beside the couch.

"Cop on cop? Not cool."

A wicked smile spread across Dex's lips, and he wriggled his eyebrows.

"You're thinking about porn aren't you?" Sloane cast him an accusing glare and Dex laughed.

"Aren't *you?*"

"No."

Looked like he'd have to change that. Dex climbed onto Sloane's lap and ground his hips, rubbing his growing erection against Sloane's. "What about now?"

"Are you saying you want me to be thinking about other guys fucking while you're doing that?" Sloane arched an eyebrow at him, and Dex held back a smile. The guy loved playing hard to get. Dex was fine with that. He loved a good challenge, especially when that challenge concerned his grumpy, sexy Team Leader, and as of four months ago, lover.

"No, I'm saying you should be thinking about us fucking while I do this. We can star in our own porn flick. I'll be the mouthy lawbreaker, and you can be the sexy officer who uses his love truncheon to teach me a lesson." It took a lot not to laugh at the deadpan expression on his lover's face.

"If you stop referring to my penis as a love truncheon."

"Love dart?"

"No."

"Portable pocket rocket?"

Sloane smiled. "Absolutely." The smile vanished. "Not."

"How about moisture missile? Peacemaker? Heat seeking missile?" He could do this all day, and his partner knew it, judging by his less-than-impressed expression.

"Dex," Sloane warned, a low growl rising up from his broad chest, the kind that made Dex feel tingly all over.

"Shut it?"

"We have a winner."

"Straight and to the point." Dex winked at him. "Old school. I like it."

"Good. Now take off your pants."

"I like that even better." Dex scrambled off Sloane's lap, pulled off his socks followed by his jeans, which proved more difficult than it should be. He got himself tangled, tried to save face by hopping on one foot, but ended up falling over onto the carpet. Kicking his jeans off, he sprang to his feet and put his hands on his hips in an attempt to play it cool. "You didn't see that."

Sloane closed his eyes and shook his head, his lips pressed together. He was trying not to laugh. Dex appreciated that. "Some things can't be unseen, but I'll try."

"Thanks." Dex quickly pulled off his shirt and dropped it on the carpet, staying in just his red boxer briefs. He took the opportunity to ogle his partner, from Sloane's black biker boots, up muscular legs clad in dark denim, the deep blue long-sleeve T-shirt accentuating his broad shoulders and tapered waist, the yellow bands on the sleeves circling his ridiculously beefy biceps. His chiseled jaw was stubbly, his black hair had grown too long again, curling around the back of his ears. Sloane Brodie was a walking wet dream, and for some unfathomable reason, he wanted Dex. Granted, Dex wasn't exactly sure in what capacity, but in the four months since they decided to secretly do something about the intense attraction between them, they'd been boinking like bunnies.

Sloane opened one eye and squinted at him. "Are you trying to blow me telepathically or something? Is this about X-Men again? Because we've established that's fiction, remember? We had, like, a three-hour argument over it."

"First, it wasn't an argument, it was an intellectual debate. Second, if Therians can happen, X-Men can happen. Third—" Sloane rose to his feet with a sigh, and Dex frowned. "Where you going?"

"To shut you up the only way I know how." Sloane closed the distance between them in two strides. He clamped a hand on the back of Dex's neck and brought him in for a kiss that was hungry, gentle, and stole Dex's breath away. Dex returned the kiss, his eagerness showing as he clutched onto Sloane's biceps. A moan escaped him at the feel of Sloane's hands slipping down his bare back, leaving shivers in their wake before his strong fingers dug into Dex's ass.

Sloane's mouth was hot, his lips soft, and his tongue tasted vaguely of the vanilla cappuccino Dex had coerced him into drinking after dinner. Without breaking a sweat, Sloane grabbed Dex's ass and hauled him off his feet. Despite being manhandled plenty of times by Sloane, Dex still let out a surprised gasp.

All his life, Dex had hooked up with Human guys. It was just the way it worked out, especially with his former position in the Human Police Force, not exactly a Therian-friendly organization. Being with a Therian was hella different. Being with a Therian who happened to also be an Apex predator in his Therian form was something else entirely. Sloane was bigger, wider, stronger, faster, and generally more powerful. As a Defense Agent for the THIRDS, Dex spent a good deal of time working out to keep up with his Therian teammates and the threats they faced out in the field. The rest of his workout came in the bedroom with Sloane. Not that Dex was complaining. If Sloane wanted to manhandle him, Dex would not only take it, he'd ask for more.

Dex closed his fingers around fistfuls of Sloane's hair as their kissing grew more desperate. He allowed Sloane to carry him over to the large couch and drop him down onto it. The weight of Sloane's body against his had him painfully hard and Dex rushed to drag Sloane's T-shirt over his head. He threw it off to the side, their breaths turning to panting as they frantically rutted against each other. Dex's need was almost overwhelming as he watched Sloane fumble with his belt buckle, unfastening it before unzipping his jeans and pushing them down along with his boxer briefs to reveal his thick, hard cock. It was leaking precome and jutting up toward his stomach. The sight had Dex whimpering. He shimmied back until he was sitting up, his back against the armrest, his gaze shifting up to meet Sloane's. When Sloane realized what he was doing, his pupils dilated, making Dex's stomach flip and his body tremble with anticipation. Sloane made quick work of his clothes along with Dex's boxer briefs so he could kneel over Dex, the tip of his cock pressing against Dex's lips.

"Open your mouth," Sloane ordered gruffly.

Dex obeyed, taking Sloane down to the root. He closed his eyes with a low moan, his fingers finding Sloane's firm ass cheeks. When he opened his eyes, Sloane grabbed fistfuls of Dex's hair, and their eyes met, those molten amber pools sending a shiver through Dex. Leisurely, Sloane moved in and out of Dex's mouth, a deep groan escaping when Dex pressed his lips against Sloane's cock. Dex loved seeing Sloane lose himself, loved when he took control and gave Dex orders in that gravelly, sexy voice of his. He let Sloane fuck his mouth, and he wrapped a hand around his own cock, stroking himself, his eyes never leaving Sloane's face even as his lover picked up the pace, his breath growing more ragged.

"Damn. I love your mouth," Sloane said roughly, pulling out and sitting back on his heels so he could kiss Dex, his tongue exploring every inch of Dex's mouth. He nipped at Dex's bottom lip, before sucking on it. When he'd kissed Dex to the point he thought they'd run out of air, Sloane pulled back, the lust in his eyes setting Dex ablaze. "I'm going to fuck you so hard, you won't be able to think about anything but my cock inside your ass all day tomorrow."

Dex huffed, pretending to be put off. "You dick. I've got training tomorrow."

"I know." Sloane's grin was positively sinful. "On your knees, Agent Daley. I want that ass ready for fucking *now*."

Oh, shit. He loved when Sloane used that tone of authority on him during sex. Dex quickly turned over, his chest pressed against the couch's armrest so he could reach into the small drawer of the coffee table next to it. Sloane snatched the small bottle of lube and condom from Dex with one hand, the other pressed to Dex's back, holding him against the armrest. Oh, damn, Sloane was going to fuck him just like this.

"Don't move," Sloane demanded in a low and husky voice. All Dex could do was remain perfectly still as Sloane parted his ass cheeks before a cool, lube-slicked finger pressed against his hole, causing shivers to rack Dex's body. First one finger, then two. Dex moved his hand to his cock only to have Sloane grab a fistful of his hair and gently pull his head back. "Did I say you could touch yourself?"

"No, sir."

"So move your fucking hand away from there."

"Sloane," Dex pleaded. God, he was so hard it hurt. Sloane took his time, prepping Dex, torturing him, his finger hitting his prostate. "Oh, shit! You asshole. Fuck me already."

Sloane leaned in, whispering against his ear. "You have an insubordinate streak in you, Agent Daley. Looks like I'm going to have to break you of it."

Oh God, yes. Just when Dex thought he was going to lose it, or punch Sloane's lights out, Sloane's cock started stretching him. Dex shut his eyes, releasing his breath slowly as Sloane sank farther in. The mixture of pain and pleasure was almost too much, and Dex gripped the armrest so tight his fingers hurt.

"That's it. Come on, Daley. I know you can take it. You can take it, can't you?"

Dex nodded.

"I can't hear you."

"I can take it," Dex replied through his teeth. "Can I touch myself? Please."

"Not yet."

"Screw you," Dex snapped, earning a chuckle. A few labored breaths later, the pain gave way to the most heavenly pleasure as Sloane started to move, his hands gripping Dex's hips as he pulled out almost to the tip then pushed in to the root with agonizing leisure. As soon as he started moving quicker, he ordered Dex to touch himself. Teeth gritted, he attempted to match Sloane's pace, at least until Sloane pulled nearly all the way out and drove himself into Dex hard. "Fuck!"

One hand went to Dex's shoulder, while the other gripped his hip, and Dex looked over his shoulder to find Sloane shifting positions, one leg going to the floor. *Oh God.* He braced himself, biting down on his bottom lip as Sloane snapped his hips while simultaneously forcing Dex back, impaling him on his cock. Unable to help it, Dex cried out, fueling Sloane's desire to do it again and again. Sloane's thrusts were deep and hard, his pace quickening as he lost himself. He folded over Dex, his chest pressed to Dex's back as he fucked him in earnest. Sloane's arm wrapped around Dex's chest to hold him firmly, hips snapping, and rotating.

"Oh God. Oh fuck, Sloane."

"Don't you dare," Sloane warned him, before telling him to get on his back. Dex hurriedly did, biting down on his bottom lip once again as Sloane shifted back and took Dex's cock into his mouth. Two hard sucks and a couple of licks later, Dex came, Sloane swallowing every drop. Dex's body shuddered, his muscles tensing as his orgasm was drawn out before Sloane released him and kissed him. He loved the taste of himself on Sloane's tongue, and it made him moan. "Open your mouth," Sloane breathed.

Dex did, his body trembling as Sloane pulled off the condom, grabbed Dex's hair, pulled his head forward, and jerked himself off. "Now," Sloane gasped, and Dex closed his mouth around Sloane's cock, sucking him hard, his finger slipping in between Sloane's ass cheeks and finding his entrance. He pressed against the tight ring. Sloane came in Dex's mouth with a feral growl, his fingers tangled in Dex's hair.

"That's it, Daley," Sloane groaned. "Swallow it."

Dex sucked and swallowed until Sloane's cock had gone soft between his lips. With a low hiss, Sloane pulled out and rolled onto his side, pulling Dex down against him and holding him close. Dex enjoyed what came after the hot sex almost as much as the sex, when Sloane was still floating in the haze of fucking him into oblivion. He tucked Dex against him, kissed the top of his head, and stroked his arm or his back, his eyes closed, and his chest beginning to steady.

With a contented sigh and a stupid smile on his face, Dex wrapped a leg around Sloane's and slipped an arm around his lover's waist. Did Sloane know he was playing with Dex's hair? Was he aware of all the tender gestures? Either way, Dex never mentioned it, simply enjoyed the moment. Sloane mumbled something about going, not having clothes, and Dex nodded, letting out a slur of sounds that in his mind was a perfectly articulate response.

What felt like seconds later was actually several hours, and Dex was startled awake. It took him a moment to orient himself and realize he was on his couch with Sloane who was in the midst of another nightmare. They'd started a few months ago and seemed to be getting worse with every passing week. Gently, he rubbed Sloane's arm.

"Sloane, wake up. Come on, buddy, wake up."

His partner stirred with a sleepy groan, his eyes fluttering open. Although it was dark and Dex couldn't see anything other than the subtle glow from the various pieces of electronic equipment around the living room and the moonlight filtering in through the curtains of his kitchen window, he knew Sloane could see him just fine with his Therian eyes.

"You okay?" Dex asked, lying back down, and huddling close.

"Yeah."

"Sloane." It was a plea, something else Dex wasn't accustomed to but found himself doing far too often lately. He wished the guy would open up. Dex had never had trouble saying what was on his mind. In fact, more often than not, it's what got him into trouble. It wasn't that Sloane was emotionally constipated. The guy was pretty vocal about his feelings, unless it meant exposing any of his vulnerabilities, or if it concerned his past. If Sloane messed up, he owned up to it every time and apologized. If he said something out of turn, he expressed his sincerest regret. If he didn't like something, he sure as hell would let it be known, and if he were pissed, well, everyone would know.

Sloane had no trouble showing Dex how much he wanted him, or how Dex drove him crazy, in more ways than one. But when it came to showing Dex the guy behind the intimidating Team Leader, nothing short of the Jaws of Life could get the guy to open up, leaving Dex to work things out through a series of elimination and guessing games. He'd swear sometimes it was like he needed Themis—the THIRDS artificial intelligence network—just to figure out what the hell the guy was thinking. Dex reached up, gently took hold of Sloane's jaw, and turned his face toward him.

"Come on. Talk to me."

Sloane smiled tenderly and turned his face to place a kiss on Dex's palm. "It's nothing. Really. Go back to sleep." He closed his eyes and pulled Dex in close. That was the end of that. If Dex pressed the matter, Sloane would get up, get dressed, and go home to avoid an argument. The next day, it would be up to Dex to show his partner everything was cool between them. The thought that he had far more invested in them than Sloane had crossed his mind on more than one occasion over the last few weeks, but he always managed to push it aside and focus on the positive of whatever they had.

What did they have? They were exclusive, but they weren't dating. They'd been sleeping together for months, and although Dex had agreed they would take things as they came, that they would go slow, there were no signs of them moving past the "sex is fun, let's do that" part. At least not for Sloane. Even so, Dex liked being with him. He enjoyed sneaking off together whenever they could, even if Dex felt a pang of guilt each time, having to hide from his dad and brother, but if they were caught, one of them would be transferred off the team, and neither of them wanted that.

It was too soon for them to have any kind of relationship talk. Dex had the feeling if he broached the subject, Sloane would balk. No point driving himself crazy over it. He'd promised Sloane they could take things slow, and he intended to keep his word.

"Sloane?"

"Hm?"

Sloane tensed slightly under Dex's touch, and Dex held back a sigh, wishing the guy would just relax. What did he think was going to happen? Knowing Sloane could see him in the dark, which was completely unfair, Dex gave him a grin despite not feeling it. "Mind if we go upstairs? My ass is cold."

Sloane chuckled, his muscles losing their previous tension. He gave Dex's ass a playful slap. "We wouldn't want anything happening to that ass."

"It is pretty spectacular," Dex teased, forcing himself to get up. His right arm was sore from sleeping on it awkwardly.

Sloane stepped up close behind him, his breath on the side of Dex's neck as his hand slipped around to cup Dex's balls and cock, making him jump. "Mm, that's pretty spectacular too."

A shiver went through Dex. "Upstairs. Soft bed." Before Dex could say another word, Sloane was hoisting him and throwing him over his shoulder. Dex flailed, his heart beating wildly. "Man, how many times do I gotta tell ya? Warn a guy when you're gonna go all Tarzan on his ass. Jesus."

"I'll keep that in mind," Sloane chuckled, carrying Dex through the darkened living room and up the stairs to the bedroom. He dropped him onto the bed, and Dex scrambled under the covers. His ass really was cold. So were his toes. He hated cold feet. Sloane joined him under the covers and didn't hesitate, pulling Dex close and kissing him. Dex had no idea what time it was, and he didn't care. If Sloane wanted to jump his bones, no way in hell he was going to say no.

The sex was hot, hard, and as amazing at it always was, with Sloane making Dex sweat, pant, and beg for it, until he was so thoroughly fucked, all he could do was lie there in a state of pure bliss and exhaustion. Dex drifted off to sleep, but to his frustration, he kept waking up every hour or so. It wasn't usual for him to have trouble sleeping, especially after an evening of Sloane pounding him into the mattress, or couch cushions. His ass throbbed as if to remind him. Dex felt the steady rise and fall of Sloane's chest beneath his hand, and he took the opportunity to study his lover's face. He was asleep, but it was clearly a troubled sleep.

It had been four months since the workshop incident when Isaac Pearce had kidnapped Sloane, chained him up, and tortured him before Dex could get to him. Four months since Sloane had discovered his ex-lover and ex-partner Gabe Pearce had died at the hands of his brother and not by a meet with an informant gone wrong, as everyone had believed. Four months since discovering the explosion that should have ended Isaac Pearce's life, he emerged as the leader of the Order, followed by the execution of Agent Morelli. And despite all that, Sloane hadn't spoken a single word of how he felt about it, other than the desire to find the bastard and bring him in, dead or alive—a sentiment they all shared.

Sloane's brows furrowed in sleep, and Dex brushed his fingers down his partner's stubbly jaw, smiling when Sloane let out a small huff but leaned into the touch. *It's only been four months,* Dex reminded himself. He needed to be more patient. Sloane had been through a hell of a lot in the last couple of years, and he'd been upfront with Dex about needing time. It wasn't fair for Dex to ask any more of him at the moment.

Gingerly, he shifted and leaned over to brush his lips over Sloane's, smiling at the faint moan he received. Wanting to ease his lover's unrest, Dex moved stealthily, roaming his hands over Sloane's body, caressing hard muscle, soft skin, until he got to Sloane's flaccid cock. With a smile, Dex stroked him, watching Sloane's face, the way he tilted his head back and moaned.

Moving the duvet, Dex delivered kisses to Sloane's thigh as he continued to stroke Sloane's hardening cock, enjoying the feel of his lover in this docile state, his heart squeezing at every tiny murmur or sharp intake of breath.

"Mm…. Gabe."

What the…? Dex sat back on his heels and ran a hand over his face. Well, that was certainly one way to kill the mood. He climbed off the bed with care and made his way downstairs, where he turned on the

TV, the glow helping him locate his boxer briefs that he slipped back on. Guess he couldn't be too surprised it had happened. If he were honest with himself, he would admit he'd expected it sooner, especially since things had quieted down. For months, Isaac Pearce's threats had remained just that, though the THIRDS was using all its resources to track him and the Order down.

They'd managed to get some information from Simon Russell, enough to deduce the whole thing had been meant to draw their attention, with Simon and the rest of the men sacrificed in the process, something they'd willingly agreed to. Well, in Simon's case, his dad had agreed for him. Dex had been true to his word, and he'd watched with a dopey grin as the brothers were reunited. Matthew shook Dex's hand, thanking him profusely for getting his little brother away from their dad. Then the two had walked off into the sunset together. Life almost seemed… good, aside from the maniac hiding somewhere in the city, plotting their demise. Dex had a bad feeling. Isaac wasn't just some brainless thug. He was an experienced, patient, intelligent ex-officer of the law.

Dex dropped down onto the couch, snatched up the TV remote, and clicked past infomercials until he got to one of the late night cartoon channels, the only station with anything remotely decent at this ungodly hour. He tried not to think about Isaac Pearce, but it was hard to shut off his brain. It was better than thinking about Sloane calling him by his former-lover's name during an intimate moment. God, Sloane had probably been dreaming of him. Great. Dex shifted his attention back to Isaac Pearce.

The THIRDS had confiscated the man's properties, although the workshop had gone up in flames as part of the guy's well-executed escape plan. Any remaining evidence was burned to a crisp, leaving only the evidence originally discovered in Isaac's home confirming he was behind the murders and the makeshift iron weapon he'd constructed to lead them off his trail. Isaac had covered his tracks well. The witnesses who'd lied for him by claiming Isaac had been with them during the times of the murders had been his followers, and they'd all disappeared by the time the THIRDS came knocking on their doors. The THIRDS had tossed out their net of confidential informants, spies, and shadows. Isaac Pearce was a ghost.

Two episodes into some weird but entertaining cartoon about a kid with rabbit ears, his dog, and some pink princess, and Dex was running through a list of excuses to give his partner if he fell asleep down here when he heard Sloane's sleepy, gravelly voice.

"Hey, what's going on?"

"Watching TV. Couldn't sleep."

Sloane came around and sat on the robust coffee table across from Dex, but not blocking his view of the TV. Dex could tell Sloane was studying him, and Dex just didn't have the energy. He was too exhausted, physically and emotionally. In a few hours, he'd have to be at work with a full day of training exercises awaiting him.

"What's wrong?" Sloane leaned in to take his hand. "Talk to me, Daley."

Funny how that street didn't run both ways. Dex thought about it, thought about every time he'd swallowed down a jab to his heart. It was getting more painful each time. He kept telling himself to pull back, not to make the same mistake he always made of falling too hard, too fast. He could see himself getting deep, but unable to get off the path to ruin. "You have any nice dreams lately?"

Sloane's endearing puzzled look made it worse.

"I was uh, giving you an impromptu hand job, and you called me Gabe." Dex pulled his hand out of Sloane's, watching his partner's brows draw together in confusion before realization dawned on him.

"Shit. Dex. I—"

"I know. You miss him. Your subconscious, your heart, it wants what it wants, right?"

"Don't, please." Sloane reached for Dex's hand again, and Dex allowed it. "What do you want from me, Dex?"

Dex didn't spend long thinking of his reply. What he wanted was unattainable, at least at the moment. The future was unclear. "I know it's selfish, but I'd like it if when you were with me, that you were with *me*." He was asking for too much. It wasn't as if Sloane could control his subconscious.

"I am. I just need—"

"Time. I know." Dex hated seeing the crestfallen expression on Sloane's face, but he couldn't summon the strength to brush his feelings aside with a joke. Not this time.

"We've been apologizing to each other a lot lately," Sloane said quietly, his thumb stroking the back of Dex's hand.

"Yeah."

"Do you… want me to go?"

Dex met Sloane's eyes, the butterflies in his stomach fluttering at the unspoken need. "Do you want to?"

After some hesitation, Sloane shook his head, his bottom lip jutted out tragically. "No."

"Good." Dex turned off the TV, tugged at Sloane's hand, and led him upstairs. He climbed into bed and lay on his side, his heart heavy. Sloane wrapped his arms around Dex's middle, and pulled Dex back against him, the gesture bringing a small smile to Dex's face. He rolled over to face Sloane, and a pang of guilt hit him for the troubled look he'd placed on his partner's face. He leaned in for a kiss, relieved when Sloane returned his soft kiss.

Maybe Dex should have gone back to sleep and not said anything. The guy had enough on his plate without Dex acting like some whiny, clingy boyfriend. Especially since he didn't even qualify for the title.

It wasn't as if Dex hadn't been in this situation before. He was always moving too quickly, but he'd never had a problem with it. Now, things felt… different. *He* felt different. Something about the guy had Dex wishing for things he'd never even thought about before. Was it because when he looked into Sloane's bright amber eyes, all he saw was a world of pain and heartache? Did he really think he could change that? Even if they had a lifetime together, would those eyes ever be filled with something… more? Not liking where his thoughts were heading, he pulled back and ran a thumb over Sloane's brow, speaking quietly. "Get some sleep."

"Dex…."

Dex put his finger to Sloane's lips, giving him as much of a smile as he could muster. "It's okay. Really. One day at a time, right?"

Sloane nodded, though his uncertainty was clear. Despite that, he closed his eyes as Dex continued to stroke his face, enjoying the feel of

Sloane's stubble, the rugged line of his jaw, the way his hair fell over his eyes. His partner was always letting it grow out until Tony threatened to take a pair of scissors to it. Dex liked when it curled around Sloane's ears, softening his features. It was a long time before Dex fell asleep, and when he did, it was restless and filled with unpleasant dreams of a madman chasing him and a lover he could never reach.

CHAPTER 3

SLOANE WALKED through the empty, white halls, the too-bright lights almost blinding. There was something familiar about the place. An icy chill ran up his spine, and for a split second, he thought he was back. Had they come for him? Looking down at himself, he was relieved to find he was no longer that frightened child, one of many occupying a room in the numerous wards. He was grown up, far stronger than he had been at the time. His rifle was in his hand, and he was dressed in his uniform. He was here on a mission. Something important. He wished he could remember what that something was.

As he advanced with caution, he did his best to control his breathing. There was a set of double doors at the end. White like the rest of the hall. He didn't know what it was, but something felt wrong. He went to press his earpiece when he heard panting, followed by a voice that brought him to a halt.

"Sloane… help me. Please…."

"Gabe?"

"Through the doors… please hurry! Oh God—"

Sloane bolted down the hall and burst through the doors, coming to an abrupt halt just inside the vast empty gray room. "Please no." He shook his head, his heart leaping into his throat and the back of his eyes stinging. Gabe knelt on the floor, his hands tied behind his back. Beside him, in the same position, was Dex. Isaac stood with a .38 in his hand. Sloane went to aim his rifle but when he lifted his arms, his hands were empty. What the hell? *What was going on? How did Isaac get hold of Gabe and Dex? Why couldn't he remember anything?*

"It's time for you to make your choice."

Sloane stared at Isaac, not understanding. Isaac cocked his gun and put it to the back of Gabe's head. "No! Please." *A tear rolled down Sloane's cheek, his hands shaking as he held them up in front of him, a terrifying sense of dread washing over him, as if he knew the outcome of this scenario.* "Whatever you want, but please, don't hurt them."

Isaac's malicious grin all but stopped Sloane's heart, and he moved the gun from Gabe to Dex and back. "Make your choice."

"Why are you doing this? Gabe's your brother!"

"Why? Because I'm a psychopath, obviously. And you? You're a coward. Five seconds."

Sloane looked from Gabe's tearful hazel eyes to Dex's pools of crystal blue before he shifted his gaze back to Isaac. "How about a trade? Me for them. It's me you want, right?"

Isaac cocked his head to one side in thought, before his lips curled into a malevolent grin. "And give up the opportunity to make you suffer? No. Five."

"I love you, Sloane," *Gabe said, drawing Sloane's attention.*

"Four."

Sloane's gaze went to Dex, his expression breaking Sloane's heart. Dex smiled tenderly and nodded. "I understand."

"Three."

"I can't," *Sloane pleaded with Isaac.* "Please, don't do this." *How could he? He loved Gabe, but that didn't mean he could let Dex go. Dex was... extraordinary. He'd never met anyone like him. There was so much Sloane wanted to learn about him, to experience with him. Dex was good to him, always there to pick up the pieces, doing so with a warm smile and tender touch.*

"Two." *Isaac moved the gun between Gabe and Dex.*

"Please," *Sloane begged, dropping to his knees, his vision blurring from his tears, and his heart breaking. He never thought the day would come when he would find himself on his knees, begging a madman like Isaac, but he would do anything for the men before him. "Please."*

"One."

The gun moved to Gabe's head and Sloane cried out. "Not him!"

A shot rang out and Sloane released an anguished cry—

Sloane gasped, choking on a fierce cry, the room around him dark. Where the hell was he? What was going on? Was he still at the research facility?

"Sloane!"

Sloane scrambled off the bed so fast, he ran into the wall with his shoulder. He spun around, his heart beating wildly, his gaze moving frantically around the room before it landed on the man in the center of the large bed, the slice of moonlight cutting through the small gap in the curtain landing on disheveled dirty blond hair, casting a glow around the man's head.

"Dex?"

Dex climbed off the mattress, his hands held up in front of him as he gingerly took a step closer, his expression filled with concern. "It's me, buddy. It's Dex."

It had been a dream. No, it had been a nightmare, a very real, very vivid one that came flooding back in excruciating detail. What had he done? "Oh God." He slid down the length of the wall, covering his face with his hands. Dex placed a hand on his shoulder, and Sloane couldn't bear to look at him. He could still see it…. Dex's limp body lying in a pool of blood, his bright blue eyes on Sloane… blood trickling from the corners of plump lips smiling tenderly at him.

"Hey, come on, talk to me. Tell me what happened."

Sloane shook his head. How could he explain to Dex what he'd done? He knew it was just a dream, but what did that say about him? About them? God, it had all been so real. He grabbed Dex and pulled him against him, hugging him so tight he heard Dex's low groan, but he couldn't let go. He had to know Dex was real, there in his arms, and alive, not executed at his words. "I'm sorry," Sloane whispered. "I'm so sorry."

"For what?" Dex wheezed, tapping Sloane on the shoulder. "You know I love a good hug, buddy, but you're kinda crushing me here."

Sloane loosened his grip, but he didn't let go. He still couldn't meet Dex's gaze, so he buried his face against his partner's neck. "That bad, huh?" Dex gently stroked Sloane's arm. He didn't deserve such tenderness.

"Yes," Sloane replied, squeezing Dex involuntarily. He felt like such a child. But he couldn't bring himself to tell Dex what he'd done. Isaac was right. He was a coward. Since he'd appeared on Dex's doorstep in December after telling him he wanted to see where things went between them, telling him he wanted to move on, he still found himself unable to. Dex was so patient, the most patient guy Sloane had ever known, but how long could that last? He'd told Dex he just needed time, and he did, but what if time didn't help? What if he could never let Gabe go? How long could he go on giving part of himself to Dex, hurting a good guy when Dex deserved so much better?

"Hey, look at me." Dex gently took Sloane's face in his hands, and Sloane lifted his gaze, a lump in his throat at the kindness in that handsome face. "It was a bad dream, okay? Whatever it was, you're here now, with me. You're safe, okay? Everything's okay."

Sloane nodded. He wished he could believe that. Despite the uneasy feeling in his gut, he allowed Dex to lead him back to bed, trying not to feel guilty over his subconscious choice. He held Dex close as he lay in bed, remaining awake long after Dex had fallen asleep. Sometimes he looked around the room and asked himself what the hell he was doing here, but then he only had to feel or see Dex beside him and a little voice in his head told him it was exactly where he needed to be. It was that feeling he drew on, allowing it to wash away the remnants of that terrible dream. It was okay. He was here with Dex. Everything was okay.

Remarkably, he managed to get in a few hours of sleep. He woke up before Dex, which was nothing new. He always did. It was kind of cheesy now that he thought about it, but not only was he always the first one awake, but he wanted to be. It had become his routine. He'd wake up, and watch Dex sleep for a brief moment, grinning like an idiot at his partner's sleeping form. The guy always looked like he'd gone three rounds with the duvet and lost. It was wrapped around his waist, one leg on top, arm tucked up against his body, the other under his crooked pillow, his hair sticking up every which way and stubble grown in. Damn he was sexy.

Sloane carefully leaned over and placed a kiss to Dex's bare shoulder, tempted by the curve of his spine leading down to that plump ass underneath the covers. God, he loved Dex's ass. Then again, there wasn't a whole lot of Dex not to love.

Love?

He quickly pushed that thought aside. What the hell was wrong with him? He cared about Dex, he did, and he had no trouble being affectionate, or showing Dex how crazy he made him, but love was another matter, one he wasn't willing to explore. He'd loved Gabe, and look where it got him. No, when Gabe died, he took all the love Sloane had with him, took a part of Sloane with him, one he'd never get back. He did care about Dex, and he was sure if he let himself, he could get attached to the guy, find himself needing and wanting to be with him, but love wasn't something he could see ever happening to him again.

Annoyed with the direction his thoughts were going, he climbed out of bed, grabbed his boxer briefs and T-shirt, and went about his morning routine. He'd have about forty minutes before Dex came ambling into the kitchen like the walking dead in search of coffee. Sloane had never met anyone who loved—or needed—coffee as much as Dex, and they worked for an organization that depended on the stuff like junkies relied on crack. If coffee became an illegal substance, the THIRDS would crumble, and his partner would likely end up a drug kingpin, trafficking coffee beans across the five boroughs.

The morning after the first time they'd had sex, Dex had been his usual self, and his enthusiasm had led to a hot blowjob for Sloane in the shower. Sloane quickly discovered it had been a one off. A mixture of medication from his injuries at the time, his excitement of getting back to work after weeks of recovery, and Dex's keenness to sex Sloane up, had been responsible for the man's alert state. After that, until his partner had his coffee, no signs of life existed.

A shuffling sound, followed by a long groan caught his ear and Sloane turned, watching in amusement as Dex took a seat at the counter. Sections of his hair stuck up in peaks, making him look like he had little devil horns, and he had a pillowcase mark across one pink cheek.

"Morning," Sloane said cheerfully.

Dex looked up at him without raising his head. He let out a grunt and Sloane chuckled. And the guy called *him* grumpy pants. Adding the hot frothed milk to Dex's coffee, he placed the bucket-sized cappuccino in front of his partner. Dex wrapped his hands around the mug, shuddered from head to toe, and rather than lifting it to his mouth, he hunched over to put his lips to the mug, and sipped.

"Oh God," Dex moaned, closing his eyes, making the same face he did during sex. It went straight to Sloane's groin. Curious, he decided to ask.

"If you had to choose between coffee and—"

"Coffee."

"You didn't know what I was going to say," Sloane laughed.

Dex shook his head. "Doesn't matter. Coffee."

"Me or coffee."

"Coffee."

"Wow. Okay, sex or coffee."

"Coffee."

"Your brother or—"

"Coffee. I would totally trade my brother for a good cup of coffee." He took a sip with a contented sigh. His gaze shifted to Sloane. "Okay, maybe I wouldn't trade him in for coffee. Although…." He pursed his lips thoughtfully then shook his head. "No, you're right, that would be wrong."

Sloane didn't mind he came second to coffee, because all he had to do was bide his time. The dark, frothy brew might dominate his lover's mind at first, but as soon as Dex was finished, they'd both have breakfast, and then the dishes would be cleared and washed. They'd go upstairs, brush their teeth, and Sloane would take off his shirt on the way to the armchair at the end of the bedroom where his clothes and toiletry bag were. As expected, he'd never make it there.

Dex pounced, arms wrapping around Sloane's waist, one hand caressing Sloane's chest, the other slipping underneath the elastic band of his boxer briefs while Dex delivered kisses to his back, the tip of his tongue licking, teeth nipping.

"Still thinking of trading me in for coffee?" Sloane asked huskily.

"I may have been a bit rash. You know I can't be trusted when the Starbucks siren gets me in her caffeinated clutches. I'm weak. It shames me." Dex's hand wrapped around Sloane's hardening cock, drawing a low moan from Sloane, his other hand tugging down Sloane's underwear. Dex's teeth bit down on the flesh of his ass cheek, and Sloane bucked into Dex's hand with a low growl. "What can I do to make it up to you?" Dex's tongue poked out to lick Sloane's ass where he'd bitten him.

"We don't have much time," Sloane replied, trying to keep his breath steady.

"How about I let you fuck my mouth in the shower? I know how much you like that."

"Like" would be an understatement. As Dex took his hand and led him to the bathroom, all Sloane could think about was how mornings were a lot more fun with Dex around.

THE THIRDS training facility was huge, occupying three buildings along York Avenue, stretching down three blocks with an outdoor facility running down the length of Cherokee Place. It was rather impressive.

For months, it seemed as if Dex was always in one training session or another. Today it was bonding with your Therian partner, a session Dex was meant to have taken months ago when he first joined, but due to everything going on with the HumaniTherians case he'd been working on with his team, it kept getting postponed. The rest of the rookies in this session were brand new recruits, making Dex the most experienced rookie there.

He waited in the huge changing bay filled with rows and rows of curtained off sections to give Therian agents privacy during and after their shift, including receiving Postshift Trauma Care afterward. Sloane had left his clothes and belongings in the equally expansive locker room next door before walking out in nothing but a towel wrapped around his waist. He'd given Dex a wink before slipping past him behind the curtain of their designated area. Dex stood dutifully in front, his hands clasped behind his back trying not to freak out at the hundreds of feral growls, roars, and howls echoing through the place.

He was used to Therians shifting, especially having grown up in a house with a Therian brother, but standing in a room filled with hundreds of them was something he was still growing accustomed to. Instead, he concentrated on his partner.

Sloane's painful groans and growls as his mass shifted made Dex wince. No matter how many times he heard it, it still got to him. The experience of shifting wasn't something Dex envied. According to his brother, it was like someone was rearranging your body from the inside out, stretching muscle and skin, popping bones, shifting organs, fur piercing skin, and then you got to do it all over again when you shifted back, with the added bonus of experiencing aftereffects equivalent to those caused by a mild epileptic seizure. Therian scientists were attempting to find a solution to that, but as of yet, had nothing. Even if they could come up with medication that would reduce the aftereffects, it would undoubtedly be accompanied by other side effects, and who the hell wanted that?

Each rookie, whether Human or Therian, was paired up with a more experienced partner, and as this training session concerned the bond between Therian and Human agents, the attendees were a mixture of Defense, Intel, and Recon agents. Dex received a nudge against his leg, and he smiled down at his partner. Sloane was as huge in his Therian form as he was in his Human form. It had taken a few weeks, but Dex could easily spot his partner among any other black jaguar Therians. Scores of little things that made it obvious to him. Those molten amber eyes, a glossy coat that was nearly pitch black with the faintest hint of rosettes coming through, all that bulk, hard muscle, the way he moved, his expressions, the way he looked at Dex as if he could hear his thoughts. There was also something in Dex's gut that told him it was his partner.

Dex stood, arms folded over his chest, trying not to chuckle at his partner doing his Felid thing, circling Dex, rubbing against his legs, the loud chainsaw-like purrs vibrating against Dex. Sloane had to rub his scent all over Dex, and Dex knew better than to interrupt or try to stop him. Well, he did now.

The first time Dex had made the mistake of moving away, not knowing what the hell Sloane was doing, Sloane had knocked him over, scared the ever living crap out of him, stood on his back, and then proceeded to make it worse by rolling all over Dex, apparently his punishment for attempting to walk away. Cael rubbed his scent over Dex while in his Therian form all the time and had been doing so since they were kids. But it was a different kind of bond. When Cael left his scent on Dex, it was so other Therians knew Dex was family, part of Cael's cheetah coalition. When Sloane left his scent on Dex, he had no idea what kind of message that was sending out.

The facility had several expansive outdoor areas surrounded by prison-style concrete walls with electrified barbed wire running along the top to keep any daredevil news folk from attempting to get an eyeful. The Human zealots loved any opportunity to show Therians as nothing but ferocious, mindless beasts, and the last thing the THIRDS needed was media footage of their Therian agents in their feral form tearing through dummies. As soon as Sloane finished rubbing against Dex, he nudged the back of Dex's legs. Every time he did that, Dex could practically hear Sloane's words in his head. *Get your ass moving, Rookie.*

As instructed, Dex headed out into Field "A." Tidy rows of mats had been placed on the grass for the Human agents to sit, their Therian partners sitting or lying on the grass beside them. Dex snagged himself a mat somewhere near the middle, not too close to the instructor, but not too far. He gave the surrounding agents a cheerful smile as he sat cross-legged, Sloane flopping down beside him looking bored already, but then again most Felid Therian agents looked bored when in their feral form. Must be a cat thing.

There were whispers and murmurs around him, and Dex noticed some of the agents were staring at him while others pretended they weren't.

Discreetly, Dex looked down at himself. Was his fly open? Nope. He leaned into Sloane, talking quietly at him. "Any idea what's going on?"

Sloane pushed his muzzle against Dex's arm over his Unit Alpha, Destructive Delta patch. Looking around, Dex noticed most of the other patches were of teams he hadn't heard of, mostly in Units Beta and Omega. "Oh, are we the only ones from Unit Alpha?" He received a fierce yawn in response. "I'm gonna take that as a yes." The attention made sense, then. From what he'd learned, Unit Alpha was the most popular unit at the THIRDS. It was also the most dangerous and the most difficult to get into.

The only way a position became available in Unit Alpha was if an agent retired, died, or messed up so bad they got transferred. And then the competition to fill that position was fierce. Dex had no doubt most of the rookies here had heard enough stories and rumors to give them that starry-eyed look. They had no idea what being an agent for Unit Alpha truly meant. Sloane could attest to that firsthand.

The instructor, a Therian dressed in khaki slacks, a white shirt, and brown cardigan, stepped up to the front. He looked more like some philosophy teacher than a THIRDS agent. He tapped his earpiece, the tiny microphone pressed against his cheek making certain everyone could hear.

"Welcome new recruits to the Therian Behavioral Science session 1.03. I'm Dr. Eldridge and I'll be your instructor. What makes the THIRDS such a unique and successful agency is its diverse nature. Here at the THIRDS we promote and embrace all cultures, religions, sexualities, genders, nationalities, and species, so that we may come together to achieve a common goal—justice for all. As you're already fully aware, for every Human agent in our organization, there is a Therian agent."

He walked as he talked, his sharp Therian gaze taking in all the recruits. The marks on his neck showed he was a cougar Therian. With a broad smile, he laced his fingers together. "Without the bond between Human and Therian, our organization could not thrive, which is why it's imperative every new recruit is paired with the right agent. However, assigning you a compatible partner is merely the beginning. Today we're going to discuss and demonstrate how to recognize certain Therian behaviors so that you might form the crucial bond needed for a successful partnership. I'm pleased that we have one of our more experienced new recruits with us here today."

Dex looked around. Sweet, so he wasn't the oldest new recruit. That should take some of the attention off him.

"Agent Daley, what can you tell us about what you've learned since being partnered with a jaguar Therian?"

Craaap. So much for that.

"Pardon me, before we get started, for those of you who may not know—though I'm certain you've heard of him, Agent Daley's partner is Agent Sloane Brodie, an agent with over twenty years field experience and the THIRDS youngest recruit to date, having joined the THIRDS at age sixteen. He's the Team Leader of Unit Alpha's first Defense team, Destructive Delta. Agent Daley, please continue. And if you wouldn't mind standing."

Well, the guy asked for it. Dex stood and addressed the wide-eyed recruits. "All right, listen up. This is serious stuff. Lesson number one: If your 240-pound Felid partner with a jaw strong enough to pierce your skull with his fangs in one bite wants to rub up against your leg, you take it and you like it.

"Lesson number two: Don't piss off your Felid partner and then think you're safe by jumping in Sparta's Olympic-sized swimming pool. Jaguar Therians love swimming, and they're better at it than you. No good can come of it, and you'll end up losing your swim trunks in the process and have to walk to the locker room naked, covering your boy bits, and nearly giving the janitorial staff a heart attack. Your fellow agents will take pictures of you, and by the time your shift is over, your ass has gone viral, and it's seen more action than you ever will.

"Lesson number three: Jaguar Therians are patient, crafty, and you will never see them coming. They're masters of skulking and pouncing. Just because you *think* you've gotten away with something doesn't mean you have. Your partner will wait months if he has to for the perfect moment to strike. He will get his revenge. So you thought attaching a cheesy 1980s Dionne Warwick song to one of his case files and disabling the audio function on his desk so he couldn't stop the hellish harmonica would be funny? Think again. Because five months later, while you're in the middle of field training, surrounded by scores of Felid Therian agents in their Therian form, you'll nearly faint from the fear of having all of them charge you at once. You'll try to run, but you won't escape. They'll knock you over, and you'll suddenly realize that your partner has stuffed catnip into every pocket, every piece of equipment, even your socks, and then you'll be rolled up in a fetal position while you're being pawed and rubbed up against by over a dozen Felids, before you get passed around like a giant Felid doobie. It's not fun."

Everyone broke into laughter, and Dex shook his head, putting a hand up. "Laugh all you want, but I'm telling you, if you have a Felid partner, you are screwed. You thought your neighbor's cat was the devil incarnate? Guess what? He ain't got nothin' on your partner. And remember, just because your partner can't maim or kill you, doesn't mean he won't make you suffer. Oh and your Felid partner will not be scared off by the rustling of a plastic bag. All it will do is piss him off. Shiny things, laser pointers, and a giant box may occasionally distract him. They love boxes."

Dr. Eldridge picked his jaw up off the floor. "Um, thank you, Agent Daley, for that… informative briefing. You may resume your seat."

"Thanks." Dex sat down, and Sloane settled in beside him. He sniffed at Dex before a sandpaper tongue licked the side of his face. "Stop it." Dex gave Sloane a small shove which was about as effective as asking Ash not to be a dickbag. Sloane continued, licking Dex, his paw thrown over Dex's arm in case he had any thoughts of moving away. "Dude, seriously, that's gross."

"Is there a problem, Agent Daley?"

Dex held a hand up. "Yeah. How do I get my partner to stop licking me?"

The instructor let out a long-suffering sigh, sounding like every teacher Dex had ever had. "He's not licking you, he's grooming you."

Tomato, tomahto. "Great. How do I get my partner to stop grooming me?"

"Agent Daley, you have a Felid Therian sibling correct?"

Dex nodded. "That is correct."

"So I assume you understand when a Felid grooms you, he or she feels comfortable around you. You are accepted as part of his or her social circle. It's a gesture of assurance and one not easily attained."

"Yeah, I know that, and it's awesome, really, but it's also weird. He's my partner. Plus it's kind of difficult working a case out in the field when your partner decides to bathe you with his tongue. And believe me when I say this, it's not as pleasant as it sounds." If Sloane were in his Human form, Dex would have had a different opinion, but while his partner was in his Therian form, it was… like he said, weird.

His instructor looked pleased by that, and Dex stifled a groan. "Ah, now if you are in the presence of someone unfamiliar, and your partner grooms you, it means he's claiming you."

Dex gaped at him. He could feel his face getting hot. "He's what now?"

"It's quite common, Agent Daley. Everyone please turn to observe Agent Daley and Agent Sloane."

This day was getting better and better. Where was a giant box when you needed one?

"When you and your partner have bonded, you'll know by your partner's behavior when he or she is in his or her Therian form. Although Humanity is present neurologically, it's also when a Therian is at his or her most feral. As you can see, Agent Brodie and Agent Daley have a bond, one of the many goals you must achieve in order to have a healthy, functioning partnership.

"There's trust there, enough for Agent Brodie to be at ease in his Therian form around Agent Daley. When Agent Brodie grooms his partner out in the field, he's letting others know his partner is off limits, under his protection. There is unfortunately, a strong instinct of possession, and you may encounter instances in which you'll need to reassure your partner there isn't a threat to his or her claim on you. Of course this will only last while your partner is in their Therian form. Now it's time for a demonstration. Agent Daley, Agent Brodie, would you please come up here?"

Dex waved a hand in dismissal. "You know what, it's cool. He can groom all he wants."

"Agent Daley."

"Right." Dex got to his feet and headed toward the front of the class with Sloane casually padding after him. Dex stood, facing the rows and rows of rookie agents, all eyes on them.

"It is exceptionally important for you to know when your partner is playing and when he or she is irate. Agent Daley, please demonstrate."

Dex arched an eyebrow at the instructor. "Which one?"

"Both."

"You want me to piss him off?" What kind of class was this?

"In a matter of speaking. Yes."

"Great." Okay. How could he piss off his partner without losing a limb? What he needed to do was annoy Sloane, *really* annoy him. Shouldn't be too difficult. Dex had annoying down to an art. He thrust a finger in Sloane's face, knowing how much his Felid partner hated that. Then he started singing. Nothing annoyed his partner like Hall and Oates.

Sloane let out a fierce roar, and Dex started dancing around him, his voice going high-pitched for certain lyrics while he snapped his fingers. Sloane pawed at him, and Dex spun on his heels, avoiding getting smacked. His partner hissed, baring his fangs before he took off after Dex.

"Shit!" Dex bolted, weaving through the rows of agents who were either laughing or watching him in disbelief while their instructor narrated as if this was nothing more than some nature video. Dex could see the title now. National Geographic presents *Predatory Partners*.

"Understand your partner's behavior. Why is he or she behaving in such a fashion?"

"Because I pissed him off?" Dex called out over his shoulder, dashing back toward the instructor.

"Very good. Thank you, Agent Daley. You may now soothe your partner."

Clearly, Dr. Eldridge didn't personally know Sloane Brodie. Dex put his hands up, walking backward slowly as he spoke to his partner.

"Hey, buddy. Just following orders, you know? You heard him. *I* wasn't the one who wanted to piss you off." Dex crouched down and held a hand out. *Please don't bite me. Please don't bite me.* Sloane blinked before jumping up on his two back paws, his front paws pushing against Dex's shoulders and knocking him onto his back. Sloane pinned him, and Dex braced himself. When Sloane started licking his face, Dex shut his eyes tight. "Okay, I get it. Payback. Take notes people." Dex pointed at his partner. "This is what I meant about payback."

"Agent Brodie, if you'll resume your place beside your partner. Agent Daley, you may return to your mat."

Sloane did as asked, and Dex wiped at his face with his sleeve before returning to his spot. He was never more grateful not to have ended up partnered with Ash than he was at this moment.

"Once you have assessed your partner and deduced he or she is irate, you will want to give your partner space. If you feel it's safe to approach, you will do so with caution. Deal with what's causing the issue. For example, Agent Fuller, please approach Agent Daley. Slowly."

The moment Agent Fuller got to his feet, Sloane's ears twitched. "Um, I don't know if that's a good idea," Dex said, watching Agent Fuller creep toward Dex, as if Sloane hadn't noticed. The Human rookie was clearly unaccustomed to dealing with Felids. "My partner's a little on the grumpy side and poking the sleeping jaguar with a pointy stick might not end so well."

Agent Fuller paused, his panicked gaze going to their instructor.

"It's all right, Agent Fuller. Proceed."

Doing as instructed, Agent Fuller resumed his prowl, while Sloane resumed his grooming of Dex, his heavy tail thumping against the floor. Uh-oh.

"As you can see by Agent Brodie's movements, he's fully aware of Agent Fuller. His tail is telling Agent Fuller to be cautious, Agent Daley is his, and he will not take kindly to any aggression toward his partner."

Dex held up a finger. "Can I just—"

"Please stand, Agent Daley."

Dex did as asked, and Sloane released a huff at having his grooming session interrupted. This was going to end badly. Dr. Eldridge had no idea what he was about to unleash. Sloane Brodie chewed rookies for breakfast and spit them out. Dex should know.

"Agent Fuller, please advance."

Dex didn't bother taking a stance or preparing for a blow that would never land. His fellow rookies looked at him as if he was crazy, but soon they'd understand. Poor Agent Fuller. The guy pulled back a fist and the moment he took a step, Sloane's roar echoed across the field. Ears flattened, fangs bare, Sloane leapt toward Agent Fuller who screamed like a preteen at a Bieber concert and made tracks across the field, Sloane on his heels looking mighty pissed.

"Thank you, Agent Brodie," the instructor called out.

Agent Brodie wiped his ass with their instructor's polite orders and chased Agent Fuller down the length of the grassy pitch. Dex glanced around. "So which of you is a medic?"

A few shaky hands went up.

"Great. Get ready for the next lesson. How to patch up a Human scratching post."

Dex was about to call his partner when Sloane came to an abrupt halt, standing exceptionally still, his ears perked up. Seconds later, the sirens around the facility went off and Dex jumped to his feet. "What the hell is that?"

Sloane came running, then pushed his head against the back of Dex's legs to get him moving. Their instructor tapped his earpiece then called out, "Unit Alpha, report in immediately." Dex didn't need to be told twice. He took off after Sloane who was nearly at the changing bays. Inside, Sloane ducked behind his assigned curtain, and Dex waited patiently. It would take some time after Sloane shifted back for Dex to administer Postshift Trauma Care, but as much as they both wanted to move quicker, you couldn't rush nature.

Several grunts, groans, and growls later, and Dex heard his name called. Sloane was especially grumpy postshift. He didn't like Dex seeing him in such a vulnerable state, but Dex was happy to remind his partner it was his job to provide him the care he needed.

Sloane was perched on the small cot with the towel across his lap, his head in his hands as the dizziness washed over him. Dex was all too familiar with the process. He removed the bottle of Gatorade from the Postshift Trauma Care kit in his backpack and waited a few seconds until Sloane was able to lift his head. His partner was stubborn, but Dex had found a way around it. He gently brushed Sloane's fallen hair away from his brow, caressing his jaw before tenderly cupping the back of his head.

After a moment of hesitation, Sloane leaned back, and Dex helped him with the Gatorade until every drop was gone. As soon as his partner was done with that, Dex unwrapped a couple of high-carb/high-protein bars and handed them over.

Maybe Dex didn't want the postshift trauma that came with being a Therian, but what he wouldn't give to have a Therian's metabolism. Therians didn't get cholesterol, nor did they get fat or unhealthy from all the meat they consumed since their bodies depended on the stuff to keep them alive, providing they were remotely active, of course. Therians had crazy high metabolic rates and burned calories by just breathing.

The expression "eaten out of house and home" had been thought up with Therians in mind. His dad could confirm that. Dex had felt for the guy. As if raising two mischievous boys hadn't been difficult enough, one of them put away enough food you'd think he was storing it away for winter, while the other ate enough to put the butcher's son through college. Dex would bet his own grocery bills were nothing compared to Sloane's.

A few minutes later and his partner was on his feet, somewhat wobbly, but okay enough to get dressed with Dex's help. He gave the waistband of Sloane's underwear a snap, drawing a playful grin from him. Soon Sloane was dressed in his uniform, looking imposing as always. It would take a hearty meal to get Sloane back up to full speed, but he'd be okay for a few hours.

"Okay, partner?"

Sloane nodded, his voice rougher than usual, as it tended to be after a shift. "Yeah, let's go. You drive." Dex nodded somberly, though inside he was pumped and doing a jig. Since Sloane was the senior officer, he always drove the huge black Suburban except during instances such as this.

Making sure his partner was all right, Dex made a quick phone call to Cael on the way to the garage, putting in a request. He climbed in behind the wheel, telling himself he was just being a good partner, but a little voice in the back of his head reminded him he was a shitty liar when it came to those he cared about. The urge to take care of Sloane and fuss over him was growing, and he had to keep a grip on that. If Sloane suspected Dex was getting too close… well, Dex had no idea what he'd do, and he didn't want to find out.

SLOANE ENTERED his badge number and security code into the Suburban's console, ignoring the hollow feeling in the pit of his stomach. His body craved meat, but it would have to wait. The console's screen lit up blue before patching them into Themis. They tapped their earpieces, and Sloane brought up the location of Destructive Delta's BearCat. The blue circle with black D's navigated down FDR Drive. "Sarge, Dex and I are en route. What have we got?"

"We received word there's an explosive device at the CDC Therian registration office on the corner of Worth Street and Centre Street."

"Do you think it's the Order?"

"We don't know. What we do know is that the call was put in anonymously, giving us one hour, so clearly whoever put in the call had something to do with it."

"Okay, thanks, Sarge. We should arrive about five minutes after you." Sloane tapped his earpiece, disconnecting the call. "Dex, take FDR Drive." He checked his watch. "Traffic permitting, that'll leave us with just under forty minutes. Haul ass, but don't get us killed."

"TMNT Party Wagon?" Dex said hopefully.

"Seriously? You do realize it's not the eighties. The world has moved on."

Dex beamed brightly. "I know."

"Do you? Because sometimes, I'm not so sure."

"How about just Party Wagon?"

"Yes, damn it!" Sloane was caught between feeling frustrated and wanting to laugh. "Fine. Party Wagon."

Dex let out a loud whoop, hitting the sirens and lights. Something was seriously wrong with Sloane. There had to be. Why else was he continually allowing Dex to name maneuvers and equipment? Especially when it was always a reference to some eighties movie, or God help him, after cartoon turtles. Maybe because arguing with his man-child partner wasn't worth the exhaustion or pouting that resulted from it. God, he'd let the guy name the Suburban after a cartoon truck. "I must be losing my mind."

Dex laughed as he maneuvered through traffic. "Variety is the spice of life."

"Is weed a spice? Because that would explain a lot where you're concerned."

His partner burst into laughter, the sound infectious. Sloane shook his head, his lips pressed together, but he couldn't stop it from bubbling up, and he started laughing. Oh God, the crazy was contagious. He sobered up, wiping a tear from his eye. "We better get our shit together, because if not, your dad's going to kick our asses."

"Welcome to the ranks of every boyfriend I've ever had," Dex said, then seemed to catch onto Sloane's startled expression. His smile fell away. "I didn't mean to imply you were, you know, um…. Forget I said that."

Sloane nodded, his heart feeling as though it was trying to escape from his chest. "It's not that I don't want—"

"Don't worry about it. It was my bad." Dex waved a hand and gave him a sweet smile. "You know me. Sometimes the wires get crossed, and my mouth is quicker than my brain."

"Sometimes?" Sloane teased.

"Dick," Dex said with a chuckle before his expression grew concerned. "You think it's the Order?"

"I don't know, but it makes no sense. They plant a bomb, then call to inform us and give us enough time to get there? Why?"

"Trap?"

Sloane shook his head. "They'd have to know we'd think that. Doesn't make any damn sense. First College Point, now this? What kind of game is Isaac playing?"

The CDC Therian registration office was situated on busy Worth Street across from Thomas Paine Park and surrounded by several other government buildings. One block over was the courthouse where Dex had testified against his Human partner, thus sending his HPF career down the pan and getting him recruited to the THIRDS.

Dex pulled the Suburban up behind the BearCat parked beside the State Office Building a block over, his expression thoughtful. No doubt, his partner was thinking along the same lines. Sloane turned to look at him. "You okay?"

"Yeah. Just thinking about how this is kind of where it all started."

Was Dex wishing he'd never left the HPF? Had his life been better? Sloane couldn't help his frown. By now, Dex would have still been with his old boyfriend Lou, or moved onto someone else, but instead he was stuck with a guy who freaked out over hearing the word "boyfriend." As if sensing his thoughts, Dex quickly spoke up.

"Not that I'm not glad to be here now, with the THIRDS and you. It just would have been nice to get here without all the bruises and threats."

How was it that Dex always knew Sloane needed reassuring without Sloane saying a word? He smiled at Dex, and took Dex's right hand in his, giving it a quick squeeze before letting go. "I'm glad you're here too, Daley. Though if you touch my radio again, you're going to see some more bruising."

"Right, sorry." Dex held his hands up in surrender. "I let the power go to my head."

"Come on, wise guy." Sloane climbed out of the Suburban with Dex following his lead. He knocked on one of the BearCat's back doors, and as soon as they were inside, Sloane took a seat to conserve his energy while Ash handed him his equipment piece by piece, starting with his tac vest. The weight of his equipment was going to be uncomfortable, but he'd simply have to endure it like so many of the other times before. As he clipped pieces of his equipment into place, he noticed Dex head straight for the front of the BearCat and the security console where his brother sat. Without a word, Cael held out a white paper bag that Dex snatched up with a broad smile and a wink. "Thanks, bro."

"No prob."

With a dopey grin, Dex handed the bag over to Sloane. "Here. I had Cael grab you a triple beef burger from the cafeteria."

Sloane took the bag, his voice mirroring his surprise. "You asked him to get me food?"

"Yeah." Dex shrugged as if it was no big deal. "I figured you'd need the boost. You're my partner, right? It's my job to help where I can."

Sloane didn't know what to say. It was true Dex was his partner, and as such, part of his responsibility was providing PSTC, but his responsibility as far as nutrition went ended with Gatorade and protein bars. Dex's job was to get Sloane on his feet. Making certain he recuperated properly, and/or healthily wasn't part of his partner's duty.

Gabe had provided exceptional PSTC, but while at work, he focused on the job, and he expected Sloane to be responsible for himself. With a "thanks," Sloane dug into his burger while Ash played the recording of the phone call put in to 911. Dex finished gearing up and stepped up to the ballistic window with a frown.

"How is no one at the registration office panicking? People are coming in and out as if nothing was going on."

The phone call didn't reveal much other than the caller was obviously using a voice enhancer. This wasn't looking good.

"I don't like this," Ash said. "Something's not right here."

Dex turned to address Cael. "Recon have any luck tracing the call?"

"No. Most likely the call was made using a burner phone."

Sloane finished eating in record time, popped a mint into his mouth, and stood to snatch a ballistic helmet off the wall. He handed it to Dex with a wink, knowing his partner would have pretended he'd forgotten it. "Cael, get a hold of the registration office's security team and get us into their system. I want access to that feed, along with all their security footage."

"You got it." Cael got to work while Sloane addressed the rest of the team.

"Let's get in there and see what the hell's going on. I want that device found." As he said the words, Hobbs grabbed one of the EOD X-Ray kits and handed it to Calvin, another to Ash. He put a hand to one of the weapon's cages and removed the large backpack containing his EOD Packbot. As soon as he'd strapped it to himself, he grabbed another EOD X-Ray kit and held it up to Sloane with a big grin, making Sloane smile. Hobbs loved his toys.

"Okay, let's go." At Sloane's signal, Letty opened the back doors and the team exited the truck, standing by while Maddock faced them.

"Recon agents are here. They're setting up a blockade around the perimeter. We'll keep you all informed. If the Order is responsible for this, I want to know about it. Keep me updated and watch your backs."

CHAPTER 4

LIKE MOST of the surrounding federal buildings, the CDC Therian registration office was a Greek revival style structure made of stone. Above all its center windows were depictions of Greek physicians, along with some Greek style ironwork on its front doors. The building had two entrances, one on Worth Street and the other on Centre Street, with more offices and windows than Sloane cared for.

Destructive Delta hurried to the building, and Sloane cursed under his breath. Goddamn revolving doors. He hated these things. He pounded on the glass on the exit door to the right of it. A confused-looking guard promptly opened it. The guy quickly jumped to one side as Sloane and his team flooded inside. Sloane motioned for Letty to lock up the front doors. The second security guard posted on the other side gave a start. Ash was right. Something was wrong. Normally when someone reported a bomb, people got gone. They didn't linger about looking more confused by the agents coming to answer the call than at the thought of being blown up. The team spread out, investigating the lobby for any possible threats, with expert speed and precision. In less than five minutes, they came back to him.

"We're all clear," Ash stated. Sloane approached the large reception desk ahead of him, and the petite redhead sitting behind it, looking on with wide eyes.

"Can… can I help you?"

Sloane leaned over, taking note of the young woman's nametag. "Ms. Beverly, I need you to listen carefully to me and remain calm. Can you do that?"

The young woman's brown eyes widened even more, but she nodded fervently.

"Good. I need you to start an evacuation procedure immediately. There may be an explosive device in this facility."

"Oh my God," she gasped, snatching up the telephone and hitting a host of blinking buttons as well as one underneath her desk. Sloane turned to his team.

"Letty, Rosa, Dex, you start evacuating the building. Hobbs, Calvin, Ash, find that damned device. Give a shout when you do." His team broke off, and Sloane turned to the numerous security guards flooding out from several directions. "Who's in charge of security?" Sloane asked. A guard in a white and black uniform stepped up.

"I am." He held his hand out to Sloane. "Allan Jeffrey. What's going on?"

"Allan, my name is Agent Sloane Brodie with the THIRDS. We have reason to believe there may be an explosive device inside the building. I need your team to help my guys get everyone out. Also, you should have received a phone call from one of my agents, an Agent Cael Maddock. I want you to give him access to your security network, its feed, and any footage we may require."

"Yes, of course." Allan turned to one of his guards. "Javier, you heard him. Get everyone out, and get Agent Maddock his access."

With Javier running off, Sloane turned his attention back to Allan. "Has anyone unscheduled come in or out of this facility?"

Allan shook his head. "All visitors either have an appointment or have to be cleared by someone in the building. There's a log at the reception desk visitors and employees fill out when they come in or out."

"I'd like to see that list."

Allan gave him a nod and led him to the reception desk where he handed Sloane a tablet. The log had six columns, one for date, name, time, species, company name, and purpose of visit. The majority were registrations, the rest employees. "Allan, can these dates and times be doctored?"

Allan shook his head. "They're automatically inserted by the system to prevent falsification. As soon as a name is submitted, the system logs the time."

"Excellent." One less thing to worry about. He scanned the list of names when one jumped out at him. A Therian registrant under the name Zeph Hyacinth. Why did that strike him as odd? He tapped his earpiece. "Cael?"

"Cael, here."

"Can you search the National Therian Database for the name Zeph Hyacinth?"

"Sure."

Sloane lifted his head in time to watch dozens of citizens come rushing out of the emergency stairwells, ushered by his team. Dex's voice rang clear above the others.

"Please exit in an orderly fashion. We're here with you, so no need to panic. That's it, follow my colleague, she'll guide you. Ma'am, please, you can come back for your belongings later, I promise, but right now your safety is far more important to me. Thank you, I appreciate your cooperation. Sir, just breathe. It's okay. Take my arm. Old? Haven't you heard? Seventy's the new fifty. Do I? Well, your grandson must be a handsome devil, then."

Sloane held back a smile. Rookie was a natural. Seconds later, Cael came back on the line. "No one under that name, no new registrants either. Themis did give me a different kind of hit on it, though. It's weird."

"What is it?"

"A Greek myth."

"What?"

"Hyacinth was lover to the god Apollo. According to one version of the tale, the West Wind, Zephyr, was also in love with Hyacinth, and in his jealousy at having Hyacinth choose Apollo over him, he blew Apollo's discus off course so it struck Hyacinth, and he died from his injuries. There's more detail, but that's the gist of it."

"That son of a bitch." Sloane gritted his teeth and took a deep breath. The bastard was taunting him.

"What does—" Cael gasped. "Oh. You're Apollo."

"Yes," Sloane replied through his teeth. And Gabe was Hyacinth. He turned to Allan, pointing to the name on the tablet. "I want to see all the footage you have on this appointment here. We're looking for a Caucasian Human male, midthirties, five-ten, one hundred and seventy pounds, light brown hair. The time beside his name is showing 2:13 p.m."

"Follow me."

Sloane stepped into a medium-sized security office behind and to the right of the reception area. It contained a wall-to-wall security console with an expansive flat screen monitor. As Allan accessed the security network searching for the footage they needed, Sloane tapped his earpiece. "Team, updates."

Rosa's voice came over his earpiece. "All top levels are clear. We're emptying out the lobby now."

"Copy that. Guys, how are we doing on that device?"

Calvin was the first to answer. "We've cleared the lobby and first floor. Ash cleared the second and third floors and is heading for the fourth. Hobbs and I are taking the stairs up to the sixth floor. There are a lot of places this thing can be. The closest substance we've gotten a read on is acetone, but that was from someone's bottle of nail polish remover. We'll let you know soon as we get something."

"Okay." Sloane turned to Allan who brought up the security footage from the timeframe they needed. The moment Sloane saw the bastard, his gut tightened. He'd lightened his hair and grown it out so it looked shaggy, the front almost falling over his eyes. He was dressed in tattered but fashionable jeans, expensive sneakers, a football hoodie, and carried a designer messenger bag. The whole ensemble had him resembling a college jock more than the maniac the THIRDS had put an APB out on, which Sloane suspected was Isaac's intent. "That's him right there. Let's see where he goes." He watched as Isaac signed in, smiling and flirting with the receptionist. She pointed to the elevator behind her on the right side of the lobby, and with a wink, he headed for it. Again, Sloane tapped his earpiece.

"It was Isaac. I've got eyes on him. He stepped into the elevator closest to the reception area, right side. I'm waiting to see what floor he gets off on." A few minutes later, Isaac stepped off on the seventh. "He got off on the seventh floor. He's carrying a messenger bag. My guess is the bomb's in there."

"We're heading to the elevator. What room does he go into?" Calvin asked.

"Hold on." Sloane watched the color screen as Isaac leisurely strolled down the hall as if he was in no kind of hurry. He opened his messenger bag, pulled out a tablet, and tapped away. Ten minutes later, he put the tablet away and headed for the end of the hall. Sloane tapped his earpiece, ready to give his team the location, when Isaac turned around and went back to the elevator. "What the hell?"

"What is it?" Calvin asked. "Sloane, we're running out of time."

"He turned around and went back down." As Isaac walked through the lobby, he took out a cellphone, said a few words, smiled, and left. What in the living fuck? Why would he ride the elevator to the seventh floor just to ride it back down, and leave? Sloane wracked his brain. The guy was smart. He was also an ex-detective. "Dex?"

"Yeah?"

"I need you in here."

Seconds later, Dex entered the room. "What happened?"

"If you were going to place a bomb inside a building knowing you were being watched. Where would you place it? He rode the elevator up to the seventh floor, walked around some, working on a tablet, then came back down, placed a phone call, and left."

Dex worried his bottom lip in thought. "I'd put it somewhere the cameras couldn't follow me."

Allan pursed his lips. "Only places with no security are the bathrooms and the elevators."

"The elevator," Dex said immediately. "They all have access panels, right? For maintenance? It's an oldie but goodie. Why try to reinvent the wheel?"

Sloane nodded. "Calvin—"

"We're enabling the elevator and calling it up now."

Sloane turned to Allan. "Can you get eyes on my team?"

"Sure thing."

They watched Calvin and Hobbs enter the elevator, the position of the camera outside in the corridor giving them an angled view. It wasn't perfect, but it was enough. Calvin hit the emergency stop, and the elevator's alarm went off, its doors remaining open. As soon as he stepped inside, Calvin's voice confirmed their fears.

"I got a read. It's somewhere close."

Allan thankfully terminated the shrilling beeping, and Sloane gave him a nod in thanks. He checked his watch. "Ten minutes. Come on, guys."

Hobbs's height allowed him to reach up, and he pushed open one of the access panels situated on the roof of the stainless steel elevator. He removed the Packbot and placed it on the floor to one side before he propped one booted foot on the railing. They all cringed along with Calvin. Sloane sure as hell hoped those things were strong enough to take the weight of Hobbs's nearly 300-pound frame. Sometimes being a Therian of that size had its drawbacks. Like when it involved small spaces or climbing flimsy structures. Hobbs tested the rail's strength before hauling himself up, his upper body disappearing through the opening in the roof and his other booted foot resting on the opposite handrail.

Calvin's stern voice confirmed their fears. "Hobbs found it."

"All right. Destructive Delta, fall back. Calvin, that includes you." With Calvin and Hobbs up on the large screen, Sloane gave Allan a pat on the shoulder. "You've been a great help, Allan. I need you to get yourself and your team out. If you wouldn't mind speaking to Agent Rosa Santiago outside; she'll take your statement."

"Sloane, the bomb's been deactivated."

"What?" Sloane turned to the screen. Hobbs was climbing back down. He held a thumb up to the camera. "Talk to me. That seemed too easy."

"Because it was," Calvin said, heading toward the stairwell with Hobbs close behind. "According to Hobbs, there were no antihandling devices, motion sensors, overrides, kill switches, or anything that might trigger the explosion, just the one wire to the power supply. None of this makes any sense."

"Thanks, guys. Get the disposal team up here." Giving his final thanks to Allan, Sloane headed out with Dex beside him. He tapped his earpiece. "Sarge?"

"Yeah, I heard. As soon as Disposal gets here, we're heading back to HQ, to see if we can't figure this shit out. I don't know what the hell is going on, and I don't like it. Lieutenant Sparks is going to like it even less."

"Copy that." Sloane removed his helmet, chucking it into the back of the truck in frustration before he climbed in, Dex behind him. "This asshole's jerking us around."

"Yeah, but the question is why?" Dex removed his helmet and dropped down onto the bench as the rest of the team climbed in. "He's got to have something bigger up his sleeve."

Sloane agreed. There was no telling what Isaac was up to and worse than not knowing was the fear of not being able to do anything about it.

"ALL RIGHT, let's run through this again."

Dex tapped files open on his desk's interface, and Sloane had to hand it to the guy; his partner was determined.

They'd been at this for hours since returning from the CDC registration office, and they were no closer to figuring any of it out now than they had been at the time of the call, yet Dex persisted. Sloane admired his partner's dedication, and went along with it. "Okay. Thanks to you and Simon, we figured out the base at College Point was a distraction to keep us busy, though at the time, we didn't know from what. Now we do. While we were there, Isaac was carrying out his plan at the registration office.

"He came out of hiding to plant a bomb in that specific office. Why, we don't know. He puts in a call, gives us enough time to get there and disarm it. The bomb itself was a quick job. Yes, it could have resulted in casualties had we not disarmed it in time, but he gave us plenty of it. He taunts me by using the name Zeph Hyacinth, knowing

I'll catch onto it and find out what it means. He knew we'd bring up the surveillance footage. So he signs in at reception, heads to the elevator, plants the bomb, walks around a bit, takes the elevator back down, and leaves. We've established the phone call he made on camera is the one placed to 911."

Dex ran a hand over his face and sat back, his frown in full force. "I would have thought it was a trap, except it wasn't. What the hell was the point? I mean, don't get me wrong, I'm extremely relieved it went that smoothly, but why bother? To taunt us? To piss us off?" He shook his head. "That dick. I can't believe I was friends with the guy."

"He fooled us all, Dex." Sloane watched Dex lean over his desk and tap away, bringing up Morelli's file for the hundredth time that week. "Obsessing over that file isn't going to add any more information to it." His partner was frustrated. Sloane understood that. He was too, but after many years of fieldwork, there was only so much you could do with the information you had until something new came up. Staring at the same files over and over wasn't going to make the case move any quicker.

The majority of Unit Alpha was working on this case, but unfortunately, information trickled down to Defense agents last, unless they came across the info themselves. Intel and Recon did the brunt of the investigating while Defense provided support and waited to be called out. Their objective was to employ special tactics in an effort to preserve life and apprehend dangerous suspects, often resulting in the use of weapons and aggressive maneuvers. Yes, they collected information along the way, interrogated suspects, and kept a clear channel of communication open with Recon, but in the end, Defense agents were the muscle, following orders and procedure. It was an aspect of the job his partner was finding difficult to accept. Sloane could see Dex going into "detective mode" every time he opened a file. It made him once again question whether Dex would be happier in Recon. He quickly pushed that thought aside.

"You're right," Sloane said, focusing on the task at hand. "It's good to talk through it. What have you got?"

"We know Morelli accessed his THIRDS file before he was killed, most likely under duress, since he signed in on his personal laptop. It's clear Isaac didn't get what he wanted and killed him. What was he looking for?"

"I don't know. Morelli tried to log in to Themis, but he would have known he didn't have access. Only Team Leaders and those with higher clearance levels have offsite access. Isaac wouldn't have known that. Maybe Morelli was buying himself more time."

Dex nodded somberly. "Other than that, I can't come up with any other reason Isaac would have picked Morelli. According to his file, the guy was a regular Lupus Therian agent. He was single, had a few girlfriends, and worked Defense before he moved to Recon. Do you know why he was moved?"

There had been rumors, but Sloane never relied on hearsay. Like any other organization, the THIRDS wasn't completely void of office politics or gossip. He gave Dex a shrug. "Something about his health. I think it got too stressful for him. That's not the first time it's happened to a Defense agent. Everyone wants to be on Defense until someone tries to blow them up."

"Glamor comes with a hefty price, huh?"

"Yep. A hefty price, a load of flying bullets, and bears."

Dex opened his mouth, and Sloane held a hand up. He knew his partner too well by now. "Not those kind of bears. Actual bears, with claws and sharp teeth." Though now that he thought about it, some Bear Therians were probably uh, bears. Trent from Unit Beta certainly was.

"My kind of bears are more fun," Dex replied with a wink, before his gaze shifted back to the file, his eyes widening. "Shit."

Sloane straightened. "What is it?"

Dex swiped his hand across his desk's surface, sending the file onto Sloane's desk and his connected interface. "Obviously we wouldn't have thought anything of it before, but look, under the 'History' section."

"Shit." Sloane stared at the familiar words. "No way in hell that's a coincidence." He tapped his earpiece. "Sarge, we found something."

Seconds later, Maddock came storming into the office, his nostrils flaring. "Give me good news, Sloane. I get one more call from the Chief of Therian Defense asking me for an update on this case, I'm gonna get an ulcer. We had video conference twice in a span of twenty minutes. What the hell was he expecting to happen in twenty minutes while I'm at the goddamn office? Other than exacerbate my growing desire to take his tacky-ass paisley tie, roll it up, and shove it up his—"

"Whoa!" Dex sprang to his feet and gave Maddock a gentle pat on the shoulder. "Easy there, Sarge. Your blood pressure's gonna go through the roof at this rate. Not to mention you've got a few new additions already," Dex said, putting a finger to Maddock's salt and pepper stubble. Sloane tried his hardest to keep himself from laughing when Maddock smacked Dex's hand away, glaring at him.

"Boy, are you crazy? I am royally pissed off, and you're telling me I've got more gray hair? Who the hell do you think gave them to me in the first place?"

Dex blinked at him innocently. "Cael?"

Maddock pressed his lips together and turned away to address Sloane. "Please, tell me you've got something before I strangle your partner."

Sloane couldn't help his chuckle. "Looks like you're going to have to leave the strangling for some other time, because it was actually Dex who found it."

Maddock glanced at Dex, groaning at his son's dopey grin. When Dex wriggled his eyebrows, Maddock planted his hand on Dex's face. Sloane cringed. Bad move. Maddock snapped his hand back as if he'd been burned by acid, clutching it to his broad chest. His frown deepened before he wiped his hand on his pants and shook his head at Dex who was still grinning. "There is something seriously wrong with you."

With a laugh, Dex dropped down onto his seat behind his desk. "I love you too."

An unintelligible growl later, Maddock nodded for Sloane to continue.

"As I was saying, Dex was looking over Morelli's file, and noticed Morelli was registered at the same CDC registration office where Isaac planted the bomb. Before today, it wouldn't have meant much, but now...."

"Now, it means he chose that office for a reason." Maddock rubbed a hand over his stubble as he considered this new information.

"Isaac planted the bomb in the elevator because he knew it didn't have cameras. Could he have done something else while in there?"

Sloane brought up the footage of Isaac at the registration office. They watched him get into the elevator and emerge a few minutes later. "I know it'd take a while to get to the seventh floor, but either this elevator is really slow, or he stopped it."

"Well, we know he was planting the bomb," Dex offered.

Something still seemed off. "True, but considering the explosive he used, all he had to do was open the access panel, plant the bomb, and flip the switch. Sarge, you might be onto something. What if he'd been doing something else? We don't even know he planted the bomb when he rode the elevator. There's no security in there. For all we know, he could have planted the bomb earlier, or had someone else plant it, and then activated it. Or maybe he had time to plant it and do whatever else he went there to do."

"Okay, all good theories," Maddock said. "So now what? Hold on a second." Maddock tapped the desk's surface, pausing the video. "What's he doing there on that tablet?"

"Cael already tried zooming in, but it's too fuzzy. We can't tell what he's doing," Dex replied with a frown. "Whatever it is, he removed the tablet from his bag after he got off from the elevator."

Sloane tapped his earpiece. "Cael?"

"Yeah?"

"We need Allan Jeffrey to grant Themis access to their security system. I want an algorithm set up to see if there's any additional footage of Isaac Pearce entering that building before today or anyone acting suspicious. It's possible the bomb could have been planted beforehand, and if not, I want to know what else Isaac was doing in that elevator. I also want Themis to run a scan on their network for any unauthorized access to their files. If Isaac didn't get what he wanted from Morelli's file, and he was registered at that office, he might have been looking for something there. Find out if Morelli has a file at that CDC office."

"Copy that."

Maddock looked thoughtful. "You think Isaac went in there looking for more information on Morelli?"

Right now, they didn't know much of anything, only that Morelli was somehow connected to all this. "We know he didn't get anything from Morelli's THIRDS file, and the guy was registered at that office. I don't understand his obsession with Morelli."

Cael's voice came in over their earpieces. "Sloane? Dex?"

"Go ahead, Cael."

"Allan says he'll get right on it, but he won't have anything before tomorrow morning. The place is crawling with CDC bigwigs. They're freaking out about security after what happened today. Obviously, they're looking to put someone's head on the chopping block."

"I appreciate that, but we really need him to get that info over to us as soon as he can, or at least grant us access so Intel can do it. If the bureaucrats are getting in the way, tell him to let us know, and I'll send Ash down there to throw his weight around."

"Will do."

"In the meantime…." Sloane gave Maddock his most charming smile. "Can you send over a glowing letter of appreciation to Allan and his security team for their exceptional and invaluable help during today's incident?"

Maddock was onto him, and he nodded with a knowing smile. "I'll get on that now. As soon as you find anything else out, you let me know immediately." He started to leave, then paused, jutting a finger at him. "And get a haircut."

"Yes, sir." Sloane gave him a salute. Damn. That meant he had at least another week before he had to get it cut. He hated getting his hair cut. His gaze went to Dex who was grinning at him.

"What?"

"You're so cute, sending a letter so Allan and his team don't get canned."

Sloane hoped his face wasn't as red as it felt. "Allan and his team did great. They don't deserve to lose their jobs because a bunch of pencil pushers need someone to blame. I mean you saw how many guards there were for a building that size, and with everything else going on, it's clear they'd made cutbacks. Security's always the first department to suffer. While poor Allan joins the ranks of the unemployed, some asshole buys a second house on the coast of France."

Dex leaned forward, his voice gruff and sexy. "Ooh, do I hear a little anti-establishment in your tone, Agent Brodie?"

With a chuckle, Sloane came to sit at the edge of Dex's desk. He leaned forward to whisper, "Does that turn you on, Agent Daley?"

Dex gave a snort. "That would imply there are moments when I'm not turned on. Okay, well, in this job there actually are moments when I'm not, but if our lives aren't in danger and you're around, it's a safe bet I've got a stiffy."

Sloane arched an eyebrow at him.

"Okay, sometimes even when we are in danger."

"That so?"

"You gripping an MP5 submachine gun, sweat dripping down your face, your tac pants pulled tight over your ass when you crouch down? Fuck, I'm getting hard thinking about it. Come on, man. I'm positioned behind you in formation, and you think my mind's not going to go there? It's your own fault."

"Jesus, Dex. We're at the office!" Sloane hissed.

"You asked."

Sloane shifted uncomfortably, his pants tighter than they'd been a moment ago. "Yeah, but… now you've got me… you know."

"So…."

"So what?" Sloane eyed him warily. "Are you suggesting what I think you're suggesting? Because we're in the middle of a case."

Dex's pale blue eyes clouded, the heat in them going straight to Sloane's dick. "We are in the middle of a case. A case with intel that won't come in until tomorrow morning, or tonight at the earliest."

Sloane swallowed hard. "Ten minutes?"

Dex grinned wickedly. "Ten minutes." He stood, his fingers brushing Sloane's thigh as he walked past.

This was insane. Sloane couldn't believe he was doing this at work. He'd never done anything with Gabe at work, not even sneak a kiss. Then again, Gabe had been a stickler for the rules, too afraid of what would happen if they'd been caught. Dex… well, Dex was a terrible, sexy—fuck, he was sexy—influence. Then again, the only time their sergeant ever suspected something was amiss was when Dex wasn't up to his shenanigans.

If Dex wasn't eating snacks when he shouldn't be, or singing in the showers, or bugging Ash, or Cael, or anyone with a pulse, Rosa was whipping out her thermometer and taking his temperature, convinced he was coming down with something. Two days ago, Dex had been straining his little blond head trying to work out a riddle Sloane had given him, and the whole floor almost went into lockdown from panic due to his prolonged silence. Their Medical Chief, Hudson, had gone so far as to insist he examine Dex, though now that Sloane thought about it, he was pretty sure Hudson might have been taking advantage of the situation. The guy was always eyeing Dex's ass.

Sloane waited five minutes then casually slipped out of the office, heading for the moderately sized lunchroom on their floor. After greeting the half a dozen or so agents who were in there, he tapped the blue numbers on one of the vending machine's smart screens. A candy bar dropped down into the tray. Sloane swiped it up and tucked it into his front breast pocket. Exactly four minutes and thirty seconds later, he was using his keycard to access his personally assigned sleeping bay.

What the hell was he doing? This was insane. This was—

Two taps on the door exactly thirty-one seconds later.

Sloane opened the door, his abdomen tightening at the sight of Dex standing there, mischief and lust in his eyes.

"You're late," Sloane said, letting him in and locking the door behind him.

"Looks like you'll have to discipline me."

Okay. He could do this. "Get on the bed and unzip."

"Yes, sir." Dex sat on the bed, kicked his feet up, unzipped his pants, whipped out his dick, and finished off by lying with his hands behind his head, a dopey grin on his face. The cocky bastard. Before Sloane could talk himself out of it, he crossed the room, and straddled Dex, their lips meeting together in a hot and needy kiss. Dex wriggling beneath him, hands on Sloane's fly, nearly made him forget his concerns. Nearly. Sloane made certain to remain alert while kissing

Dex, letting out a low groan when Dex pulled at Sloane's hardening cock.

With a nip to Dex's bottom lip, making his partner groan, Sloane rolled onto his side. He motioned down toward the other end of the bed, his blood drumming through his veins, filling his cock at the sight of Dex's tongue poking out to lick his bottom lip. "Get down there and be quiet. The walls are insulated, but I don't want to take any chances."

Dex's enthusiastic nod almost made Sloane laugh, until he was forced to throw an arm up to keep himself from getting kicked in the face as Dex scrambled to turn his body around. The man was a disaster, nearly falling off the bed in the process. Sloane threw an arm out, grabbed him by the belt, and yanked him down so his cock was in front of Sloane's face.

"You're damn lucky you're pretty, Daley," Sloane growled quietly.

"Aw, you think I'm pretty?"

"Shut up and suck my dick."

"You're lucky you're damn sexy," Dex countered, inhaling sharply and bucking when Sloane closed a hand over Dex's cock and squeezed. "Sweet Jesus."

"Yeah, less talking, more sucking." He let out a low hiss at the feel of Dex's hand on him.

"Anyone ever tell you you're bossy?"

"I'm sorry, I was under the impression we came here for blow jobs and not to discuss my people skills." Dex's hot mouth enveloping him put a stop to both their grousing, and Sloane returned the favor, taking Dex down to the root. He closed his eyes, humming around Dex's cock, sucking, licking, and trying his damn hardest to keep himself in control.

Dex dug his fingers into Sloane's ass cheeks, his gorgeous mouth making it difficult for Sloane to concentrate on what he was doing. Damn, the guy knew how to drive him over the edge. As excruciating pressure began to build up inside Sloane, he quickened his pace, his hand on Dex's hips to keep him still. He loved the taste of Dex, and he expressed it as best he could, his tongue circling the head, pressing into Dex's slit, making Dex buck. Dex hummed around him in warning, and

Sloane doubled his efforts, sucking him harder and faster until Dex stiffened before he came in Sloane's mouth. He swallowed, his muscles tightening as the heat spread, and with a low moan, he shot his load into Dex's mouth.

Sloane gently pulled off Dex, and as soon as Dex did the same, Sloane rolled onto his back, his breath coming out heavy. Damn, that was good. He lay there for a moment, staring at the ceiling. The bed moved, and Sloane held back a smile at Dex snuggling up close, his arm around Sloane's waist. Sloane's hand found Dex's hair, and he absently ran his fingers through the dirty blond locks, a smile breaking through. After a few heartbeats, Sloane nudged his partner.

"We need to go before someone comes looking for either of us."

Dex let out a groan, but rolled over and got up, unaware of Sloane watching him tuck himself back in. He zipped up and straightened out his clothes and hair. Damn, he was cute. Pale blue eyes shifted up and Dex cocked his head to one side, that brilliant smile stealing Sloane's breath away.

"What?"

Sloane shook his head. "Nothing." He got up and sorted himself out before pulling Dex into his arms, delivering a kiss to his head. "Come on." He didn't know where the tenderness came from, and he refused to dwell on it. He made his way to the door, and with Dex out of sight behind him, Sloane peeked out of the room. At his signal, Dex slipped out and Sloane followed, closing the door behind him. They quickly made their way to the end of the hall, slowing down to a casual stroll when they reached the corner.

They walked past the male locker room when Ash stepped in front of them, scaring the hell out them. Lucky for them, Ash was too annoyed to notice their less than innocent reaction.

"Where the hell were you two?"

Sloane and Dex produced a candy bar from their front breast pockets in unison, answering simultaneously, "Lunchroom."

Ash looked genuinely horrified. "You two are spending way too much time together. Seriously, that was creepy as fuck." He snatched their candy bars. "For the psychological trauma you've just inflicted."

Dex pouted. "Hey, I was gonna save that for the next briefing."

"Briefings are not snack time." Ash crowded Dex, who looked genuinely perplexed.

"But…. How else am I supposed to get through them?"

"I don't know, by paying attention? I can't believe Lieutenant Sparks lets you get away with it."

Sloane pushed himself between the two. Well, there was little pushing involved. He only had to slip a hand between them, and Dex took a step back. Sometimes it surprised Sloane how responsive Dex was to his every touch. Even when the guy was focused on something else, he always seemed to be aware of Sloane and his movements. "All right you two, that's enough. What did you want, Ash?"

"We're going to Bar Dekatria tonight. Cael says if one more Intel guy calls him to add another algorithm to the case, he's going to lose it and take everyone with him." Ash chuckled. "You should have seen him. He got all red in the face and started stomping around. At one point he got so mad, he knocked over someone's empty soda can."

"Did he pick it right up and apologize profusely?" Dex asked with a grin.

"It's Cael. Of course he did. Then he offered to buy the guy a new one."

Dex shook his head with a laugh. "You should have seen him when he was a kid, and he'd get pissed off in his Therian form, chirping all over the place, his little cheetah fuzz at the top of his head sticking up. It was adorable."

Ash actually laughed along with Dex. It fascinated Sloane how the two were always arguing, annoying the hell out of one another or wishing fiery pain upon each other, except when it concerned Cael. Then they were a couple of mother hens, clucking away over their little chick. It was sweet, and at times, frightening, especially where Ash was concerned. If it weren't for Cael, Sloane would never have guessed his friend possessed any kind of nurturing instinct. Something moved behind Ash and Sloane coughed into his hand. When that didn't work, he elbowed Dex, only to be once again ignored.

"Guys," Sloane warned.

"What are you two talking about?"

Ash and Dex stopped abruptly, both turning to Cael who stood there, a deep frown on his boyish face. Dex waved cheerfully. "Hey, little brother."

Cael folded his arms over his chest. "You were talking about me, weren't you?"

"Us? No." Dex's grin got wider.

"You're a shitty liar. I'm not in the mood for you, Dex. Stupid Intel with their stupid algorithms, and their stupid stupidness." Cael sighed, looking embarrassed. "I'm sorry. They're not stupid." He looked up at them with a pout. "What?"

Dex threw his arms around Cael's neck, petting his head and murmuring softly. "You're so precious. So, so precious."

"Get off." Cael pushed Dex away from him. "So are we going to Dekatria tonight or what? I need alcohol."

"Of course we are," Ash replied, throwing an arm around Cael's shoulders. "First drink's on me. What do you say?"

Cael perked up. "I say awesome!"

"Hey, I'm cute, too," Dex protested as they followed Ash and Cael to the bullpen. "Why don't I get a free drink?"

Ash flipped him off, calling out over his shoulder, "You're not cute, Daley."

"Screw you. I'm fucking adorable!"

Sloane leaned into Dex, whispering. "I think you're cute."

Dex smiled at him and batted his lashes. "Do I get a free drink?"

"No."

"Damn." Dex craned his neck and waved his arms. "Hey, Rosa! I have to ask you something." He ran off and Sloane chuckled, hearing Dex calling out after her. "Where are you going? I want to ask you if you think I'm cute. You do, right? Rosa?"

Well tonight should be interesting to say the least.

CHAPTER 5

Scratch that. This wasn't going to be an interesting night. It was going to be horrifying.

"Oh no." Sloane tried pushing Cael back out the bar's entrance, but Rosa and Letty were crowded around him with Hobbs blocking the doorway. "Get out. Everyone out!"

"Why?" Cael stood on his toes, trying to peer around Ash and Sloane.

Damn it, there was no time. "Just get out—go, go, go." He grabbed Ash's arm, hissing in his ear. "Threat Level Fuchsia. Fuchsia!"

Ash's eyes widened and he turned to usher everyone back out. "Shit. Everyone out before—"

"What?" Dex swept past them, God knew how, slowing when he saw what Sloane had been trying so hard to avoid. He turned and threw his arms up with a loud "whoop" in victory, followed by a sing-song, "Karaoke night!"

Ash delivered a punch to Sloane's arm. "What the fuck, man? You couldn't have said something sooner?"

"Damn it, Ash." Sloane rubbed his arm, glaring at his best friend. "I didn't see the equipment until it was too late." He returned Ash's punch to the arm. "You're the one who wanted to come here."

"I didn't know they'd started doing that shit. Now what?"

"Now we get drunk. He's already checking out the playlist. It's too late."

Ash thought about it for a moment. "We could knock him out."

"That's your answer to everything isn't it?" Sloane lowered his voice to mimic Ash's growl. "Dex is singing in the shower, you want me to knock him out? Dex is eating gummy bears during the briefing, you want me to knock him out? Dex is napping during the assembly, you want me to knock him out?" Sloane shook his head. "How can you knock him out if he's already out!"

"Chill, man. Don't get your fucking panties in a bunch. I suggest you skip the beer and go straight to the vodka." Ash strolled over to the bar and held a finger out to signal one of the barmen. "Also I could have woken him up and then knocked him out. Just saying."

Sloane chose to ignore his friend, offering a noncommittal grunt when Bradley, the handsome Therian bartender with an armful of tattoos and tight black T-shirt, greeted him with his cheerful smile. Bar Dekatria was a Therian and Human friendly bar that had quickly become a team favorite, especially for Dex. It was less than a fifteen-minute drive from THIRDS HQ. The place was tastefully decorated in a classy retro-style with rich dark woods, dark accents, a black, tufted leather bar, and leather seating, and had a spacious dance floor opposite the bar that Dex always managed to hijack along with his male and female groupies once he'd had a few drinks in him. The guy was a total lightweight when it came to booze.

"What'll it be, Sloane? Beer? Or my 'It's Going to be One of Those Nights' special?" Bradley leaned on the bar, his eyes sparkling with mischief. By now, Bradley had come to know Sloane and his team pretty well, and he had a bad habit of finding Dex amusing, among other things. The bartender had no sympathy for Sloane whatsoever. Bastard.

Sloane shook his head pitifully. "Karaoke night? Really? How could you do this to me?"

Bradley let out a pleasant laugh. "I'm sorry."

"No you're not," Sloane muttered. "You just want to see him shake his ass."

"He's actually a good singer. At least this time he'll have lyrics to follow when he's too drunk to remember them. Besides, who doesn't want to see your boy shake his ass?" Bradley gave him a wink and called out over his shoulder as he walked away. "I'll get you that special."

Bradley seemed to have gotten it in his head a few months ago that Sloane and Dex were meant to be together. Little did he know, they already were. Sort of. Sloane tried not to put a name to whatever it was he and Dex shared. All he knew was that for all his griping and grumbling, he liked being with Dex. He liked who he was around him, liked how Dex made him feel, and the sex was damn hot. Things were good between them. That was enough for him.

"Here you go."

Sloane lifted the tall shot glass with the foggy concoction, a mix Bradley had put together just for him. "Should I be worried you refuse to tell me what's in this?"

The speakers came on, along with the small stage's spotlights. Crap. It was starting. He threw back the shot and shook off the sweet, tangy taste before placing it on the bar's sleek black surface. "Better give me one more," he wheezed. "And a beer." A minute later, Bradley returned with his order, and Sloane made quick work of the shot. He thanked Bradley before making his way over to the small cluster of tables his team occupied in front of the stage Dex was walking up to. His partner took the microphone, that cheeky thousand-watt smile aimed at the growing crowd.

"Hi there," he said, his voice throaty. The regulars who were already familiar with his antics cheered and applauded. Wherever his team went, Dex seemed to pick up a fan following. Something about the guy fascinated Humans and Therians alike. Sloane was still trying to work out what it was. Especially since the guy was… well, kinda weird. Then again, crazy had a way of attracting crazy.

"For those of you who don't know me, I'm Agent Dexter J. Daley, but you can call me Dex when I'm not on duty. I am literally, licensed to kill." He held a hand up to stifle the cheering. "Don't let that scare you. That's just the day job. At night, I'm—" Dex grinned wide and wriggled his brows. "—licensed to thrill."

Sloane covered his face with his hand and groaned. He should have had at least two more of Bradley's "specials." Maybe three. No, four. Oh, sweet Jesus, what had he gotten himself into?

"That's my team. Say hello, team."

Sloane peeked through his fingers, watching Letty, Rosa, Cael, and Calvin wave enthusiastically, receiving a round of applause and catcalls. Hobbs ducked his head in an attempt to hide behind Calvin, and Ash looked pissed. Nothing new there.

"Yeah, they're pretty awesome," Dex added. "Especially that guy there. Agent Keeler. He is the biggest, squishiest teddy bear you'll ever know."

Sloane burst out laughing, much to Ash's annoyance. His friend let out a low growl, his murderous glare on Dex, who smiled wider. "Kidding. He's an asshole. But, next to him is my partner and Team Leader, Agent Brodie. Say hello, Agent Brodie."

Although it wasn't said, it was in Sloane's expression. *I'm going to kill you.*

"He's shy," Dex said, removing the microphone from its stand. "This one's for you, partner."

"Oh, dear God." *He wasn't…. He wouldn't….* Sloane sat mortified. The piano started on a power ballad. *He would.* Sloane groaned when he recognized the song. "Oh God. It's Journey. He's going to sing Journey." Dex owned every Journey album imaginable and was always driving him nuts with those damn songs. He recognized this one. "Faithfully."

Rosa and Letty swayed with the music, whooping, and waving their arms in time to the ballad. Ash's glare was deadly. "Really?"

"Leave the guy alone. He's a good singer, and unlike some grumpy jackasses, he knows how to have fun." Rosa didn't bother looking at Ash, whose frown deepened.

"You're saying I don't know how to have fun?"

Rosa rolled her eyes. "There are other ways to have fun that don't involve shooting things."

"I agree, but you and your girlfriend keep turning me down."

"*Cabron*," Rosa muttered under her breath, smiling brightly at Dex who returned her smile with an added wink.

Ash shook his head, his expression one of disbelief. "I don't get it, man. How can Butt-Boy have more game with women than me?"

Sloane turned to look at Ash, his expression deadpan. "It's a mystery."

"Fuck you and your boy toy."

That made Sloane laugh. "How are they not falling at your feet? Clearly there's a conspiracy at work here."

Ash glowered at him, his bottom lip jutting out tragically. "He's turning you against me."

Cael patted his bicep, reassuring him sweetly. "I think you've got game."

"You do?" Ash perked up and flipped Sloane off. "Cael thinks I've got game, so you can bite me. Keep it up and you're getting demoted from BFF to BF."

Sloane held back a smile and saluted him with his beer. "Duly noted."

Cael hung his head in shame. "He's doing the grabbing air thing."

It wasn't so much the grabbing air thing that made Sloane cringe as the lyrics harping on about love affairs and strangers falling in love again. Why the hell did Dex have to look at Sloane when he sang? Sloane tried not to fidget in his seat, pretending the lyrics didn't mean anything, or that Dex's throaty singing didn't go straight to his dick. His jeans were starting to get uncomfortable.

"Aw, he's serenading you," Ash teased.

Sloane gave him a daggered look. "Fuck off."

My God, when will it end? How long was this damn song? He snuck a peek at the rest of the audience, a good deal of whom were swaying and gazing dreamily at Dex. How the hell did the guy do that? Okay, so maybe he could sing, and he did know how to move. Damn, but he knew how to move. Dex was dressed in his usual black and white Chucks, a pair of scruffy jeans, a gray T-shirt with aviators hanging off the chain from his dog tags, and a black leather jacket. Damn, okay, the guy was fucking sexy. His dirty blond hair was ruffled, his jaw stubbly, he had a smile that was slightly crooked and dopey, and an infectious laugh. He could be as perceptive and sweet as he was frustrating and over the top.

"Hey, Sloane."

Sloane snapped himself out of it, his gaze shifting warily to Ash. "What?"

"Your gay is showing."

"Screw you." He snatched Ash's beer. "Just for that, this is mine now." Stupid Ash. Maybe Sloane was spending too much time with Dex and his brother; he was starting to sound like Cael. Ash leaned over, though for what purpose, Sloane had no idea, considering he didn't bother lowering his voice.

"Admit it, you'd hit that."

"That's a stupid question," Letty pitched in with a snort. "Who wouldn't hit that?"

Rosa perked up, turning to her friend. "Letty. Fuck, marry, kill."

This night just got better and better. Onstage, Dex was singing away, playing to the crowd, and now his team was going to start playing the worst game ever. Maybe Sloane could slip away, pretend he was going to the bathroom, and run. He considered it, until Letty offered her choices.

"Too easy. Fuck Sloane, marry Dex, kill Ash," Letty said.

Sloane's embarrassment was superseded by Ash's expression of disbelief. "Wow. Thanks, partner."

Letty shrugged. "Rosa?"

Rosa took a sip of her beer, considering her choices carefully. "If I was into cock? I'd totally fuck Dex, marry Hobbs, and kill Ash."

"Seriously?" Ash threw his hands up, and Sloane tried not to laugh. The girls didn't bother. Poor Hobbs went red in the face to the tips of his ears, and Rosa gave him a wink. For a moment, Sloane thought Hobbs was going to run. Like hell he was. Not without taking Sloane with him.

"Calvin?" Letty asked.

Their blond friend toyed with his beer coaster. "Um…."

Letty gave him a playful slap in the arm. "Come on, Cal, it's only a game. Besides, you and Hobbs act like an old married couple anyway."

Calvin scratched his head, looking embarrassed. "Okay, uh, I guess fuck Dex, marry Hobbs, and kill Ash."

"I hate all of you," Ash grunted, his beefy arms folded over his chest as he leaned back in his chair. Letty ignored him and moved on.

"Hobbs?"

Hobbs whispered in Calvin's ear, and Calvin's face went as red as his partner's. "Um, same for Hobbs. Fuck Dex, marry me, kill Ash."

"You too, bro?" Ash shook his head at Hobbs who gave him an apologetic smile and a shrug of his big shoulders. He shifted his chair, so he could hide behind Calvin, but unless Calvin suddenly gained an extra foot and a half in height, that wasn't going to work. Seeming to realize that, Hobbs let his chin rest on the top of Calvin's head with a sigh. Calvin was so accustomed to it, he took a sip of his beer as if he didn't have a tiger Therian twice his size using him for a prop.

When Letty turned to Sloane, he shook his head. "No way. I'm not touching this."

"Come on, don't be a wuss. Say it. You'd totally fuck Dex."

Already have. In the kitchen, bedroom, living room, bathroom, car, work… "Not touching this."

With a pout, she moved on. "Fine, Ash?"

Ash scoffed. "I wouldn't fuck or marry any of you, but I'd have the time of my life killing your asses. All of you. Assholes."

Beside him, Cael huffed, giving Ash's bicep a prod. "Hey, what did I do?"

"Not you. Cael's the only one who gets to survive. The rest of you can kiss my ass."

"Cael?" Rosa wriggled her brows. "Come on, *gatito*. Who makes you purr?"

Cael shifted uncomfortably in his seat, his whole face going pink. "I don't know that I want to—"

"Come on," Rosa teased.

"Leave him alone." Ash threw an arm protectively around Cael's shoulders. "He doesn't want to play your stupid game."

"Touchy. Fine, who do you think Dex would choose?"

Ash got that look in his eyes and Sloane groaned. He fortified himself by downing half his beer in one gulp. Dex was on his third song. Something about being wanted dead or alive. The part about being a cowboy had Sloane picturing Dex in nothing but torn jeans and a cowboy hat. He didn't know what was worse, what was happening on stage or at their table. His choices were watching Dex and possibly getting an erection, or listening to his team argue over who they'd imaginary fuck, all of which led back to Dex. He was far too sober for any of this.

"Easy," Ash said, far too happy for his own good. "He'd clearly kill me, and he's already Sloane's wife, so there you go. Two for one right there."

Sloane finished the rest of his beer and pinned Ash with a glare. "And you wonder why everyone wants to kill you."

Ash shrugged. "What? It's the truth. You want proof?"

Dex finished singing and the crowd erupted into cheers. When he got to their table, he pointed to Sloane's empty beer bottle. "Want me to get you another one?"

"While you're at it," Ash said sweetly, "why don't you fetch him a snack and when you're done, bend over. Hubby's had a long day and needs to unwind."

"I don't know what you're talking about, but I bet a 'bite me' is in order." Dex snatched up Sloane's empty bottle and stormed off. Sloane shook his head at Ash in disbelief.

"Why do you have to be such an asshole?"

"Aw, isn't that sweet? Defending his honor. Want me to tell him? It might get you a blow job at the very least."

Dex came back, handed Sloane a beer, and took a seat next to him. "So what's going on? I take it Ash's pleasantness stems from something besides life in general."

Rosa chuckled, her gaze checking out the waitress in the tight black jeans. "He's pissed because everyone wants to kill him."

"How is that different from any other day?" Dex asked, following Rosa's line of sight before arching an eyebrow at her. She gave him a guilty smile and answered his question.

"We were playing fuck, marry, kill. It was pretty unanimous we would fuck you and kill Ash."

Dex put a hand to his heart. "Aw, you guys. That's so sweet. I'm honored you'd all choose me as the one to bang."

"So, how about you, Dex?" Rosa asked, leaning in keenly, followed by Letty. Everyone's attention was on Dex, and Sloane told himself if there was ever a time to run, now would be it. He looked over his shoulder and waved a hand to get Bradley's attention. Soon as he had it, he made the universal sign for "shot" then held up three fingers. Bradley laughed, and with a nod, walked off to make him his order. While he waited for his shots, Sloane took a swig of his beer.

"Easy," Dex said. "I'd fuck Sloane."

Sloane nearly choked on his beer. He snatched up a napkin to wipe the dribble from his chin. *Smooth. That wasn't obvious at all.*

"Don't worry, I'd be gentle," Dex purred, patting Sloane on the back and oblivious to Sloane's glare.

"As for marry. I'd marry Ash."

Sloane and Ash sounded off like a couple of echoes. "What?"

"Explain," Rosa demanded.

"See, you all should have put more thought into your answers. I'd marry Ash, make him fall in love with me, convince him to take out a million dollar life insurance policy *then* I'd kill him. Bam! I'm rich and free to keep banging Sloane." The table burst into laughter and Dex wriggled his brows at Sloane. Dex leaned over to take his hand. "Will you wait for me, darling? We can start new lives down in Rio de Janeiro. I'll become a card shark, and you can be my sexy cabana boy."

Sloane couldn't help his laugh. "You're such an ass."

"An ass with a million dollars. It'll be painful, but I'm willing to do this. For us." Dex gave him a wink, and Sloane felt him squeeze his fingers before releasing them. For a split second, Sloane wished he hadn't let go. Dex took a deep breath, straightened, and met Ash's gaze.

"Ash, you're looking... less murderous today."

"Fuck you."

"See that," Dex said, slapping a hand against the table in victory. "I've already got him wanting to fuck me. We're half way there. Rio de Janeiro, here I come." He reached into his back pocket, pulled out his wallet, and took out a ten-dollar bill. With a wink, he slid it over to Sloane. "Here you go, baby. Buy yourself something nice that'll set off your tan."

Sloane snatched up the bill and stuffed it in his jacket pocket.

Dex blinked at him. "You're not going to give me my money back, are you?"

"Nope."

"Damn, I should have thought that through."

Cael shook his head at his brother. "Dude, how much money have you lost to Sloane for the sake of your jokes?"

Dex looked to Sloane for an answer that Sloane cheerfully provided. "In the last month? Enough to pay my next cable bill."

"Seriously?" Ash gaped at him then turned his attention to Dex, leaning forward. "So, if I go along with your stupid jokes, will you pay my cable bill?"

"Nope."

"What the hell?"

Dex shrugged. "He's my partner. And he's pretty."

Everyone laughed, and Bradley appeared beside Sloane with the three shots. "Perfect timing. Thank you so much." Sloane handed Bradley a ten-dollar tip.

"Wait a second...." Dex waited for Bradley to leave before smacking Sloane in the arm. "That was *my* ten-dollar bill."

"No, it was mine," Sloane corrected. "You gave it to me to buy myself something nice, remember? I did. I bought myself alcohol." He downed the first shot, cringing as the foggy liquid burned down his throat.

"What the hell's in that?" Dex asked, eyeing the mysterious brew warily. "And how come he made it up just for you?"

Was that jealousy Sloane heard slip into Dex's tone? He had to admit, it gave him a tingly feeling, or maybe that was whatever Bradley slipped into his shot. He moved one of the small glasses in front of Dex. "I have no idea what's in it. He won't tell me. Give it a try."

Ash took the shot glass and moved it away from Dex. "I don't think that's a good idea, bro. He's already had a beer. Add a shot like that to the mix, and he'll probably end up with alcohol poisoning."

"Fuck you, Simba." Dex snatched up the shot and threw it back. Sloane let out a groan. His partner had played right into Ash's hands. Dex wheezed and coughed. "Jeeesus! What the...." He pounded on his chest, his voice hoarse. "What is that shit? Acid? It's burning a hole in my fucking throat! Oh my God, it burns!"

Ash laughed and waved at Bradley, putting up three fingers. "Next round's on me, Dex."

While Dex wheezed and Rosa patted his back, Sloane leaned over to grab his friend's arm. "What the hell are you doing?"

"Just buying my teammate a drink." The evil in Ash's eyes annoyed Sloane. No one knew Ash better than he did.

"Bullshit. You're trying to get him shitfaced."

"I hate to break it to you, but your boy's already well on his way to being shitfaced. With whatever the hell was in there, I give him twenty minutes before he's doing something extraordinarily stupid, and I'm going to be around when he does it."

Bradley arrived with the shots, and with a "thank you," Ash took one for himself before pushing the other two in front of Dex. "Time to man up, Daley."

"Ash," Sloane warned.

Rosa turned to Letty. "Let's go dance before they start whipping them out to see whose is bigger."

"I'm coming with you," Cael said, jumping to his feet. "I don't want to be here for whatever chaos is about to ensue." He joined Rosa and Letty, following them to the dance floor where the DJ was getting ready. The lights dimmed, the dance floor lit up, and the music started thumping.

Dex settled back in his seat, his arms folded over his chest. "I don't have to prove myself to you."

With a wicked grin, Ash shifted his gaze to Sloane. "What's it like having a blond partner? Do you have to remind him which end of the gun the bullets come out of?"

Calvin looked on unimpressed. "A blond joke? Really? That's pretty sad, even for you, Ash."

"You two still here?" Ash waved a hand in dismissal at Calvin. "Why don't you and your toy tiger go play pirates or something? Leave the drinking to the big boys. And Dex."

Hobbs vacated his seat so quickly, his chair toppled over. He took a step toward Ash, only to have Calvin put a hand to his chest. "Forget it, Ethan. You know he's just being his usual dickhead self. Come on." Calvin straightened Hobbs's chair and ushered his partner toward the bar.

"I don't know whether to be comforted or disturbed that you're as much of a dick to the rest of your team as you are to me." Dex gave a snort of disgust. "Look at you. Your biceps have biceps. What's your problem, Ash? You've been an asshole since I joined. Or is that part of your charming personality?"

Ash shrugged, looking unfazed. "I don't have to have a reason to dislike you. I just do."

"At least I have a reason," Dex muttered. Sloane felt Dex's leg slip in behind his, rubbing against it. He took another sip of his beer. What he wouldn't give to be somewhere dark and quiet where he could strip Dex, push him onto his knees, and make him beg for it.

"And what's that?" Ash asked, throwing back one of the shots in front of them.

"You're an asshole," Dex replied. The "duh" was implied in his tone.

Ash opened his mouth to answer, when a soft gasp got their attention. Sloane tilted his head up, puzzled by the slender, good-looking guy with dark hair, a rich tan, and big hazel eyes standing beside their table, staring at Dex.

"Oh my God. Dex?"

Dex stared right back. "Lou?"

The name hit Sloane like a punch to the gut. It took everything he had to school his expression and appear mildly interested, instead of his initial thought of *what the fuck?* This was just perfect. What the hell was Dex's ex-boyfriend doing here? Sloane watched Lou round the table, his too-tight designer shirt and equally tight designer slacks accentuating his sinewy frame and tight ass. His heart-shaped face lit up when he looked Dex over, his wide smile exposing perfectly straight, bright white teeth. Sloane disliked him even more than he previously had. Ash arched an eyebrow at Sloane, who gave him a pointed look. There was no telling what would come out of Ash's mouth, and things were awkward enough already.

"Wow, look at you," Lou gushed. "You look amazing. Must be all the training they've got you doing."

Seriously? The ole "have you been working out" chestnut? Was that still in circulation? Did guys go for that? Dex patted his stomach, his cheeks flushed. Apparently they did. Or it could be his idiot partner.

"Thanks. Yeah, it's pretty intense," Dex replied, looking embarrassed. "What are you doing here?"

"I'm not normally down this side of town, but we landed a big client and wanted to celebrate. One of the staff kept raving about this place. Something about some cute guy who's always singing here and…." Lou's eyes went wide and his hand flew dramatically to his lips. "Oh, hell. He's talking about you, isn't he?"

"Um…." Dex cleared his throat. "I'm sure I'm not the only guy to sing in here, with or without a Karaoke machine."

"Oh my God, I'm so embarrassed. I should have known, especially when he mentioned the eighties songs." Lou giggled and Sloane gritted his teeth. Under the table, Ash kicked him, and Sloane's glare was enough to get his friend to back off.

Dex cringed. "Yeah, okay, he was probably talking about me."

"This is so awkward. I'm probably the last person you wanted to see in here. I'll grab my friends and go." Lou turned, when to Sloane's surprise, Dex caught his arm.

"Hey, listen, it's cool. You and your friends have fun. It's no big deal."

It was Sloane's turn to clear his throat, and he held back his aggravation at Dex's startled expression, as if he'd forgotten he wasn't alone.

"Shit, sorry. Lou, this is my partner at the THIRDS, Sloane Brodie, and my teammate Ash Keeler. Guys, this is Louis Huerta."

"The guy who dumped you after you got beat up by your cop buddies, right?" Ash said pleasantly, a big grin stretching across his face.

With a heavy sigh, Dex turned his attention back to Lou. "Ignore him. He only has one setting—asshole."

Lou looked nervously from Ash to Sloane, offering a tentative smile. "It's nice to meet you." He shifted his gaze to Dex. "You think we can talk a sec?"

"Okay." Dex excused himself and followed Lou over to a small standing table toward the end of the room, away from the dance floor where it was conveniently atmospheric, with most of the lighting coming from the amber wall sconces and the candle in the center of the table.

"Well, well. Look who came crawling back," Ash drawled.

Sloane decided he was definitely too sober for this evening. "What are you talking about?" Did he want to know?

Ash leaned forward, nodding toward the corner of the room where Lou and Dex were chatting. "Come on, man. Look at him. He can't keep his hands off Dex."

Sloane discreetly followed Ash's gaze and frowned at Lou playing with Dex's dog tags. He was obviously flirting. His hand went to Dex's bicep, giving it a squeeze. Dex said something and Lou laughed, slapping Dex playfully on his side, making Dex wriggle. His partner was ticklish under his arms and down his ribs. Clearly, Lou was aware of the fact as well. It struck him then how Lou had more intimate knowledge of Dex than Sloane did. The thought brought a sour taste to his mouth.

"He might have bailed when the shit hit the fan, but Dex is a THIRDS agent now. His pretty-boy face has been all over the news since he joined. Love him or loathe him, he knows how to work the room and play to the crowd. Why do you think Lieutenant Sparks keeps loaning him out to the Community Relations Department? He's got the PR agents practically wetting themselves."

"Careful, Ash. Those are starting to sound like compliments." Sloane couldn't help his smile. It was rare moments like this one when Sloane wondered if deep down, Ash didn't hate Dex as much as he said he did. His best friend was frustratingly hard to read at the best of times, much less when he was purposefully keeping something from Sloane.

"Fuck off. I'm just saying, Dex is in a whole new league and some people are bound to take notice, including those from his old life."

"And you're telling me this because?"

Ash shrugged, averting his gaze. "You've stopped moping. For the most part. I think you're mopey by nature. I'd hate for something or someone to come along and mess your shit up again."

"I don't fully understand what you're trying to tell me, and it's probably best I don't." Worse than Ash being a dick, was Ash being concerned. It happened so rarely, that when it did, Sloane didn't know what to do with it.

"I'm saying, he's your friend, and he's helped you. He's good for you."

"So you keep telling me. Are you saying I should stop him from hooking up with someone, and the possibility of being in a happy relationship because he's good for me? Is that what you're saying?"

Ash blinked at him, looking truly confused. "Well, yeah."

"You are… astounding."

"I know."

"That wasn't a compliment."

"Tough shit, that's how I'm taking it." Ash looked over his shoulder, a deep scowl coming onto his face. "That shitbag."

"Who?"

"Some jackass is coming onto Cael and doesn't seem to understand the meaning of the words 'fuck off.' Sometimes Cael's too polite. How come he can rip a guy to shreds when it concerns his brother, but when it's about him, he's so damned nice about it."

"Cael's a nice guy," Sloane replied with a shrug. "Besides, he can take care of himself."

"It's not him I worry about. That guy's got 'sleaze' written all over his face."

Sloane leaned to peer around Ash. His friend was right. The guy crowding Cael was definitely a creep. No matter how many times, Cael pulled away, the guy kept getting all up in his personal space.

"Excuse me." Ash got up and Sloane hoped his friend wasn't about to get them kicked out. When it came to Cael, Ash had little control. It wouldn't be the first time Ash had gotten into a brawl over Cael, despite Cael's protests that he didn't need rescuing. Sloane could sympathize with the younger Therian, but it was hard stopping a train once it was going full speed with no brakes.

Sloane found himself on his lonesome at their table. He discreetly sneaked another peek over at Dex, his heart hammering as he watched Lou dance with Dex. To Dex's credit, the guy looked uncomfortable, and he seemed to be trying to talk to Lou, who of course was distracted by other things, like Dex's lips. Lou reached out to cup Dex's cheek, and Sloane got out of his seat. He'd had enough fun for one night.

"Fuck this." He'd just about made it to the door, when someone grabbed his arm.

"Hey!" Dex pulled him past the coatracks, through a door on the right, and they ended up in an empty hallway with a set of stairs leading down to the basement and at the far end, a supply closet. "What the hell, man? I turn around and you're leaving without me?"

Sloane shoved his hands into his pockets and shrugged. "I'm sure you could have found a ride. Lou's probably dying to give you a lift home." He knew he sounded like a jerk, but he couldn't help it. He was pissed off. Whether at himself or Dex, he wasn't sure.

"Whatever you're thinking, stop it. We were only talking."

And flirting, and dancing, and touching. This was stupid. What's more, this wasn't like him at all. He'd never had bouts of jealousy where Gabe had been concerned. Maybe because he'd never worried Gabe would leave him. Gabe had also never fraternized with any of his ex-boyfriends or ex-girlfriends. The idea that Dex would so easily dismiss what he'd been through with Lou, and let the guy waltz back into his life, aggravated Sloane. "How can you act like nothing's happened? He dumped your ass when you needed him most, and now he shows up out of nowhere, flirts with you, and you accept it like you're old friends?"

"Like I said, we were talking. Why are you pissed off with me? You're the one who was going to bail on me."

Sloane could see Dex growing angry with him, and he really couldn't understand why. What the hell did Dex have to be angry about? Sloane wasn't the one with his ex's hands all over him. He leaned a shoulder against the wood paneling and shrugged. "I figured if you wanted to give Lou another chance, who am I to stop you."

"Oh, fuck you." Dex shook his head, his face growing red. Before Sloane had a chance to ask Dex what he was getting so pissy about, Dex met his eyes, his gaze intense. "Is that it? That's all it would take for you to walk away? You don't bother asking me what that was about, or what's going on, just 'hey, have a nice life with your ex.' You dick."

"You're the one acting like he's back in your life. Like it's no big deal. You even stopped him from leaving," Sloane spat back. Why was he allowing this ridiculous situation to get under his skin?

"What did you expect me to do? Punch him? Tell him to fuck off?"

Sloane ran a hand through his hair and took a deep breath, trying to get a grip on himself. "I don't know. I didn't know what to think." This was all so new to him. He kept telling himself not to get so close, despite knowing it was too late.

"That's why there's this thing called communication, Sloane. Let me demonstrate. 'Sloane, does what we have mean so little to you that you would walk away just like that?' Now you answer."

Sloane gave Dex a warning look. "Don't patronize me."

"You're right. I apologize. I'm pissed off and that foggy shit Bradley made is getting to me. Now answer the question."

"I fucked up, okay?" What else did Dex want from him? It seemed like lately all Sloane did was either apologize to Dex or explain himself. He didn't like it.

"Try again."

"Fuck off." Sloane crossed his arms over his chest. Maybe he was being childish and defensive, but he didn't appreciate Dex's tone. He appreciated the fact that Dex was right even less. Dex stepped up to him and gently moved Sloane's arms away from his chest. Sloane allowed it, watching Dex intently as he closed the distance between them, his pale blue eyes pleading.

"Sloane."

Sloane was contemplating another evasive answer, but studying Dex's expression, his slightly parted lips, and handsome face, he couldn't do it. "No, it doesn't mean that little to me." He could feel his anger melting away. Dex had a point, and Sloane wasn't so egotistical he couldn't admit when he was wrong. "I got upset and didn't think things through. I figured an offer at a real relationship with someone you cared about would tempt you. I wouldn't blame you."

Dex's brows drew together. His expression filled with anger and what Sloane suspected was hurt, before he moved away. "You're such a dick. My God, are you taking lessons from Ash?"

The unexpected hostility stunned Sloane. "What did I do now?" He watched Dex pace around before his partner finally stopped, his shoulders slumping. He seemed to deflate, and Sloane felt shitty for bringing that look onto Dex's face.

"Next time, talk to me, please. If I didn't want to be with you, I wouldn't be. Or do you think I'm biding my time with you until something better comes along?"

"I don't think that. I fucked up." Sloane pulled Dex into his arms, aware of the slight hesitation. If he kept this up, one of these days Dex was going to be the one walking away. He didn't like how the thought made him feel. He wrapped his arms tightly around Dex and kissed his temple, inhaling Dex's scent. "I'm sorry," he said quietly. Dex's arms circled his waist and gave him a squeeze.

Knowing their teammates were busy and most likely didn't know where they were, Sloane took a chance, stealing a kiss. It started slow, Dex's mouth tasting sweet from the shots, his lips soft and sending a rush of blood down to Sloane's groin, but it quickly turned heated. Sloane slipped his hand under Dex's T-shirt, his fingers stroking smooth skin over hard muscle. He dug his fingers into Dex's ass, reveling in the low moan Dex let out against his lips, loving the shiver that Sloane could feel go through his partner. He reminded himself he was responsible for that. His thoughts went to Dex writhing underneath him, the way he stole Dex's breath, left him speechless, in a sweaty, panting mess. His mouth demanded more from Dex, and he pulled Dex hard against him, his erection rubbing against Dex's.

"Dex? Is everything—Oh wow."

Sloane pulled away with a start, his breath heavy and his eyes wide at Lou standing there, his mouth hanging open. *Shit.*

"Shit." Dex thrust a finger at Sloane. "*You*, don't you dare disappear on me. I'll handle this." He took Lou's arm and led him outside, leaving Sloane standing there with nothing but the muffled sounds coming from the dance floor and the taste of Dex on his lips. *Fuck.* He rubbed his hands over his face as he considered his next course of action. Okay, he was the Team Leader of a tactical team operating under the military branch of the United States government. He could handle one ex-boyfriend.

Sloane went over his options. Not that he didn't trust Dex to handle the situation. After careful consideration, he came up with two choices—threaten Lou into silence, or use this situation to his advantage. The first one sounded fun, but the latter was the smarter choice. He'd give Dex a few minutes, then he was going in. One way or another, their secret had to remain that.

CHAPTER 6

THIS NIGHT was turning into one spectacular clusterfuck. Lou ordered a JD and Coke and Dex ordered a beer. He took a quick survey of the place. Calvin and Hobbs had disappeared. Ash was over in the corner with Cael, having an animated conversation that Cael seemed to find particularly amusing for some strange reason, while Letty and Rosa were on the dance floor busting some serious moves. Relieved his team was none the wiser to his disaster of a love life or more likely, life in general, he turned to Lou, who was looking both embarrassed and startled. Seeming to snap himself out of it, Lou spoke up.

"He's…."

"My partner at the THIRDS and my Team Leader," Dex replied in a hushed tone, though there were enough people crowding the bar and enough noise to drown out their conversation from eavesdroppers.

Lou nodded. "I was going to say scary, but okay."

"That too. I need you to keep what you saw to yourself. I could get into trouble if my superiors, including my dad, found out, not to mention I'd be transferred from the team. Please, Lou." To his surprise, Lou stiffened, looking affronted.

"Dex, I'd never be so vindictive. Especially not with you."

"Thank you."

"So, he's a Therian."

"Yes." He knew Lou had a thing against Therians, though he'd only discovered it while in the process of being dumped. It had been an unexpected revelation to say the least.

"Is…." Lou swallowed hard, his eyes falling to his drink. "Is that why it didn't work between us? Because I wasn't—"

"No! Jesus, Lou." Dex put his hand to Lou's shoulder. "I really cared about you. I still do. What happened between us had to do with us not being right for each other and nothing to do with you being Human. I wasn't making you happy, and you deserve to be happy."

Lou nodded. "Does he make you happy?"

That was the million-dollar question. Or was it? "When I don't want to strangle him, yes, he makes me happy." A sad smile came onto his face. "Even if he has a hard time believing it."

"Sounds like you two have issues to work out."

Issues? More like subscriptions. Dex took a sip of his beer in an attempt not to give it too much thought. "Yeah, but I think we'll get there. He's a good guy."

There was silence between them, both taking sips of their drinks until Lou got that mischievous look in his eyes. "I guess he's kind of hot, for a Therian. I bet he's huge."

"Oh my God, Lou!" Dex nearly spit out his beer. He wiped his mouth with the back of his hand and stared at his ex-boyfriend. Lou gave a delicate snort.

"You're such a prude. Well, is he?"

He knew Lou wasn't going to let up until he got his answer. Dex had never been shy about this sort of thing, but talking about Sloane's sexy parts with his ex was wrong on so many levels. "It is proportionate to the rest of him."

"In other words, he's hung."

Dex pinched the bridge of his nose, resigned to the absurdity that was this evening. "Yes. I can't believe I'm discussing my guy's dick with my ex."

Lou's face went beet red, and Dex wished he'd ordered Bradley's "special" instead of beer.

Over his shoulder, a gravelly voice sealed the deal. He should have expected it, really. "That makes two of us. But I guess I should be glad you approve."

Lou held his hand out to Sloane, a wide smile on his face. "You clearly know who I am. Thank you for not punching me."

Sloane accepted the handshake with some hesitation. "I'll admit, I was tempted, but I guess if you hadn't dumped Dex, he wouldn't have given me a chance."

"He's an amazing guy."

"Having second thoughts?" Sloane cocked his head to one side, his expression guarded.

"He's happy, and that's all I ever wanted for him."

Dex noticed the way Sloane peered at Lou. Did he not believe Lou? Then again, he didn't know Lou and therefore had no reason to. "You were flirting with him."

"Before he told me he was seeing someone. Look, I know you're probably expecting me to be the evil ex who comes swooping in trying to dig my claws into him, take back what I think is mine, and all that campy drama, but I'm not. I respect him, and I would never come between him and someone he cares about. I had my chance, and I blew it. So take it from me. Don't blow it. I would, however, like to be his friend. Would that be acceptable to you?"

Dex had to admit, he was surprised. Not that he had anything against being friends with Lou. He was a good guy, despite the dumping, but Lou had been adamant about Dex not contacting him, and Dex had obliged, deleting Lou's details from his life. He recalled Lou's answer on having second thoughts, or rather the fact he hadn't given Sloane a direct answer. Had Lou been having second thoughts? He'd never tried to get in contact with Dex. Not that it mattered. There was only one guy who made Dex's toes curl, and that guy was currently giving thought to Lou's offer. What the hell?

"Remember," Lou added with a wicked grin, "I know everything about him. Like his fear of goats."

Dex's jaw dropped. "Seriously, Lou? That's what you're going with?"

"Deal." Sloane held his hand out, and Dex watched, stunned, as his ex-lover shook hands with his current lover. With an arched eyebrow, Sloane turned to Dex. "So, goats, huh?"

"Have you seen their eyes? The way they climb up the side of mountains or perch on branches like gravity doesn't apply to them? They're evil! Evil I say!" An image of the hairy beasts with their freaky eyes made him shudder. Sloane and Lou both laughed, and Dex let out a groan. "I think I liked it better when you wanted to punch him." Sloane ignored him, giving Lou a pat on the shoulder.

"Let me buy you a drink."

This couldn't be happening. Why was this happening? This night had started out so well. "Why? Why are you buying him a drink? Are you going to ask him stuff about me? What happened to getting to know someone? The thrill of the chase. The mystery."

"Overrated," Sloane replied sweetly, not bothering to look at Dex. "So, this zombie thing he has going on in the morning before he's had coffee. How long do I have to get away with something before he's awake enough to know what's happening?"

"What?" Dex squeaked. That was his most guarded secret. How could Lou betray him like this? Dex pinned his ex with a glare, which only resulted in a knowing smile from Lou.

"Ah, the Waking Dead."

Sloane let out a laugh and Dex gasped. He quickly recovered and slammed a fist down on the bar. "You can't tell him about the Waking Dead! I forbid it! I'm demanding you adhere to the ex-boyfriend code of honor."

"There's no such thing," Lou stated. "So, the Waking Dead. From the moment he gets his ass off the mattress until he takes the first sip—providing he hasn't showered, you're in the clear. After the first sip, you have exactly twenty-three minutes."

"Oh my God, you timed me?" Could this night possibly get any worse?

"Of course. How else do you think I got you to say yes to the white antler chandelier?"

"I knew it!" Dex thrust an accusing finger at Lou. "I knew there was a reason I couldn't remember saying yes to that hideous monstrosity. I'd like to say, this is not cool, and you're both dicks." He sulked all the way to their table where most of his team had regrouped. "Rosa, I need your maternal bosoms." He flopped down onto the chair and let Rosa wrap him in her embrace, his head pressed against her breasts as she petted his head. Ash's expression would have been hysterical if Dex wasn't so busy being miserable.

"Let me get this straight."

"Did you intend that to be a pun?" Cael asked in amusement, obviously knowing what Ash was about to say. Hell, they all knew what Ash was about to say.

"Quiet, you." Ash turned to address Rosa. "So because he's gay, he can get all up in your boobs and that's okay? What is it with gay guys and boobs? You don't even enjoy them!"

"Not true," Dex said, snuggling against Rosa. "They're very comfortable."

Rosa rolled her eyes, her attention returning to Dex. "Aw, poor baby. What's the matter?"

Dex threw a hand toward the bar. "My life is ruined."

"Is that your ex talking to Sloane?"

"Yep."

"They're laughing together."

"Yep."

Rosa cringed. "Ooh, your ex is spilling the beans, isn't he?"

"Apparently, in exchange for being my friend, Lou gets to tell Sloane whatever he wants to know. Sloane knows about the Waking Dead, Rosa! The Waking Dead!"

"I… I don't know what that means, but I'm going to assume that's bad." She looked to Cael with a shrug.

"That's bad," Cael said, looking concerned. "He really told Sloane about the Waking Dead?"

"Yes!" He needed a drink. "I need a drink. Someone get me something that'll get me shitfaced. I need to soften the blow of this heinous breach of the ex-boyfriend code of honor."

"No such thing," Letty chipped in.

"Et tu, Letty?"

Ash pushed his whiskey glass containing a clear drink in front of Dex. "Vodka and lemonade. You wanna inhale the fumes? That should be enough."

"Screw you." Dex snatched up the glass and threw the contents back. "Damn it, Ash," Dex wheezed. "You dickhead. There was no lemonade in that at all, just vodka!"

Ash let out an evil cackle. "I know. I really enjoy watching you get shitfaced." Cael let out a fierce yawn and rested his head against Ash's shoulder. With a chuckle, Ash wrapped an arm around Cael. "Looks like someone might be ready to call it a night."

"Damn. I really wanted to get more drunk. Drunker. My brain's given up." Cael sat up, his hair sticking out on one side of his head. He grinned sleepily at Ash. "I'll pick you up in the morning."

Dex arched an eyebrow at his brother, his face feeling flushed. Looked like the vodka was doing its job. Sweet. "You pick Ash up for work?"

"Yeah, we carpool. Saves on gas," Cael replied with another yawn. "So what? You and Sloane carpool."

Dex opened his mouth then quickly shut it. He and Sloane carpooled because they were more often than not waking up after a night of horizontal poking. "True," he muttered, though it didn't exactly scratch the particular itch he got when he thought about his brother carpooling with Ash. Neither had to worry about scrimping on gas money. He doubted Ash was the environmentally conscious sort. They weren't even partners. What was the real reason they carpooled, and whose idea was it? Could it be possible his brother actually—gasp—*enjoyed* hanging with Ash? Ash caught him contemplating and scowled at him.

"Don't hurt yourself, Daley. My apartment's not far from Cael's, and it's on the way to work. Plus sometimes we hang out if it gets late, or we have a few too many, and the last thing I want to do is worry about facing morning traffic. I am not a morning person."

Dex blinked at him. "You? Grumpy in the morning?" He jumped from his chair and held his hands out. "Stop. Everyone stop what you're doing." The people seated closest to them stopped to observe in amusement. "This is serious news. Ash Keeler, the warm, fuzzy bunny you see before you, is not a morning person. He is, in fact, grumpy.

You might want to tweet that. The world shouldn't be deprived of this shattering revelation. Thank you for your time." He resumed his seat, a wave of fuzziness washing over him and making him all tingly. Yay, vodka. He grinned broadly at Ash, who ignored him to address Cael. Pfft. Rude.

"Ten squads, Cael. Your dad could have put him on any other squad, but no, he sticks Dudley Do-Right on ours. Be honest with me. Your dad hates me, doesn't he?"

"Everyone hates you," Dex muttered, looking down at his shirt. Was it inside out? Hey, sunglasses. He put on his aviators and smiled at Ash. "That's why everyone wants to kill you, remember? Why's it so dark in here?" He looked around with a frown. "Rosa? Something's wrong with the lights. Is it closing time? No, wait, the lights would get brighter not darker." Where the hell was Sloane? He looked up and gave a start. "Whoa! Hey, partner, I was wondering where you were." Why was Sloane looking at him funny?

"Why are you wearing sunglasses?"

"What?" Dex touched his eyes. "Oh. I don't know. Why not? Where's Lou?" A thought struck him and he chortled. "Skip to my Lou."

"Oh God. Yeah, it's time to go," Cael said, getting up, making Dex momentarily sad.

"Why?" He stood, the world spun, and he threw a hand out, hitting something hard that suddenly steadied him. Man, it was dark in here. "Come on, little bro. I'll buy you a drink."

"I don't think so. You've had enough for the both of us and I'm tired. Sloane, can you take him home before he ends up drooling on the bar? Again."

Sloane chuckled. "Sure."

Mm, sexy rumbly chuckle. No, not sexy. Dex whispered to himself in his head, *the team is here. Play it cool.*

"Hey," Dex thrust a finger at Ash. No, wait, he meant to point at his brother. He moved his arm over. "There you are. I did not drool on the bar. I spilled my drink and then fell asleep on it. It was sticky. Get your facts straight."

"Okay, then. Good night, everyone." Cael waved and Dex waved after him, smiling broadly.

"Ash, take care of my precious baby brother, or I will drug you and shave off your mane. Have you ever seen a lion without his mane? Not so majestic. Either that or you'll look like a lady lion." He turned to Sloane. "Help me out here. Lady lion?"

"Lioness," Sloane offered, a dimple forming on his cheek. Dex was tempted to put his finger to it, but controlled himself.

"Right. Lioness." He turned back to find Ash and his brother gone. With a snort of disgust, he turned to Sloane. "That guy is sooo fucking rude. I'm hungry."

"All right. Time to go."

"Yeah, yeah." Dex turned and blew a kiss at Rosa and then Letty. "*Hasta luego, mis ermanas, or is it companeras?*" Dex let out a gasp. "Oh my God, you guys! Why didn't you tell me I sounded like such a douche speaking Spanish?"

"It's *hermanas and compañeras*," Rosa corrected, but kissed his cheek anyway.

"I love you, Rosa. You're so good at kicking Ash's ass." He hugged her tight until Sloane started pulling him away. "Love you, Letty! Your gun skills make angels cry 'cause it's so beautiful."

"Okay. Let's get you out of here before the public loses any more respect for our organization."

Dex allowed Sloane to lead him outside into the cool night air. "I'm hungry. And why's it so dark?" Something moved in front of his eyes and it got brighter. He looked up at a handsome smiling face. "You're so hot. I'm hungry." Sloane. Food. Sloane. Food. How was he supposed to decide? Unless… "Can I have both?"

"I think you left the other half of that question in your head," Sloane said with a chuckle as he walked Dex down the street, his big, strong, beefy arm around Dex's shoulders. He liked Sloane's arms. And other things. "I'll make you a sandwich soon as I get you home," Sloane added.

Next thing Dex knew, he was sitting inside some car. "Whose car is this?"

"It's a taxi," Sloane said, handing him something cold and wet. "Here. Drink this."

"I'm not thirsty." He took a swig and scrunched his nose. "This doesn't taste like anything."

"Because it's water. Just drink it."

"All of it?" Dex's eyes widened. "It'll make me pee."

"Then you pee."

"You're so smart." Dex leaned into Sloane and inhaled deeply. "God, you smell good." Dex opened his eyes and found he was standing on the sidewalk in front of his house. Damn. That taxi was astoundingly fast. Like… the Doc's DeLorean. Now that was a cool car. He closed his eyes for a moment and took a deep breath. He was still hungry, but the water Sloane had given him had helped clear his head some. He heard Sloane talking and turned to find the taxi driving away. The fact it was driving away without Sloane left butterflies in his stomach. He should be feeling happy about it, knowing there was probably some sexy time in his near future, but he started thinking about other things that weren't sexy. He'd tried to keep it to himself, but he couldn't any longer. With a pathetic frown, he came out and said it.

"Am I a sucky partner?"

SLOANE CAME to an abrupt halt at the murmured words. "What?"

This was usually the part where Sloane ended up at Dex's for some hot, drunken sex, except tonight, something was off, namely Dex. Sloane wrapped his arm around his too quiet partner as he helped him up the front steps. Before getting in the cab, he'd managed to walk Dex around in an attempt to sober him up and made him drink a whole bottle of water. He'd expected some more of Dex's drunken ramblings, but not the serious concern on the man's face and certainly not the question he'd spouted.

"Am I a sucky partner?" Dex repeated. His voice was barely audible, and his words came out slurred.

"Okay, sit down with me. The night air will do you some good." Sloane sat Dex down beside him on the top step, and he held Dex against him so he couldn't fall forward. He smiled as Dex turned into him, nuzzling his neck, and snuggling close.

The street was quiet, lined with trees, and the lighting dim enough to conceal them from any curious passersby. He ran a hand over Dex's head and through his hair, speaking softly. He reckoned the night hadn't gone exactly as planned for Dex. He felt guilty now for leaving Dex to get information from Lou. Considering what he'd found out, maybe not so guilty. He'd make it up to Dex, but first things first. "Now what's this whole sucky partner business?"

"What if I'm kidding myself? I'm a detective, not a soldier. You, Ash, Hobbs, you're tough as bricks, Therians who bench press busses, or at the very least a Volkswagen Beetle. Letty was in the army. Rosa, I'm pretty sure, is the next evolution of Terminator. Calvin can shoot the wings off a fly with his eyes closed, and Cael can program algorithms in his sleep. What the hell do I do, besides sing karaoke and win at laser tag?"

Sloane turned to cup Dex's cheek, wondering where this sudden bout of insecurity was coming from. Dex never showed the slightest hint of being anything other than confident in nearly everything he did. Maybe Sloane didn't know as much about his partner as he thought he did. "Dex, just because you haven't had the training we have, or the experience, doesn't mean you're not a good soldier. You never hesitate to go out there and do the best job you can. You're smart, clever, enthusiastic, driven. You never give up, and you lift everyone's spirits. If we didn't have you to pick us up, to pick *me* up, I don't know where we'd be."

"Bored," Dex muttered. "So I'm the comic relief?"

"No. You're an important member of this team. They love you, Dex. You're the perfect fit and exactly what we needed. After I lost Gabe… I was so sure I was going to lose them too. It was unbearable, watching them retreating into themselves, not being able to do anything about it. Rosa kept to herself. Letty spent more time around guns than she did people. Calvin was always moping around. Hobbs barely said a word."

"If that's a joke, it's in poor taste. Hobbs is awesome."

"No, I'm not kidding. I know it looks like he doesn't talk, but he talks to Calvin all the time. I mean, you never hear him, but you can see him talking. After Gabe died, Hobbs didn't even do that much. It really got to Calvin. Ash was even more unbearable, and your brother? He stopped smiling, stopped being playful, and holed himself up in his office, hiding behind his computers. At first, I thought they were grieving. I had no idea how bad it really was. Before you came, I was losing my team, Dex. You changed that. You, with your amazing smile. Even when I tried to push you out, you never stopped being you. You showed them it was okay to keep on living."

"What about you?" Dex asked murmured.

"You showed me that too. I know it's been… difficult with me in particular, but I promise you, I'm trying." He ran his thumb over Dex's bottom lip and leaned in for a kiss, tasting the alcohol on Dex's tongue. Dex shivered beneath him and when Sloane pulled away, he received a warm smile.

"Thank you."

"I'm the one who should be thanking you. And you're a great agent, trust me."

"You're just saying that to be nice."

"Think about that for a moment. When do I ever say anything to be nice?"

Dex chuckled. "True. Grumpy pants."

Sloane let his head fall against Dex's and sighed. "I didn't know you were so worried about your position. Why didn't you tell me?"

"Because you're my Team Leader. You got real shit to deal with. I wasn't going to bother you with my pathetic whining."

"It's not pathetic whining, and if you're going through a rough patch, I want to know about it, as your Team Leader, your partner, and… more."

Dex pulled back, his gaze searching Sloane's. "Really?"

"Yes, really. And please don't let Ash get to you."

"That guy," Dex let out a frustrated groan. "I really want to shoot him. Next time we're at the firing range, if I promise you a blowjob, can I shoot him? Just a nick. He'll barely feel it."

With a laugh, Sloane helped Dex to his feet. "Come on, let's get you inside."

"We can pretend it was an accident. A ricochet."

"I'll think about it." Sloane walked Dex to his door and waited until he had it open. He paused before going in, and Sloane held his breath. Despite how many nights he'd spent at Dex's, he still got butterflies in his stomach when Dex said that one word.

"Stay?"

Sloane nodded and followed Dex inside. He couldn't find it in him to say no to Dex, and what's more, he didn't want to.

Dex locked up, and they walked in companionable silence upstairs to get ready for bed. In no time at all, they were huddled close under the sheets. Sloane wrapped Dex in his arms, softly stroking his back as Dex's warm breath hit Sloane's shoulder. This night hadn't turned out as disastrous as he thought. Dex was out within seconds, and Sloane shouldn't have been far behind, but he couldn't stop thinking about Dex.

Lou had confessed to Sloane his regrets on hurting Dex as he had and walking out on him. He'd been certain things wouldn't have worked out, and Dex had agreed, but the longer he spent away from Dex, the more he realized the mistake he'd made. Lou admitted he had taken Dex for granted. He'd gotten scared and instead of turning to Dex, he bailed. He warned Sloane not to make the same mistake.

It was easy to get caught up in the job, in the past, in life, and without realizing it, end up putting everything before those you cared about, until one day you looked around to find yourself alone. Sloane had spent a good deal of his life alone, and he'd grown accustomed to it. He had been fine being alone. Then he'd met Gabe, and he'd stopped being alone. He'd taken Gabe for granted, believing he'd always be there, but then Gabe had done the same. How much had they missed out on? Sometimes they'd been so scared of being discovered, so scared to take the most minimal of risks, that at times, Sloane worried about their future. He'd convinced himself everything would turn out fine. They'd worry about it later. And then there was no later.

Dex let out a soft huff and mumbled something unintelligible in his sleep, his brow creasing with worry. It wasn't like Dex to have unpleasant dreams, and Sloane was certain he was partially responsible. He ran his fingers through Dex's hair and kissed his head, hushing him tenderly.

"It's okay. Everything's okay."

Dex hummed and snuggled closer, his bare leg slipping between Sloane's so he was all but wrapped around Sloane, pressed against him from head to toe. It made Sloane smile. He'd never been much of a snuggler, but Dex had a way of bringing it out in him, and he happily surrendered. Giving in to the feel of Dex in his arms, for the first time in a long time he drifted to a sleep devoid of nightmares.

That didn't mean he wouldn't be facing a different kind of nightmare in the morning.

"Oh shit!" Sloane bolted upright, cringing at the loud thud that followed, accompanied by a slew of sleepy groaning. He leaned over the side of the bed, wishing he had more time to soothe his groggy, dazed partner. "Sorry, but you need to get your ass up. We're going to be late!" They'd both forgotten to set their alarms, and although Sloane was usually pretty good with waking up before it went off, today he hadn't. Luckily, they weren't already late, but they definitely had no time for their usual morning routine, and if he didn't rush his partner out the door, they wouldn't make it. "We're going to have to shower at work. Brush your—Oh my God, are you sleeping?"

Scrambling out of bed and nearly tripping over himself when his leg got caught in the sheets, he stomped over to Dex and grabbed him by the waist to haul him to his feet. Dex was fast asleep. "Unbelievable." He dragged Dex over to the bathroom, held him in front of the sink with one arm and with his free hand filled a cup with cold water, and splashed it in Dex's face. His partner gasped and flailed, sputtering water.

"Why you trying to drown me?" he grumbled, still half asleep.

"Because we're going to be late, and I'm *never* late!" He took Dex's toothbrush and shoved it at him. "Now brush your teeth. We'll shower at work."

"Coffee?" Dex asked, looking like he might pass out.

"You have an addiction," Sloane said, grabbing his toothbrush. "We'll get coffee on the way there, but you need to move your ass."

Dex nodded and went about brushing his teeth. While he was doing that, Sloane managed to brush his teeth, take a piss, change, and grab Dex's clothes. "To hell with this. You're changing in the car." As soon as Dex finished using the bathroom, Sloane snatched Dex's backpack from the armchair and stuffed a pair of jeans, a T-shirt, socks, and Dex's Chucks inside. He slung the backpack over his shoulder, grabbed Dex, practically carried him downstairs, swiped Dex's keys from the bowl near the front door, and pushed Dex outside to lock up.

Dex stood yawning next to him. Either he wasn't aware he was standing outside barefoot, in nothing but his boxer briefs and a T-shirt or he didn't care. A little old lady walking her tiny dog gasped as she shuffled by. Dex waved at her, another yawn escaping him.

"Hi, Mrs. Bauman."

"My God, how have you survived this long?" Sloane ushered Dex down the stairs toward Sloane's Impala parked in front.

"Coffee."

Sloane pressed his lips together to keep himself from responding. He shoved Dex in the car, thrust his backpack at him, ordered him to get dressed, then climbed behind the wheel. At this rate, after picking up some drive-through coffee and a breakfast sandwich, they'd have enough time to hit the showers and dress before heading to their morning briefing. He took a deep breath and pulled out into Barrow Street. Provided traffic wasn't too bad, they could make it in under twenty minutes. They were okay. He hated rushing, but he hated being late even more. Dex changed in the seat beside him, albeit somewhat awkwardly, and they'd had a close call when Dex almost smacked Sloane in the face trying to get his jacket on.

Not long after, Sloane's panic had eased, they'd had their coffee, and eaten, with Dex insisting on feeding Sloane his Tater Tots so Sloane wouldn't have to take his eyes off the road. The whole thing was very couple like. Sloane had even let Dex tune into *Retro Radio,* laughing at his partner's antics as Dex played air guitar and sang along to "My Sharona." Dex made stupid sex puns to go with his lewd gestures, and Sloane went along with it. He'd never had this much fun driving to work.

Luck was on their side and they made it on schedule. Soon they were on their floor's male locker room, showered, and getting dressed. Dex was in his baby-blue boxer briefs, and Sloane did his best to concentrate on tying his bootlaces and not his partner's ass, which happened to be at eye level.

"Shit. I left my toiletry bag in the showers. Be right back." Dex headed back to the shower as Agent Taylor was heading toward Sloane.

"Hey, Daley."

"Hey, Taylor." Dex gave the Therian agent a nod as he walked past him, and to Sloane's surprise, Taylor's eyes followed Dex. Sloane finished tying his boots and stood, rounding his shoulders.

"Damn. How do you work around that ass and not want to pound it?"

"Excuse me?" Sloane closed his locker, his glare pinned on the back of Taylor's auburn head. Taylor turned to him with a leer.

"Come on, Sloane. From one Team Leader to another, I'm not even into Humans, but I'd tap that. And those lips? That mouth was made to have a dick in it."

Sloane shoved Taylor up against the lockers. "Show some respect."

"Hey, what the hell, man?" Taylor tried to move, but Sloane held him in place with an arm to his chest.

"Dex is my partner and my friend. I hear you talking shit about him to anyone, I see you trying to fuck with him, and you and me are going to have problems. Understood?" Taylor had a reputation for being a player and a certified asshole, not that Sloane cared who the hell Taylor fucked, but if the guy was getting any ideas about Dex, Sloane was going to put a stop to it right here and now. Taylor eyed him warily, as if he wasn't sure if Sloane was kidding or not. Sloane was far from kidding. "I asked you if you understood."

Taylor threw his hands up. "Yes! Fuck, man. I didn't know you two were so close."

"We don't have to be close. Like I said, he's my partner. You want to get laid, do it on your own time and away from my fucking team."

"Can you believe Howell was using my shampoo? Dude doesn't even have any...." Dex's voice had Sloane moving away from Taylor. His partner looked from Sloane to Taylor and back. "Hair. Everything okay?"

Taylor grinned widely, his intense gaze on Sloane. "Everything's copacetic, Agent Daley. See you on the field."

"Sure." Dex watched Taylor stroll off whistling to himself, before he turned to Sloane. "What was that about?"

"Just straightening something out. You gonna get dressed, or you plan on hanging out in your undies all day?"

Dex pulled his uniform out of his locker and gave him a wink. "Don't want other dudes checking out my sweet ass?"

Despite his jokes, Sloane knew his partner was oblivious to the ogling he received from both his male and female coworkers. For all of the THIRDS' rules on fraternizing, the place was incestuous. It wasn't so much that their employer didn't know agents were sleeping together, but as long as there was no evidence of it, they could pretend it wasn't happening. "Come on. Cael should have something from Allan and the CDC registration office by now. I want to see—"

The panic alarm blared through the locker room, the emergency lights flashing. Something serious had gone down.

"Shit." Dex finished tying his bootlaces, and they made a run for it, rushing through the bullpen and out into the hall toward the elevator. On the way down, Sloane fastened his earpiece and connected. It beeped once and he tapped to answer.

"What's going on?"

Maddock's deep voice answered somberly. "There's been an explosion."

"Where?"

There was a slight pause and for a moment, Sloane thought he'd been disconnected. "Sarge?"

"Sorry. At the Therian Youth Center on the corner of East Tenth Street and Avenue A, by Tompkins Square Park. I don't know for certain, or how many, but there may be casualties. Suit up. We're heading out."

Sloane stood numb for a moment, before turning and slamming a fist into the stainless steel elevator wall. "*Fuck!* That piece of shit!"

"Hey, calm down." Dex's gentle words had Sloane taking a deep breath. His partner's hand came to rest on his shoulder, and Sloane shook his head.

"Kids, Dex. He put a bomb in a kids' center." Sloane pressed his head against the wall, his hands curling into fists. No matter how much he'd seen, how long he'd been on the job, there was no preparing for something like this.

"Do we know if it was him?" Dex asked as the elevator pinged. Sloane stormed out toward the armory with Dex at his side.

"I know it is. I can feel it in my gut. There's a special place in hell reserved for Isaac Pearce, and I'm going to be the one to put him there."

"Hey." Dex grabbed Sloane's arm before they reached armory's huge metal doors. When Sloane didn't turn around, Dex stepped in front of him. "We all want this bastard as much as you do, and we're going to get him, but I need to know you're going to be able to face him and not lose your shit."

Sloane wanted to snap at Dex that he didn't know what the hell he was talking about. No one wanted to get his hands on Isaac Pearce the way Sloane did, but his partner was right. As much as he personally wanted to bury Isaac, he had a job to do. His badge weighed heavily on him, and with a grunt, he stormed into the armory to suit up. He had to keep a level head. Something told him he was going to need it.

As soon as the team geared up, they headed out to the BearCat where Maddock instructed Hobbs to take FDR Drive. Hobbs gave Maddock a curt nod and dashed around to the driver's side, with Calvin joining him on the passenger side. They all climbed into the BearCat, the doors slamming behind them before they took their seats and buckled up. The BearCat's engine roared to life, and they were soon weaving through traffic, sirens blazing and lights flashing, though their sirens weren't the only ones that could be heard. Maddock tapped away on his tablet, most likely bringing up their target location.

"Cael, what can you tell me about the center?"

Cael followed Maddock's lead, scrolling through the information Themis was providing him on his THIRDS issued tablet. "It's a nonprofit organization providing emergency and transitional housing for Therian youth. Their funding comes from either direct donation via individuals, fundraising, or businesses, with some private grants. They also have a strong educational program, with over two dozen staff, from a couple of physicians and psychologists, to art directors and social workers."

"Structure?"

"Five floors, including a rooftop court. We're talking a hell of a lot of rooms. Recreation rooms, dormitories, swimming pool hall, classrooms, lunchroom...."

"That son of a bitch," Ash growled, shaking his head. "A kids' center. When I get my hands on that sick fuck, I'm gonna—"

"Take it easy, big guy. We know." Cael gently patted Ash on his leg, and Sloane saw the gruff agent give Cael a sad smile. It was amazing how Cael was the only one who ever got through to Ash and didn't come out of it verbally pummeled. Even Sloane would get a coarse reply or growl from Ash. Though right now, Sloane knew how Ash was feeling.

If this really was Isaac's doing, no matter what rock he tried to crawl under, Sloane wouldn't give up until he found him and made him pay.

CHAPTER 7

HE COULD do this.

Dex jumped down from the BearCat after his partner, turned the corner, and was stricken by the sight before him. The air was thick, a muddy gray, with debris, ash, and fragments of burning paper raining down like confetti, the sidewalk littered with crushed glass and branches from the once lush trees now standing crooked and splintered. Humans and Therians alike looked on in horror and confusion. Some huddled together, others helped those around them, some ran in a panic, fear etched on everyone's dirt- or blood-smudged face.

Bodies were scattered all around, some moving, some still. Sloane appeared before him, his bright amber eyes behind his helmet's visor filled with concern as he spoke, though Dex couldn't hear a word, only see his lips moving, as if someone had pressed the "mute" button. A shake to the shoulder and the world around him exploded with noise and uproar, sirens wailing, car alarms blaring, kids shrieking, adults crying, shouting, utter chaos.

"Dex! Come on, partner, snap out of it!"

Dex nodded fervently. "I'm okay. I'm okay."

"Good." Sloane turned, pulling Dex with him as he shouted over the noise into their earpieces. "Letty, Rosa, you know the drill, tag by priority, get the rest of Unit Alpha up here. Calvin, Hobbs, Ash, Cael, we're going in."

They rushed through the main entrance, its three colorful doors streaked with gray, past the clouds of dust and billowing smoke. Dex almost ran into Ash who'd stopped dead cold. Stepping around him, Dex gasped. "Oh my God." Kids were everywhere, on the floor crying, screaming, some bloodied, some looking dazed, a few who weren't moving, all scattered among chunks of stone, bits of glass, fallen segments of plaster, and ceiling, waiting for someone to tell them what to do or where to go.

"Shit." Sloane grabbed Calvin and Cael. "Start getting these kids out of here."

Maddock appeared with a dozen agents behind him. "I put out a call to the other divisions requesting assistance. Emergency services are already here and Beta Ambush is ready for their orders. Where do you want them?"

"Okay, I want one agent per floor along with my team, the rest down here and outside helping Rosa and Letty until the other squads arrive. I'll take this floor, Ash you take the second. Dex, you and Hobbs evacuate the third and fourth floors, Beta Ambush, you're on your own for the fifth floor and the court on the roof. Let's get everyone out of here. I want updates as you get them and watch your step!"

They broke off, Dex running after Hobbs as they took the stairs two at a time while simultaneously checking to make sure it was safe. Exposed wires hung from the ceiling, but not low enough to reach them. The fallen ceiling panels snapped under their boots as they rushed through the fire door. Dex tried not to think about what they might find. From the looks of the place, the ground floor was in worse shape, which told him the explosion had originated there. Every time Dex thought about the man behind this, he had to quickly push it from his head to keep his anger in check. If he thought about the sick fuck who'd done this, he'd be no good to anyone. He had a job to do and terrified kids depending on them.

Kids ranging from young to teens huddled together in small groups or pairs, looking stricken, their dirty cheeks stained with trails from their tears. They were lost, and scared, and when they spotted Hobbs, they flooded over en masse. Hobbs was a huge Therian, a golden tabby tiger in his Therian form, but unlike Ash, Hobbs had a kind face and a tender smile. He knelt down as the kids all tried to talk to him or climb into his arms at once. He hugged them close to reassure them, whispering at them and doing his best to soothe them. Some of them eyed Dex warily, and he couldn't blame them. They were in this center because they'd been shunned or mistreated by Humans, whether by their parents or other Humans. Hobbs must have said something, because they turned their tearful gazes toward him, uncertain but willing to take Hobbs's word for it that Dex was one of the good guys.

"We need to get out of here, okay?" Dex approached one of the bigger boys. "What's your name?"

The kid rounded his shoulders, his gaze unwavering, though Dex could see past the bravado to the fear he was trying so desperately to hide. "Kurt."

"Okay, Kurt. These fellas need your help. Take the smallest ones, lead them downstairs. Our guys are in the lobby. They'll make sure you get out safe." Kurt hopped to it while Dex and Hobbs rounded up the others and saw them down the stairs, waiting while they made their way out to the lobby. Dex tapped his earpiece. "Sloane, we've got thirteen kids on the way down. I'd send Cael for them. Anyone else will scare them, especially Human agents."

"Copy that. Good work."

When the last of them had disappeared out the door downstairs, Dex turned to Hobbs. "Why don't we start at the west end and make our way down, then take the stairs up to the fourth."

Hobbs nodded and they hurried to the other end of the corridor, checking each room. The third floor was all dorm rooms. They were painted in cheerful colors, some with rows of bunk beds, some with rows of single beds, while others had fewer beds. The rooms with bunk beds were clearly for the younger kids, judging by the scattered toys, picture books, and cartoon bedding. The rooms with single beds were most likely for the preteens with posters of young pop stars and superheroes on the wall. And the rooms with fewer beds were for the teenagers as they were mostly solid colors, included desks with computers, and bookshelves piled high with books ranging from Algebra to Harry Potter. Dex was glad to see all the rooms were clean, everything freshly painted. As far as youth centers went, the place was top notch.

Dex made sure to check under, inside, and over any space where a kid could wedge him or herself. Everything was clear by the time they got to the end. He tapped his earpiece. "Sloane, third floor is clear. We're heading up to the fourth."

"Copy that. From the intel I'm getting, it seems the worst of the damage is down here. Still, keep your eyes peeled up there."

"Copy that," Dex replied, joining Hobbs on the stairwell to the next floor. This one was quiet, and he assumed at this time of day, the kids had been involved in other activities. The fourth floor was mostly classrooms for different age groups. One had a huge rug with a map of the United States with each state and name in a bright color. All kinds of maps were pinned against the walls, waist-high bookshelves running along the walls all around the room filled with books, DVDs, and games. Finding that room clear, they moved into the next room, which was some kind of recreation room filled with game tables—Ping-Pong, foosball, paddleball, a pool table, and air hockey. They checked the art room, library, computer room, and finally reached the last classroom. It was a huge room behind a large set of fire doors at the end of the hall.

It looked like any other children's classroom filled with colorful tables and chairs, a teacher's desk that was made of some kind of durable stainless steel or aluminum, shelves filled with books, chalkboards, corkboards displaying colorful pictures, and science diagrams hanging from the ceiling. There were shelves displaying projects, hooks for school bags, and a section for educational toys. They checked behind every piece of furniture, inside every cupboard, and even behind all the raincoats. They were about to head out when Hobbs stopped in the middle of the room.

"Hobbs?"

Hobbs put a finger to his lips and cocked his head to one side. That's when Dex heard it too. Faint sniffling. Hobbs walked to a medium sized toy chest filled with stuffed animals and got down on his knees. He picked up two bright bears with numbers on their tummies and smiled. Putting the bears on the floor, he tapped his name badge, his smile making wrinkles form at the corners of his green eyes as he held his gloved hand out. A second later, a small chubby hand slipped into Hobbs's much larger one. A small boy with big brown eyes, an

Iron Man T-shirt, and paint-spattered jeans stood up. He threw his arms around Hobbs.

Dex tapped his earpiece. "Sloane, we've got one more."

"Copy that. I'll send someone up." Moments later, a Therian agent from Beta Ambush came running, and Hobbs handed the boy over. With a nod, the agent was off, disappearing through the stairwell. Dex tapped his earpiece. "Sloane, Agent Simmons is heading down with the last one. We're going to do one last sweep of the floor, but I think we might be clear...." His voice trailed off when Hobbs stopped to study the vent up near the ceiling at the far end of the room. "Hobbs?"

"Dex? What's going on?" Sloane asked.

Hobbs pulled off the vent screen, stood on his toes, and peeked in. The rest happened so fast, Dex barely had time to register what the hell was going on. Hobbs sped straight for Dex, shoving him so hard he went stumbling through the fire doors. The last thing he heard was the slam of metal and an explosion that shook the floor beneath him when he hit it.

Dex curled up on himself, arms thrown over his helmet as the blast reverberated around him. Debris, ceiling panels, chunks of plaster, and brick falling on him, banging against his helmet as a cloud of heavy smoke and dust threatened to choke him. He rolled onto his side, coughing and hacking, his body covered in a layer of gray dust. When he inhaled, his lungs burned, and sitting up made him wince. His left thigh stung. Checking his leg, there was a long gash where a piece of something sharp had sliced through his tac pants, but lucky for him, it wasn't deep. When his ears stopped ringing, he could hear Sloane shouting through his earpiece.

"Dex, goddamn it, answer me!"

"I'm okay," he wheezed. "Are Simmons and the kid okay?"

"Yeah, they're fine. The stairs are blocked. You'll have to make your way down the stairs on the other side of the building. What the hell happened?"

"There was another bomb. We were about to sweep the area, when Hobbs—" Realization slammed into Dex's chest, and he pushed himself to his feet, ignoring the pain in his leg. "Oh, God. Hobbs!"

Calvin's anxious voice came over his earpiece. "What happened to Hobbs? Where is he?"

"That son of a bitch!" Dex slammed his fist into the wall. "He pushed me through the fire door. He… he stayed inside the classroom." There was silence on the other end of his earpiece until Sloane spoke up.

"Can you see the room?"

Dex turned, cursing under his breath. "Negative. Part of the corridor collapsed in front of it."

More silence, followed by Sloane's quiet voice. "There's nothing you can do. Get down here."

Dex shook his head, tears stinging his eyes. No. That bastard was not dead. "Hobbs, if you're in there, you better answer me, or I swear I will kick your ass." One of the doors had been blown off its hinges and was lying like crumpled paper to one side; pieces from the corridor walls, cement blocks, bricks, and clusters of wires blocked the only way into what was left of the classroom. Live wires sparked, sizzled, and popped from somewhere to his right. Dex limped over to the debris. "Hobbs, answer me!"

"Dex…." Sloane began.

"He's a tough bastard. He's not dead," Dex ground out angrily. "Hobbs, you answer me right fucking now!" He grabbed a piece of cement block and tossed it to one side, shoving and moving bricks. "Hobbs!" Through the silence, there was a low groan. "Hobbs?"

The softest gasp met Dex's ears, followed by what Dex could have sworn was his name.

"I'm coming, buddy. You hang in there."

"Negative. Dex get out of there," Sloane ordered. "We don't know how stable the building is."

Dex shoved at a small pile of debris and thanked whoever was watching out for him. There was a tunnel large enough to get Hobbs through. "I found an opening. I can get him out."

"That structure is unstable. You go in there, and you might not come out. Wait for backup," Sloane ground out, his frustration becoming evident.

"There's no time." Dex pushed tentatively against the makeshift tunnel walls. "It's stable." *For the most part.*

"You don't know that. Fall back, Agent, Daley. That's an order!"

"I can't leave him in there to die." Dex got down on his stomach and crawled through the tunnel with caution, ignoring Sloane's curses in his ear. His partner was going to tear him a new one, but Hobbs was alive, and if his friend was going to make it out of this, Dex would have to get him out now. He didn't know how he was going to get the nearly three-hundred-pound agent out of there, but he'd worry about that later. For now, he worked on controlling his breathing and refused to think about the throbbing in his bloodied leg. God, he sure as hell hoped the other end of this wasn't blocked. It was dark and cramped, leaving enough room for him to maneuver Hobbs through once he did get his fellow agent in here. It was going to be a tight fit, but he'd get it done.

Something crumbled above him, knocking against his helmet before rolling off. Dex stilled, sweat dripping down the side of his face as he listened for any indication the tunnel was about to collapse on him. Sloane would really be pissed at him, then.

After what seemed like an eternity, he reached the end. It was dark and he pushed out ahead of him with his hand, letting out a sigh of relief when it gave way. Crawling out into the smoke-filled room, Dex could only be grateful the bomb had been small scale, taking out half the classroom and not the whole thing. He searched through the mounds of debris and thick fog, spotting a bloodied hand poking out from behind the teacher's desk, which had toppled over, the heavy metal taking the brunt of the explosion judging by its dented and blackened surface.

Dex limped over, sucking in a sharp breath as he knelt down beside Hobbs. He checked his friend's vitals before running his hands over and under Hobbs, checking for any broken bones, embedded objects, or bleeding. Hobbs was covered in scratches, dirt, dust, and blood, but he was in one piece, on the outside at least.

"It's okay, buddy, I'm here." Dex unclasped his backpack, removing his coil of rappelling rope, and hurried to secure the rope around Hobbs, looping it through straps on his tac vest, around his chest area, until he got a firm hold. Testing the rope and feeling confident it wouldn't come undone, Dex slipped his arms under Hobbs.

He dragged his friend toward the tunnel and stopped twice to catch his breath. It was hard enough to breathe as it was in here, but Hobbs's massive frame didn't help. "Why are you Therians so goddamn heavy?" With some serious teeth gritting and determination, Dex managed to get Hobbs over to the tunnel entrance. He patted Hobbs's arm and took hold of the ropes.

"I'm getting you out of here, okay? You think about Calvin. How pissed will he be if you leave him hanging? Where would Calvin be without his best bud Hobbs, huh?" He tied the rope securely around his waist and lay down on his stomach, crawling back through the tunnel. At one point, he had to pause long enough to reach in under his visor and wipe the sweat from his face so it wouldn't fall into his eyes. It was so damn hot and his equipment was weighing him down, but he kept going. He had to get Hobbs out of there.

Once on the other side, Dex unfastened the rope from his waist and braced his feet to either side of the tunnel before he started to pull. Calvin's voice came over his earpiece. "The EMTs will be with you any minute, Dex. We've managed to clear a way up the stairs."

"Copy that," Dex replied through his teeth, every muscle in his body straining while he pulled and dragged Hobbs closer. It felt like a lifetime had gone past, although it was only a few minutes. As Hobbs's helmet came into view, Dex heard the calls of the EMTs not far behind. "Over here!" He gave another pull, relieved when Calvin dropped to his knees alongside Dex and snatched the rope to help him. They both moved out of the way as the half a dozen EMTs grabbed Hobbs and carefully pulled him out from the tunnel and onto a stretcher.

"Ethan...." Calvin put a gloved hand to his partner's shoulder and leaned in. "Ethan, can you hear me? It's Cal." There was no reply from Hobbs. Calvin's bottom lip trembled, and his eyes grew glassy, but he pulled himself together.

"He'll be okay," Dex said, putting a hand on Calvin's shoulder. "You'll see."

Calvin nodded, though Dex wasn't sure how much Calvin had heard, much less believed. He took his partner's hand in his, talking to him in soothing tones as the EMTs got to work. When it was time to take Hobbs away, Calvin stepped up to Dex, trying his best to remain composed. "I know I already said this, but thank you. You saved his life."

"He saved mine first."

"Yeah, but if you hadn't persisted in going back for him...." Calvin shook his head.

"Don't mention it." He threw an arm around Calvin, limping along, and shooed away the EMT that started buzzing around his leg. "This can wait. It's only a scratch. Go help someone else who needs it more." The woman ran off, and Dex gave Calvin a broad grin. "There is one thing you can do for me."

"Anything."

"When your partner wakes up, talk to him about going on a diet. Seriously, I think I pulled something."

Calvin blinked at him before letting out a laugh. "I'll do that."

As Calvin helped him to the stairs, Dex braced himself. "So on a scale of one to diva, how pissed off is Sloane at me right now?"

Calvin winced. "I'd say…. Mariah Carey pissed."

"Shit. Mariah? Really? You sure he's not Tom Cruise pissed, demanding a hotel be cleared out for him and his dinner?"

"Nope. Definitely Mariah pissed."

"Damn it." Maybe he should play up his injury. No, that would probably blow up in his face. He had no idea what lay in store for him, as it was the first time he'd gone against Sloane's orders. But Dex had been right to do so. If he'd waited until backup arrived, waited for them to clear the area, before going in for Hobbs…. He'd rather not think about it.

"Calvin? Dex? Where the hell are you two?"

"Speak of the devil," Dex murmured. "We're on our way." Calvin helped him down the stairs and the moment he stepped foot in the lobby, Sloane was waiting for him, and he was most definitely pissed off.

"What the hell—" Sloane took in his bloodied leg, his face going red as he pulled off his helmet and thrust it at some poor agent within arm's reach. "I told you it was dangerous. Did you get that looked at?"

"It's fine, just a scratch. I'll go now." Dex thanked Calvin, who couldn't mask his relief at being able to run off, and Dex made his way outside the building. The sidewalk and street were littered with agents, EMTs, firefighters, news vans, reporters. It was a nightmare. Outside, Sloane pulled Dex to one side.

"What the hell did you think you were doing?"

"My job," Dex replied, making certain no newspersons heard him. The last thing they needed was the press reporting how the THIRDS couldn't even manage their own teams. They were going to be crucified for this. Didn't matter that they weren't clairvoyant, that they didn't have enough evidence, or information to go on. All they would see was that the THIRDS had failed and innocent kids were hurt. A part of him believed they were right. The last thing he needed right now was to be chewed out by his Team Leader.

"No. Your job is to follow orders, and you sure as hell weren't doing that."

Dex limped over to their BearCat and tossed his helmet inside the open back doors. Rosa was at the console connected to dispatch, updating the various THIRDS units on scene. Instead of helping, Dex was stuck arguing.

"You really thought I was going to walk away when there was even the slightest chance of going in there and saving him?"

"I expected you to wait for backup," Sloane insisted.

"There was no time to wait for backup!"

"Dex!"

You've got to be kidding me. He really was not in the mood for Ash. Dex turned to snap at him. "What?" At Ash's stricken expression, Dex knew something was wrong. "What happened?"

"It's Cael."

"What about Cael?" Ash's hesitation, coupled with the pain on his face, scared the hell out of Dex and he grabbed Ash's vest. "Ash, where's my brother?"

"He got knocked out during the blast. Part of the ceiling collapsed in one of the rooms he was in. The EMT that checked him over says they won't know how serious it is until they get him back to the hospital. They're loading him up in that ambulance there." Ash pointed out one of the ambulances, and Dex started for it when Sloane caught his arm.

"We're not done here."

"Are you serious?" Dex gaped at Sloane. "That's my brother."

"I know that," Sloane replied, clearly attempting to summon patience he didn't have left. "I know you're worried, but we have a job to do. *You* have a job to do."

Ash put his hand on Sloane's shoulder. "Can I talk to you?"

"Not now, Ash."

"Sloane."

"Fine." Sloane released Dex, jabbing a finger in his direction. "I expect a debriefing later, Daley."

"Yes, sir," Dex ground out through his teeth before he made a dash for the ambulance calling out to them. "Wait!" He reached one of the EMTs before he could close the door. "I'm coming with you. That's my brother." He climbed into the back of the ambulance, taking a seat on the bench as the doors closed.

"Cael." Dex ran a hand over his brother's head, hating the look of him covered in grime and blood. He'd been so lost in his thoughts he hadn't heard the EMT talking to him. "I'm sorry, could you repeat that?"

The guy pointed a blue-gloved finger at Dex's leg. "Would you like me to take a look at your leg?"

"Please. Thank you." He brushed Cael's hair away from his head. "Is he going to be okay?"

"We won't know if there's any internal damage or the extent of it until we get him x-rayed and scanned." Something in Dex's face must have given the guy pause, because he gave Dex a sympathetic smile. "His vitals are good. He received no lacerations, or severe injuries from what we can see. It's likely his brain was rattled around a bit from the impact. We're probably looking at a couple of nights of observation and rest before he's cleared. It's a good thing your brother's Therian. It's the only reason there hasn't been any loss of life."

"None of the kids...."

The EMT shook his head. "No. Don't get me wrong; we're transporting several children in critical condition, but they're going to pull through. There are plenty more with serious injuries, but being Therian has saved their lives. If they'd been Human, there'd be fewer flashing lights and not enough sirens."

"Thank God for small miracles," Dex muttered. He thanked the EMT, letting him go about his business patching up Dex's leg. On the way to the hospital, countless questions went through Dex's head. Had Isaac known the Therian kids would be more resilient? How would he know there wouldn't be casualties? Why the hell would he pick a youth center? If he'd really wanted to cause loss of life, why hadn't he? Something in Dex's gut told him there was more to this than what was on the surface. There had to be a reason behind the bombing, just as there had to be a reason behind Isaac targeting the CDC Therian registration office. If only they could figure it out before Isaac ended up destroying the city.

DEX HAD spent the rest of the afternoon and early evening hovering outside Cael's room at the New York Presbyterian Hospital waiting for the doctors to tell him about his baby brother. He'd managed to stop seething a few hours ago, after being forced to fight his way through reporters and angry mobs the moment he'd stepped foot off the ambulance. It was lucky the THIRDS had assigned agents to the hospitals receiving the wounded, or Dex would have ended up in jail for assault. Despite limping and looking like he'd been to hell and back, the villagers had their pitchforks out, demanding he be burned at the stake for his failures. Despite arriving earlier, Calvin hadn't fared any better with the crowd, but managed to make it inside without punching anyone's lights out.

Two doors down, his teammate had waited for word on Hobbs, who was in worse shape than Cael. After a bunch of x-rays and scans, Cael's assigned doctor had assured Dex his brother looked worse off than he was. He'd been knocked out but nothing was broken, fractured, or concussed. They would be keeping him a few nights to observe him and keep running a few Therian tests to make sure. Apparently his brother had a hard head, and lucky for them, that hard head had been protected by an even harder helmet.

As soon as Tony was able to get away, he was thundering through the hospital, voice booming, and boots stomping like Godzilla through Tokyo. Dex had heard him from Cael's room. His dad deflated the moment his gaze landed on Cael, his gaze going from Cael to Dex and back. The two of them had blubbered like a couple of babies, despite knowing Cael was going to be fine. Then his dad put his game face on, told Dex to call him if anything changed, and stalked off. That had been an hour ago.

After tucking his brother in, Dex decided to check in on Calvin and Hobbs. Lieutenant Sparks had authorized Dex and Calvin to take a couple of personal days, and had even allowed the rest of their team to come visit in shifts. Rosa had kissed Cael's head, called him her poor *gatito*, and left with what Dex had been certain were teary eyes. Letty had squeezed the life out of Dex, brought him lunch, and kissed Cael's head, telling him he'd better be on his feet soon. Neither Sloane nor Ash had made an appearance, but he didn't hold it against them. Headquarters was on lockdown, trying to sort out the chaos from the bombing, deal with families, address the media, and put every available agent out there on the streets in an attempt to track down Isaac or someone who could lead them to Isaac.

"Hey," Dex said quietly, closing the door behind him. Calvin stood with Hobbs's hand in his. There were IVs and tubes everywhere. They'd cleaned Hobbs up, revealing the countless scratches and nasty bruises.

"Doc said it's a good thing he's a Therian. His size helped. Plus he was wearing his gear and a helmet. If he'd been Human…." Calvin bit his bottom lip then nodded. "He's going to be okay. He's got a few cracked ribs from where he landed." Calvin followed Dex's gaze to the tubes in Hobbs's nose. His voice was rough when he spoke. "Smoke inhalation. They're giving him antibiotics. Luckily, there was no damage to his lungs."

There was a sudden loud commotion outside, and Calvin's eyes widened. "Oh hell. It's them."

"Who?" Sounded like a damn war had broken out. Dex was sure he heard a chair clattering somewhere. He edged away from the door.

"Rafe and Seb."

"I still don't know who that is." Should he be worried? By Calvin's expression, it appeared so.

"Hobbs's big brothers."

Dex arched an eyebrow at him. "Like, big as in older, right?"

"Big as in older and *big*."

"How much bigger can they get? Hobbs is already the size of the fuckin' Chrysler building." Dex looked down at himself. "How do you not get an inferiority complex being around these dudes?"

"Dex, we're Human. You can't compare yourself to them. Once you accept that you'll never be as big, strong, fast, or resilient, it gets easier. And it's not because you're not trying hard enough, or not good enough; it's in their blood. Why do you think the THIRDS recruits them?" Calvin ran his hand tenderly over Hobbs's head. "It might seem like a gift, but some don't see it that way."

"I never realized." He never would have suspected Hobbs to have any hang-ups about being Therian. Cael had plenty growing up, but with Tony and Dex to support him, he'd grown out of it, even if his little brother occasionally felt inferior to his Felid teammates. Dex knew the feeling. "Wait, you said 'recruit *them.*' Are you telling me Hobbs's brothers are—"

The door to the room slammed open and Calvin jerked back. Dex opened his mouth to tell off the two Therians, but when they stepped in the room, he quickly shut it. Rafe and Seb were not only bigger than Hobbs, they were tougher and meaner looking. They were also in THIRDS uniforms. Crap. Hobbs's brothers were Defense agents as well. Why the hell hadn't he known that?

"Ethan...." One of the brothers ran over to the bed and when his expression softened, Dex immediately spotted the resemblance. The guy couldn't be that much older than Hobbs, with short black hair interspersed with gray, same with his stubbly jaw. The lines at the corners of his eyes were the same as Hobbs's, showing he smiled often. The second brother was a whole other story. It was clear he was the eldest, and by the looks of it, not the friendliest. His expression was stern, revealing nothing. As opposed to his brothers, he had fairer hair, a few permanent nicks and scars here and there on his clean-shaven face, and had a lightly crooked nose that had clearly been broken one too many times. He had a stoic, military air about him.

The younger of the two gently put his hand to Hobbs' head. "What happened?"

Calvin swallowed hard and looked to Dex. Where the hell was Sloane when you needed him? Shouldn't the Team Leader be the one to explain why their brother was in a hospital room? "We were clearing out the youth center when we found a lost kid. We got him out and were about to make another round, when Hobbs came across a bomb hidden in a vent. There wasn't enough time. He shoved me through the fire door and was left behind."

The oldest turned to Dex, his amber eyes pinning Dex to the spot. "Who the fuck are you?"

"Oh, uh, I'm Agent Dexter Daley. I joined the team about eight months ago." Dex held his hand out, but when the guy left him hanging, he shoved it in his pocket.

"A rookie? Are you the reason my brother's lying there?" he growled, crowding Dex.

"Whoa, hey, take it easy." Dex put his hands up and took a step back, not appreciating the accusation, but understanding how hard this probably was for the guy.

"Don't you fucking tell me to take it easy, Rookie. If you screwed up, I swear I will—"

"Rafe, stop!" Calvin wedged himself between Dex and Rafe, pushing the larger Therian away. "Dex was the one who got Ethan out. He risked his life to save him. If he hadn't gone in there, the paramedics might not have made it in time."

Surprise flashed through Rafe's face, but within seconds, the stern mask had returned.

"Wait, you're Dex?" Seb came over, shoving past his older brother as if he wasn't there, and took Dex's hand. "Ethan's always talking about you!"

Dex's jaw dropped. "Hobbs talks?"

Seb laughed. "Of course he talks. Can't get him to shut up sometimes. He's told me so much about you, it's like I know you. I swear, every time I talk to him he's telling me about something funny you did or said."

"Hobbs talks? Talks out loud? I had no idea."

"Yeah, but only to Seb," Rafe grunted. "With the rest of us, it's like he's a fucking mute."

Seb rounded on his brother. "Maybe if you weren't such a dick to him all the time, he'd talk to you too."

O-okay. Obviously some family issues needed resolving here. Rafe gritted his teeth, his jaw muscles clenching, but he said nothing. He walked over to Hobbs's bedside, Calvin joining him to speak quietly.

Seb gave Dex a weary smile. "Ethan was diagnosed with selective mutism when he was a kid. Social situations were impossible for him. The anxiety was rough. Thanks to years of cognitive-behavioral strategies and therapy, he got the help he needed to get through it, but he's still shy. He has trouble talking to certain people or during certain situations."

"And it's never impeded his job?" Dex asked, wondering how Hobbs ended up a Public Safety Bomb Technician for the THIRDS.

Seb shook his head. "Ethan loves what he does. Always has. When it comes to the job, he's confident. When he needs to relay information, he's speaking into a headset, so for him, the way he manages, is that his job is dealing with machines, not people. It's people who are the problem." Seb looked over his shoulder at Rafe and shook his head. When he spoke, his voice was quiet. "Don't feel bad, though. He doesn't talk to our parents much either. Just me and Calvin." He smiled warmly. "Thanks, for saving his life."

Dex returned his smile. He liked Seb a whole lot better than Rafe.

"Our brother's in the hospital and you're looking for a place to park your dick?"

Yep. A whole lot better.

"You know what, Rafe? Fuck you."

The brothers started arguing when Sloane came thundering into the room. His laser glare was set to stun and pissed off seemed to be his new modus operandi. "What the hell is going on here?"

"What kind of team are you running, Brodie?" Rafe marched up to Sloane and gave him a shove. "How could you let this happen?"

Sloane put his hands up in front of him, his voice calm. "Rafe, take it easy."

"If one more asshole on your team tells me to take it easy, I'm going to put a bullet in them. You didn't answer my question. How could you let this happen?"

"Rafe, leave him alone," Seb warned. "I'm sure Sloane did everything he could."

Rafe turned to his brother with a glare. "Tell me, bro. Is there someone in this unit you don't want to screw?"

"What the hell is your problem?" Seb spat out, giving his brother a shove.

"You're my problem. If you'd kept it in your pants, you wouldn't have been transferred from Destructive Delta, and you would have been there to have his back. But you couldn't, could you? And now look at him!"

"You love throwing it in my face. I'm sorry we can't all be fucking perfect like you, Rafe. Whatever happened, you can't pin this one on me, you asshole."

"I've had enough of this." Dex fished into his utility belt pouch and grabbed his Ultra Sound Device. He held out the small black device and pulled out a couple of earplugs that he tossed to Calvin. "Get those in Hobbs's ears. Sloane, get the hell out."

Sloane's eyes went wide and he bolted from the room. As soon as Calvin had the earplugs in Hobbs's ears, Dex clicked the small black button. It seemed as if nothing was happening, at least not to Dex and Calvin. Hobbs's brothers dropped to their knees, their hands over their ears as they writhed in pain. Dex clicked off the device and put it away, knowing the two would remain stunned for a few seconds. He grabbed each one by the ear and hauled them to their feet.

"If you two insist on acting like a couple of Felids throwing a hissy fit, I'm going to treat you that way. Come with me." He dragged them out of the room, ignoring Sloane's startled expression as Dex strode by with the groaning and squirming Therians in his grip. The brothers were too affected by the ultrasound device to do much about it.

He led them a couple of doors down and pushed them inside, turning them so they faced the bruised and battered agent.

"You see that? That's *my* baby brother."

The two agents swallowed hard, their surprised expressions quickly growing remorseful.

"You don't see me blaming everything that has a fucking pulse. He was doing his job. Yeah, I'm pissed off. I'm hurt. I want to scream and beat the living shit out of something, but I won't. Why? Because he needs me to keep my shit together so I can catch the sons of bitches who did this to him. Now you two can keep throwing your temper tantrums, see how far that gets you. Or you can do your damn jobs and make your brother proud. Now get the hell out. It was a pleasure making your acquaintance. Let's do it again, perhaps never." Dex headed for Cael's bedside and took a seat on the sky-blue couch. The two brothers lingered silently for a moment before Rafe stormed out. Seb came around and took a seat next to Dex.

"I'm sorry about your brother."

"Yeah, well, you two aren't the only ones with something to lose."

"Hobbs mentioned you were Cael's older brother. I didn't know he'd been hurt. He's a good kid."

Dex couldn't help his smile. "He'd punch your lights out for calling him that. He hates to be called a kid." It was hard not to think of him that way. Although Cael was in his late twenties, he looked much younger, and his sweet, playful disposition had him coming off as younger than his age as well. To Dex, Cael would always be his little brother.

"Thank you, for what you did. I'm glad you're on the team, Dex. Makes me feel better knowing Ethan's got you to watch his back."

That reminded Dex. "I didn't know you'd been on Destructive Delta."

Seb averted his gaze, his green eyes looking at nothing in particular. "Yeah, reassignments are usually kept on the down low since it tends to happen most often when an agent fucks up rather than anything else."

"But from what I've gathered, except for Sloane, no one on Destructive Delta has had any previous partners."

"You're right. Originally, Team Leaders worked solo. When I was reassigned, they restructured all the squadrons and Team Leaders were given partners, so each team had an equal number of Therian and Human agents. My partner applied for Recon, so they hired Gabe to fill the position and assigned him to Sloane."

Dex nodded, waiting for Seb to continue. Judging by what Rafe had said, Seb had gotten involved with someone on Destructive Delta, and Dex couldn't help wondering who it was. It had been before Gabe's hiring, so it could have been Sloane. The only other options were Calvin and Cael. As far as Dex knew, Cael dated, but they were mostly casual hookups from his college days, and it had been a while since he'd heard Cael mention anyone in particular. Having a secret forbidden relationship with your partner wasn't the only challenge to an agent's love life. "So, what happened? If you don't mind my asking."

"I fucked up." Seb shook his head, a deep frown coming onto his face. "Never fall for a teammate, Dex. It'll only end in heartache."

Don't I know it. Dex swallowed hard. "Sounds like you really cared about him."

"If I'd cared about him, it would have hurt, but… It's been five years and I can't get him out of my head. He's something else. Gorgeous, funny, sweet, such a nice guy, and I messed it all up. I tried to talk to him after—"

A knock sounded at the door, and Dex looked up, smiling at their visitor. It had been a while since Dex had seen Hudson around. Their team's Chief Medical Examiner had been on loan to the rest of the unit and snowed under with backlogged cases. Just because Destructive Delta was working on finding the Order didn't mean homicides stopped happening.

"I came as soon as I could—" Hudson came to an abrupt halt, his eyes widening, and his face going red at the sight of Seb. "What are you doing here?"

Seb got to his feet, his hands shoved in his pockets. "I was visiting my brother."

Hudson's expression softened. "Oh, yes of course." Hudson gave him an apologetic smile. "I do apologize. How is he doing?'

"Resting. You know Ethan, tough as nails."

"I can assure you, he's being well cared for." Hudson gave a tentative smile, and Dex looked from one to the other. Awkward didn't cover it.

"So, uh, how are you?" Seb asked, running a hand absently through his cropped hair.

"Good, considering. You?"

"Same."

An uncomfortable silence stretched between them as they both tried their hardest not to look at the other one. Guess there was no question who Seb had been involved with. Poor guy. It was obvious he was still crazy about Hudson.

Seb finally broke the silence, motioning toward the door. "I should get back. Rafe is probably driving Cal crazy."

At the mention of Rafe's name, Hudson stiffened, and his jaw clenched. "Would you mind not telling him I'm here? I'd rather avoid one of his oh-so-pleasant encounters."

Rafe's reputation certainly preceded him, Dex thought wryly. Bet he and Ash were best buds. If Rafe was hostile with his brother concerning what happened, he could only imagine he wasn't too fond of Hudson. Dex didn't blame the Englishman for avoiding the guy.

"I'm sorry," Seb said sincerely.

"Not your fault your brother's… difficult."

That made Seb chuckle. "Still so polite."

"One of my many faults." Hudson smiled sadly at him. "Please take care of yourself."

"You too." With a wave at Dex, Seb left, and the room was once again plunged into awkward silence.

"So, you and Seb…."

"It's not up for discussion," Hudson snapped.

Dex held his hands up. "Sorry. Didn't mean to pry." Wow. It must have been bad. Hudson was nothing if not polite at all times. After a few months, Dex learned there was more to their Chief Medical

Examiner than he'd first thought. Hudson was exceptionally well spoken, composed, and polite, but he had a mouth on him that would make a nun keel over. The wolf Therian could swear with the best of them and far more creatively. Dex was always learning fun new words from him. He'd even learned how to make English tea. Of course the cookies, or biscuits, or whatever the hell Hudson called them, didn't hurt in making the experience more enjoyable.

Hudson let out a weary sigh. "I apologize. It was a rather disheartening experience. Seb is… a wonderful bloke."

"Seems like he still cares about you," Dex added carefully.

Hudson's cheeks flushed, and he pushed his trendy, black-framed glasses up his nose. "The feeling would be mutual."

"Then why not—"

"It's in the past, Dex." Hudson went to Cael's bedside and put his hand to his forehead. Seeming unable to help himself, he checked Cael's vitals, the IV bag, and the chart tucked into the pocket at the end of the bed. "I'm glad to see he'll be okay. Nina's been so worried. The whole Unit is worried. Your brother's very much cared for."

"He's a great guy," Dex stated proudly.

"Well, if you need anything, do give me a shout."

"I will. Say thank you to Nina for me."

"Will do."

Dex grabbed the change of clothes Tony had brought him earlier and headed for Cael's bathroom. There was a small shower stall and some towels. Once inside the shower, his muscles relaxed. He'd managed to clean up some while he waited to hear about Cael from the doctors, but now he was finally able to wash away the remaining dirt, grime, and blood. He wished his worries would wash down the drain with the rest of it. Besides coming into Hobbs's room to see what all the noise was about, Dex hadn't run into Sloane, and that wasn't a good sign. This was the first time Dex had done something to really piss Sloane off. Oh, he'd made his partner angry before, but not nostrils flaring, you-done-fucked-up angry. He was not looking forward to whatever awaited him.

After toweling off, he pulled on a clean pair of boxer briefs, socks, his comfy jeans, and a loose charcoal gray, long sleeve T-shirt.

He dropped down onto the couch, fluffed up the pillow given to him by a cute little Therian nurse, and stretched out for a much-needed nap. His leg protested, but it wasn't too bad since he'd been given some painkillers. With his arms folded over his chest, and his stocking feet crossed at the ankles, he forced himself to clear his mind, hoping this whole thing with Sloane would blow over. Maybe by the morning, everything would be back to normal.

CHAPTER 8

DEX

The faint sound of his name being called woke Dex with a start. He rubbed his eyes and sat up when he remembered where he was. Jumping to his feet, he ran to Cael's bedside, his heart squeezing at the sight of his little brother smiling at him.

"Hey, you're awake," Dex said, putting a hand to his brother's head. "How are you feeling?"

"Like shit," Cael replied, his voice raspy. "Can I have some water?"

"You can have all the water you want." There was a jug of water, along with some plastic cups on the small table beside the bed, and Dex poured some, handing it to Cael then pausing. "Can you hold it?"

Cael rolled his eyes and took the cup from him. Well, it looked like his baby bro was going to be fine. He drank down the whole cup and passed it back to Dex. "Thanks. How long have you been here?"

Dex looked at his watch. "A few hours. Dad brought me some clothes, and I used your shower. You know, if this is to get out of programming more algorithms, there are better ways to go about it than getting yourself blown up."

"Screw you," Cael said with a laugh, then winced. "Ow." He frowned, his expression giving way to panic. "Hobbs? Is he okay? I heard you say he was trapped just before I got knocked out."

"Take it easy. Hobbs is fine. He's pretty banged up, but he was lucky. They're treating him for smoke inhalation."

Cael nodded somberly, his eyes welling up. Dex carefully took a seat on the edge of his bed. "Hey, what's wrong?"

"Hobbs is okay because he's a Therian. What if he hadn't pushed you out of there?"

Dex's close call hadn't even crossed his mind until now. He'd been so busy worrying about his brother and his teammate, he hadn't given it much thought. He swallowed hard and gave his brother a reassuring smile. "You know me. I got a hard head."

"How can you joke about this? You could have been killed!"

"It's my job, just like it's yours. You think I wasn't going out of my head, thinking the worst when I heard about you?" Dex had known from the moment he was recruited how much more vulnerable he was to the rest of his team. Not only were his teammates Therians, they were more often than not facing Therian threats. His Human teammates had the advantage of experience over him, but Dex couldn't spend his time worrying about what ifs.

"Yes, but I'm a Therian. I know I'm not as strong as Sloane, or Ash, or Hobbs, but I can take more than you, and you're on Defense."

"Hey, don't work yourself up. I'm fine. What about when I was in the HPF? I was just as likely to be hurt there as here."

"That doesn't help," Cael muttered pathetically. "Promise me you'll be careful?" He narrowed his eyes at Dex. "You're not really John McClane, you know."

"Thanks for bursting my bubble." Dex could see Cael trying not to smile, but he failed miserably.

"Ass hat."

There was a soft knock at the door, and Dex called for them to come in, surprised to find it was Ash, though he was more surprised by Ash's behavior. It almost resembled… insecurity. That couldn't be right. It would mean the guy possessed feelings other than anger and disdain.

"Ash," Cael said cheerfully, his smile stretching from ear to ear. Dex still couldn't fathom how these two were such close friends. It was like a bunny becoming friends with an anaconda.

"Hey." Ash returned Cael's smile and held up a thermal lunch bag. "Rosa made you dinner. She's convinced the only way you'll get better is if she gets some of her Boricua food in you." He walked over to Cael's bedside and handed him the bag.

"Ooh, did she make me some *arañitas*?"

Ash chuckled. "Of course she did. She knows how much you love those things. A bit too greasy for my taste, but they're not bad."

"Are you kidding? They're awesome! Fried shredded plantains with the right amount of garlic. Besides, Rosa's cooking is the shizzle."

"You and your brother, man. What is it with you two and food?"

"Um, it's tasty." Cael motioned over to his right and Ash followed the movement, giving a start when he saw Dex. What the hell? Seriously?

"Daley. I didn't see you there."

"Yeah, I must have been real difficult to spot with all the other people not in the room," Dex muttered. Jerk.

Ash opened his mouth then seemed to think better of it. When he turned his attention back to Cael, he was smiling again. "Did you want to eat now?"

"In a minute. Thanks for bringing it."

"No problem. How are you feeling?"

"Better, now that you're here."

Dex's stunned expression mirrored Ash's. Cael carried on, obliviously.

"Yep. Letty came by—"

"Wait a second." Dex held a hand up. "I've been here the whole time. When did she come by?"

"While you were sleeping, a.k.a. dead to the world," Cael said with a snort. "She tried to wake you up, but you rolled over and mumbled something about having coffee first."

Dex had no recollection whatsoever of someone trying to wake him, but he knew his brother was speaking the truth. Hence, his ex-boyfriend getting away with horrendous home furnishings for the house. "Makes sense. Carry on, then." Cael rolled his eyes and turned back to Ash.

"Anyway, as I was saying. Letty came by earlier today, said she was worried about you. Apparently, you've been acting like an ass." Dex opened his mouth and Cael put a finger up without glancing in his direction. "Shut it."

Dex made a zipping motion over his lips.

"She called me an ass? What the hell?" Ash pouted, his beefy arms crossed over his chest.

"No, I'm calling you an ass," Cael corrected.

"What for?"

"For blaming yourself. This wasn't your fault, Ash. And before you say anything else, you were on the other side of the damn building. There was nothing you could have done. You know that, right?"

"I know, I just…." Ash let out a long breath.

"Come here, big guy." Cael carefully shifted over and patted the bed. After some hesitation, Ash sat down beside him with exceptional care. Dex tended to forget how big Ash was, since whenever Dex saw him, the guy was usually standing around Sloane, Hobbs, or other Therian agents closer to his size, but next to Cael, the difference was staggering, especially since Cael was shorter and slighter than Dex. Cael's size and Therian qualities weren't suited for Defense, but they were an exceptional fit for Recon. His size, stealth, speed, agility, and smarts made him perfect for the reconnaissance position. "Bring it in. Time for a hug."

Dex watched flabbergasted as Ash gently pulled Cael into a hug. His brother tilted his face toward Ash's neck, his fingers slipping under the collar of the larger Therian's uniform. With a smile, Ash pulled back, giving Cael a wink, followed by a playful nudge on the cheek.

"I gotta go. If you need anything, and your bro's busy, or sleeping on the job, call me."

Cael grinned widely. "Okay."

With a grumbled "good-bye" in Dex's direction, Ash left the room. Dex waited until he'd closed the door behind him before taking a seat on the edge of Cael's bed. His brother wisely avoided his gaze, his eyes dropping to his fingers.

"What?"

"Christ, it's that bad?" Dex said, running a hand through his hair. He got up and started pacing. "Cael, we went through this. Remember your senior year in high school? You remember what I told you?"

Cael nodded somberly. "Yes."

"What did I say?"

Cael swallowed hard, his voice quiet. "Never fall for a straight guy."

"And what happened with Shane? He broke your heart into tiny pieces."

"Yes, I remember." Cael lifted his chin defiantly. "Thank you, Dex."

"And out of everyone, you're gonna fall for *him*? The guy's an asshole!"

"He's not!" Cael snapped, startling Dex. Damn, it really was that bad. "I know he might seem that way, but he's really not. I don't know why you two can't get along. He's outspoken, and yes, crude sometimes, but underneath all that, he's really…. He's a good guy."

"Okay, look, as much as the guy annoys me, you know I'd support you in anything that made you happy, with anyone who made you happy, but Cael—"

"Yeah, he's straight. I get it. But you know what, sometimes, I'm not so sure."

"Cael…." Dex let out a sigh and resumed his seat beside his brother. He wanted nothing more than to see his brother happy, even if it was with, God help him, Ash, but his brother was looking for something that wasn't there. "Don't confuse affection for something more. He cares about you. I know he does. It's obvious. He treats you differently than he does everyone else. I admit, it amazes even me, but I don't think it's more than that. Have you ever seen him do anything with anyone that made you think he might be interested in males?"

Cael shook his head, his bottom lip jutted out. "But maybe it's different with me. Maybe it's the first time he's thinking… he might want to." He worried his bottom lip, when he suddenly seemed to think of something. "You could ask Sloane."

"What?"

"Don't tell him it's for me, but ask him if he might know something about Ash that maybe we don't. They've been best friends since they were little. If anyone knows anything, it'd be Sloane, right?"

"Things are tense at the moment between us, what with my going against his orders." Cael nodded dejectedly, and it was too much for Dex. "But as soon as we sort it out, I'll talk to him."

"You will?"

"Of course I will. You know I'd do anything for you, bro."

Cael smiled sweetly at him, before letting out a yawn. "Thanks, Dex."

"Why don't you get some sleep, huh?" He gently pulled Cael in for a hug and planted a kiss on his brother's head. "We'll sort it all out." As soon as Cael drifted off to sleep, Dex lay back down on the couch. He should have seen the signs sooner. Why hadn't he paid more attention? Cael had a bad habit of falling for guys who weren't good for him, and now he'd fallen for the mother lode. Even if there was the slightest probability Cael was right, Ash was so deep in the closet, he was taking Aslan's place in Narnia. Whatever the outcome, it was going to be one hell of a tough road for his baby brother.

IT HAD been two days since Sloane had spoken with Dex, and he'd genuinely believed he would've simmered down by now, but when Dex undressed beside him in the locker room, the bandage around his leg glaringly white against his fair skin, Sloane was far from calm. The more he thought about it, the more he could feel his anger rising. He recalled the way Dex had limped out of the building, leg bloodied, face dripping with sweat, and smudged with muck from the explosion, an explosion that had happened mere feet away.

Dex finished getting dressed and turned to him with a sigh. "Look, I know you're pissed off—"

"Pissed off?" Sloane slammed his locker shut, the rest of the agents in the locker room gathering their belongings and bolting. "I'm not pissed off, Dex, I'm fucking furious."

Dex swallowed hard and stood his ground, rounding his shoulders. "I was doing my job."

"No, you were disobeying orders. You not only put Hobbs's life in danger, but your own."

"He would have died. How much more in danger can he get?"

"Don't—" Sloane caught himself and tried to pull his anger in check. "I'll see you upstairs." He needed to cool off, but every time he closed his eyes, all he could see was Dex lying on the floor in a pool of blood. Since the explosion, Sloane had been sleeping at work in his sleep bay, and both nights he had the same nightmare he'd had back at Dex's place, with the same outcome, except instead of Isaac pulling the trigger, Sloane had watched a mirror image of himself doing the shooting. Disturbed didn't begin to cover it.

His team was his family. If he lost one of them.... Goddamn it, he had a job to do. Protocols were put in place for a reason. If the structure had given way.... What the hell would he have told Cael? How would he have faced Maddock? How would Sloane have explained to Maddock he'd let his son die because he hadn't the balls to put his foot down and take control of the situation? Dex was a good agent, but emotionally, he was too green. Maybe in the HPF, Dex could get away with running headfirst into the fray, but not at the THIRDS, and certainly not on Sloane's watch. He'd make Dex understand, one way or another.

When he walked into their office, he went straight to his desk, where he brought up the files he needed and typed in the time and date, as well as a quick and brief description of the incident. Afterward he would attach his notes and the appropriate reports. As soon as Dex walked through the door, Sloane tapped a code into the side panel. The door swished closed, and the room went into "privacy" mode, the frosted white walls turning solid white so no one could see inside or overhear any conversation.

"Sit down," he stated calmly. Dex pressed his lips together and did as asked. There was no telling how Dex would react, but Sloane reminded himself he was doing his job, and although his partner would most certainly disagree, he was doing it for Dex's own good. Sloane would have done the same had he been facing any other of his teammates. Pressing the "record" button on the panel of his desk's interface, Sloane began.

"Team Leader Sloane Brodie, badge number 0102, issuing a verbal reprimand to Agent Dexter J. Daley, badge number 2108, for direct violation of Policy 2-3, Failure to Follow Procedure."

Dex gaped at him. "You're taking disciplinary action?"

Sloane paused the recording. "Were you expecting special treatment?"

"You mean because we're fucking?" Dex hissed quietly, though with the room in "privacy" mode, Dex could shout at the top of his lungs and no one would hear a word. "No, I didn't expect any special treatment for that. What I did expect from you was guidance."

"You knew exactly what you were doing," Sloane ground out through his teeth. He leaned his arms on his desk and met Dex's stubborn gaze. "That wasn't a rookie mistake and you know it. You deliberately went against direct orders!"

Dex jumped to his feet. "And I'd do it again! I'm not about to stand by and watch one of my teammates die when I can do something about it."

"The structure was unsound!"

"It was sound enough. I was there and you weren't. This isn't about not following orders. It's about *you* not trusting me on the job, or outside of it."

"What?"

"You don't trust me."

What the hell? "Bullshit. You're my partner. I put my life in your hands every time we go out in the damned field."

"Only because you're taking the lead. You're not risking a part of yourself."

"I don't know what the hell you're talking about. I take the lead because I'm the Team Leader and that's my job! Like it's your job to do whatever the hell I tell you to do!" If he wasn't careful, he was going to lose it. Dex had a talent for getting under his skin and that angered Sloane further. "Why are we having this ridiculous conversation?"

"Argument," Dex corrected. "We're having an argument. And we're having it because you can't open up and trust me. I know my eight months on the job are shit compared to your twenty-something years, but I'm not an idiot. That structure was sound. What's more, you know I'm right. That's why you're shouting."

"You're not thinking objectively and *that's* what this is about." He hit the pause button again to resume the recording. "Performance improvement to a satisfactory level is required to prevent further disciplinary action which may impede the course of your training and development, or lead to punitive action which may result in your dismissal. You have a right to contest to this reprimand, under THIRDS Policy 6-2, and are permitted three weeks in which to do so." He took a deep breath and braced himself. "Do you have anything you'd like to add?"

"No," Dex replied through gritted teeth.

"Verbal reprimand concluded." He hit "stop," wishing he could do the same with the shitty feeling turning his stomach. What the hell had gotten into him? He'd never shouted at any of his coworkers. He'd never shouted at Gabe, and they'd had plenty of arguments at the office.

"Are we done?" Dex asked.

Sloane was tempted to keep arguing, but instead, he nodded, not trusting himself to speak. Dex stood, typed his code into the panel and marched out. Just Sloane's luck, seconds later, Ash walked in.

"You okay?"

Again, all Sloane could do was nod. He dropped down into his chair, hearing the swish of the door, and watching the walls go white once again. Ash came to stand beside him, and stared at him in disbelief.

"You gave him a verbal reprimand? Why?"

Sloane glanced up at his friend. "What do you mean, why? He disobeyed orders."

"We disobey orders all the time. Orders aren't always right. You know that better than anyone."

"Are you going to tell me how to do my job too?"

"What the hell's going on with you? You wouldn't have reprimanded Gabe."

Sloane jumped to his feet to confront his friend. "Gabe would have followed orders."

"Don't bullshit me, man. Gabe would have done the same. Hell, any one of us would've if we'd been in Dex's place, and I *know* you wouldn't have resorted to disciplinary measures."

"He has to learn he can't go off half-cocked, disregarding his safety, like everything will turn out fine."

"So this is about Dex."

"Yes, it's about Dex. It's about him thinking he can do whatever the hell he wants without having to face the consequences. He thinks he's goddamn indestructible."

"No, I meant this is about how you feel about him."

"What the hell are you talking about?"

"You think I don't see how close you two have gotten? It's fine. No one's going to hold it against you." Ash took a seat on the edge of Sloane's desk and shrugged. "It was bound to happen. He's your partner."

Sloane's frown deepened. There was no way Ash could know.

"You two have become close friends. You work together, hang out together. No one said you can't be friends with your partner. Look, the guy annoys the ever-living fuck out of me, but I can see why you like to hang out with him. You're too serious, *were* too damn serious, and he changed that." Ash let out a heavy sigh and tapped away at Sloane's interface as he spoke, bringing up several online news sites. "After what happened to Gabe, I thought… I really thought that was it for you." Sloane's surprise must have shown, because Ash glared at him. "Don't look at me like that. Of course, I was worried. You're my best friend, but let's face it, you're different with him, in a good way. He makes you laugh, drags you along to do stupid shit. He's like an excited puppy that never sits still, which makes me want to punch him."

Sloane peered at his friend. "You want to punch puppies?"

"I'd never punch a puppy. What's wrong with you? Dex I'd punch."

"So what's your point?"

"My point is, before he came along, all you had was the job. I could never get you to fucking relax outside of it. I can't believe I'm saying this—and I swear if you tell him, I will deny it to my dying breath, and then I will beat the shit out of you. Don't screw this up, Sloane. Talk to him. He'll listen to you. The guy practically hangs off your every word." He tapped the desk and the board to Sloane's right filled with news articles, all concerning Dex.

Sloane came to stand before the digital board, looking over at various photos of Dex captured by photographers spanning from Detective Walsh's trial, to the bombing at the youth center. He stepped forward and double tapped the image of his partner and lover emerging from the smoke filled building, his arm slightly forward as if he were reaching for Sloane who was walking ahead of him. The tagline read, *Human agent, Dexter J. Daley saves Therian teammate in the aftermath of tragic events.* Sloane swallowed hard. The irony wasn't lost on him.

"Talk to him," Ash insisted, the swish of the doors the only indication Ash had gone, leaving Sloane standing there in the silence of his empty office, staring at pale blue eyes.

"Damn it." He walked back to his desk and closed the window containing all the articles, leaving the reprimand glaring back at him. His finger hovered over the "Submit" button before he tapped the screen and hit "Delete" instead. It asked him if he was sure and he let out a scoff. "I don't know what the hell I'm sure about anymore." Tapping "Yes," he logged into his partner's communication device. Dex was in Sparta. Fucking fantastic. This wasn't going to end badly at all.

He headed down to Sparta, mumbling a greeting to his fellow agents as he searched for Dex. Just his luck, he found his partner in one of the training bays set up for boxing. Dex was down to his snug, black undershirt, his tac pants, and bare feet. He was taking his frustration out on the battered leather bag swaying in front of him, with wraps around his hands instead of gloves. He didn't bother looking at Sloane when he spoke.

"What? Did you come to grade my performance? I'm not wearing shoes. Have I breached protocol again?"

"You gonna throw a hissy fit every time I have to do my job?" Yep. Not going to end badly at all.

Dex delivered a fierce left hook to the bag, followed by a right. "You weren't doing your job, you were being a dick."

Calm. Remain calm. "There are protocols and you failed to adhere to them."

"I'm really starting to hate that word," Dex muttered, delivering another right hook to the bag. "The structure was safe."

"You don't know that." Sloane tried his hardest to summon patience, despite knowing he wouldn't last much longer, especially with Dex's punches growing angrier. The sweat dripped down his face, and Dex stopped long enough to swipe the back of his hand across his brow.

"What if it had been Ash or Cael?"

Sloane rounded his shoulders, answering tersely. "My orders would have been the same. You're letting your emotions cloud your judgment."

"Well excuse me for having any," Dex spat out.

That got Sloane's hackles up. "What the hell's that supposed to mean?"

"Nothing." Dex turned back to the punching bag, but Sloane wasn't about to let him off the hook, not with what he was implying.

"It's too late. It's out there now, so own up to it."

"You want me to own up to it? Okay. I know it's your job not to let things get to you, but sometimes I wonder if you have an off switch. Don't you get tired of being *the* Sloane Brodie all the fucking time?"

"Is that what you think?" The remark cut deep, but Sloane didn't want him to see that. At least Dex hesitated, which told Sloane maybe his partner's words were more out of anger than anything else. Still. He didn't appreciate the remark.

"Sometimes." Dex shrugged. "Look, the job is important. Believe me, I know. But you know what? So is family. If it came down between my teammate's life and my job, fuck the job. They'll stick some other agent in my place, but my friend, my brother, my dad, will never be replaced."

"Losing our teammates is the risk we take. That's why you're here." How could he make Dex understand? Surely he'd faced similar situations with his fellow officers at the HPF? Sloane was aware it was slightly different with a team. When one was out of commission, the rest suffered. When one was lost, the rest grieved. They laughed together, cried together, waded through scandal and death, and a river of toxic shit, protecting each other, caring for one another, at times falling in love. But they were also soldiers, officers, defenders for the public. They took an oath to put the citizens of the city before themselves.

"I'm here to prevent loss of life. *Prevent*. Or have you forgotten? And that's what I did that day. Yes, sometimes a situation will be out of our hands, and lives will be lost, but if I have a choice to do something about it? Guess what I'll be doing?" Dex went back to punching the bag, and Sloane grabbed his arm.

"Damn it, Dex. Will you look at me when I'm talking to you?"

"Let go of my arm," Dex warned, his hand curling into a fist at his side.

"Seriously? We're going to do this?" Sloane nodded and took a step back, motioning for Dex to advance. "All right. Come on. If it'll get it out of your system, I'll oblige."

"Now who's being patronizing?"

"Why do you have to be so goddamn unreasonable?"

"*I'm* unreasonable, Mr. It's-your-job-to-do-what-I-say?" Dex's jaw muscles clenched and he put his hands up. "You know what? Screw this, and screw you."

Sloane scoffed, his voice a low grumble so only Dex could hear him. "Yeah, you won't be doing that any time soon."

"You can be such an asshole." Dex made the mistake of thrusting his hand out toward Sloane. He might have been going to poke Sloane, or shove his shoulder, but Sloane's instincts kicked in and he caught Dex's left wrist, twisting his arm and forcing Dex to double over. The hold didn't last long, as Dex twisted his body toward Sloane, bringing his right fist with him.

Sloane caught Dex's fist and swiped his leg out from under him. He stood back, watching Dex push himself off the mat with a frustrated growl. Dex came at him with everything like he did during their training sessions, with the added bonus of being truly pissed off. Sloane wasn't too proud to admit he had to watch himself. Dex's skills had improved dramatically since he'd joined, and Sloane could no longer take Dex's rookie status for granted. The guy was a fast learner.

determined, and quick to adapt. He was also frustratingly good at mimicking Sloane's movements. Sloane reeled backward, getting clipped on the chin by one of Dex's right hooks. He'd had enough of this.

Dex charged him, and Sloane used his size, weight, and strength to his advantage, grabbing Dex, lifting him off his feet, and slamming him down onto the mat. Then he rolled his partner over, and pulled his arms behind his back. "Calm down." Sloane swiped a zip tie off his utility belt and looped it over Dex's wrists, giving it a tug. He got to his feet and took a step back, surprised when Dex started laughing. "What the hell's so funny?"

With a shake of his head, Dex rolled onto his side and sat up. His expression darkened as he rose. "One, I resent the fact you don't think I can still kick ass with my hands tied behind my back, and two...." Dex bent over and thrust his arms down. The zip tie snapped and fell to the floor. He swiped it up and tossed it at Sloane's feet. "I grew up in two cop houses. You think I don't know how to get myself out of a fucking zip tie? You want me down and out, you're going to have to do better than that." Dex stormed off with Sloane staring after him. What in the hell just happened? He snapped himself out of it, the agents around him pretending they hadn't seen a thing. Well, some of them were pretending.

"What are you all looking at? Get back to your training." He turned and ran into Ash. "Now you're babysitting me?"

Ash looked unimpressed. That made two of them. "Maybe I should have explained how talking works."

With a grunt, Sloane swept past him. "I didn't realize I was talking to the expert on communication." To his frustration, Ash followed him out of the training bay, out of Sparta, and into the busy corridor.

"Don't get pissy with me. You gave him a reprimand, lectured him, and then restrained him? I would have been surprised if he *hadn't* tried to kick your ass."

"Ash, go away."

"Not gonna happen. Didn't happen when we were kids, ain't gonna happen now. Get your shit together, bro." Ash walked off, and Sloane put his hand to the elevator panel. Had someone drugged the water around here? Released some toxic gas into the vents he hadn't become aware of? How had he ended up the bad guy in all of this, with Ash defending Dex, no less? Had the world gone crazy?

"Screw this." He had way too much shit to do to go chasing after Dex. His partner needed time to cool off and come around to the fact Sloane was right. In the meantime, he would head to the Recon department and try to get some answers from someone. This whole case wasn't sitting right with him. Not so much from Isaac's end. The man was a lunatic bent on vengeance. That Sloane understood.

What he didn't understand, was why everything was moving so goddamn slow around here. Something was going on, and he had every intention of finding out what it was, with or without Dex.

CHAPTER 9

OVER AN hour later, Sloane was in even more of a foul mood, if that was possible.

According to Recon, Allan's information from the CDC Therian registration office had come in seconds after the Therian Youth Center bomb went off, meaning it had been put aside, priority falling to the youth center, as it should. Themis had run its algorithms, showing Isaac Pearce had visited the center a few weeks before planting the bomb. He had signed in under a random name, worn a different disguise, and done exactly what he had the second time he'd visited. Sloane's guess was he'd been casing the joint, doing a test run of sorts. Isaac was smart. He wouldn't have gone in blind. Themis also found what Isaac had been doing on his tablet. He'd been accessing the registration office's network and their files, namely Morelli's.

Sloane stalked toward his office and tapped his earpiece. "Rosa, Morelli's registration file led Isaac to the Therian Youth Center. Apparently, Morelli had spent some time there when he was a teen. I'm willing to bet he had a file there as well, and Isaac accessed it before he set off the explosion. I want to know what was in that file."

"I'm on it," Rosa replied.

Maddock's voice came over his earpiece. "I want everyone listening to this to meet in briefing room 'A' right now. Don't care what the hell you're doing, get in here."

Sloane hurried to the briefing room, his eyes instinctively landing on Dex. Their eyes met before Dex turned away to face the front of the room. Ignoring the jab, Sloane took a seat behind him. He wouldn't let his partner's brooding stop him from getting on with his job. The room filled with agents from Beta Pride and Beta Ambush, including Agent Taylor. Although plenty of seats remained empty around the huge semicircle conference table, Taylor decided he was going to sit in front of Dex.

"All right everyone, settle down." Maddock stood behind the podium at the front of the room and tapped his tablet. A video player appeared on the large flat screen TV positioned high on the wall behind him. "This video was uploaded on a Humans 4 Dominance forum that popped up a couple of days ago. Intel has been monitoring it since it launched, but until now, it was mostly a bunch of idiots talking trash. A few minutes ago, Themis sounded the alert." He tapped his tablet and the video played.

They all watched in uncomfortable silence as what started as a sunny, serene day on a quiet street turned into a war zone. Every minute of the horrific Therian Youth Center bombing was there in gory HD. At the end, Maddock switched over to the forum.

"Have you read the comments?" Ash asked from across the table, shaking his head in disgust as he scrolled through the forum on his tablet.

"Don't," Dex said, his jaw muscles clenching. "It's better if you don't. Let Themis read that shit. It'll only make you want to hit something, preferably one of those assholes' faces."

"What kind of sick bastards get off on watching shit like this?"

Dex turned his attention back to Maddock. "More importantly, whoever uploaded this was there. Do we know who it was?"

Maddock brought up a large black screen with undecipherable white text scrolling at unreadable speeds. "Themis is trying to pinpoint a location, but it looks like it was uploaded via cell phone. We should have the owner any second now. There we go."

The screen flashed and a second narrow screen slid in from the side with a John Doe avatar instead of a photograph, along with a name. Themis continued to scan for more information, but came up with nothing.

"Looks like we've got a name. Dr. H Freedman. No visual, driver's license, or social security." Maddock frowned down at his screen.

Damn. Sloane sure as hell hoped they got something. A GPS setting, IP address, something. Whoever had uploaded the video knew what they were doing.

"We've got an address," Maddock declared.

Maybe not. One mistake, that was all they needed, and they could nail this bastard.

"All right. Everyone, suit up, and head out. Destructive Delta, you're going in. Agent Taylor, Agent Stone, you and your teams are going in as backup since Destructive Delta is down three agents since Agent Simmons won't be in until tomorrow. "Keep me informed. I want this Dr. Freedman brought in."

Sloane hurried out of the room along with everyone else, aware of Dex close behind. They'd yet to say a word to each other. Rosa came running up to him and he welcomed the distraction. "Give me something, Rosa."

"This isn't looking good. According to the Therian Youth Center's head organizer—Dr. Michaels, the network was completely fried by the explosion, and the backup files would be accessible through their corporate office, but when I called the corporate office, I was told they no longer had access due to security restrictions and were waiting for clearance from the founder. I decided to cut the middle man and get a hold of the founder, except, whoever they are, they don't exist."

Sloane stopped in his tracks. "What do you mean they don't exist?"

"Well, they exist on paper. Everything is meticulous and thorough. All the paperwork is legit, except there doesn't seem to be a body to go along with the information provided. Every phone number I call leads me to another number, which leaves me to another message. One big loop de nada."

"So suddenly there's a lockdown on the files and the founder goes missing, if he or she ever existed. Fantastic." He hurried out of the department to catch up with the rest of their agents, annoyed when his eyes continually strayed to Dex, as if his body couldn't stand not making some kind of contact with him, even if it was just visual. "Rosa, I want you to tell Intel to keep trying. I want some goddamn answers." The elevator was full, but Sloane pushed in, finding himself squeezed in against Dex, the top of his head under Sloane's chin. Sloane closed his eyes, silently urging the elevator to get moving. It didn't help that he could smell Dex's shampoo, or feel the softness of his hair when Dex shifted. It especially didn't help when someone decided to squeeze in at the last minute, forcing Dex back against Sloane, their bodies pressed together.

Sloane hated how he was starting to doubt himself. Had he made the right decision? Was he willing to give in to see Dex smile again? *Get your shit together, Brodie.* He wasn't going to stop being Team Leader, or running his team the way he always had because he'd gotten into a fight with his lover. If he gave in now, what kind of message would he be giving Dex? That he could get away with what he wanted because they were sleeping together? The elevator pinged, and Sloane all but fled. He had more pressing matters to deal with. The rest would have to wait. At least that's what he kept telling himself.

DR. FREEDMAN'S house was located on the Upper East Side of Manhattan in a residential neighborhood lined with fenced-in trees, expensive brownstones sporting flowerbeds in bloom, and luxury cars parked alongside pristine sidewalks. Agents from Beta Ambush approached the house while the rest searched the perimeter, and each end of the street was blocked by their backup teams' BearCats. Sloane waited with his team in formation behind the safety of their own truck, rifles in their hands. The moment Beta Ambush breached the front door, Sloane gave the order, and they rushed up the steps and into the house. They spread out, checking all the rooms, under beds, in closets, anywhere anyone could hide. One by one, his team confirmed their status until the house was declared clear.

Sloane scanned what was once an elegant-looking living room. The large room was decorated in cream and brown hues with dark accents. The windows were light and airy, expensive rugs covered the hardwood floors. Bookshelves were tucked into the walls to each side of the fireplace, though it was empty of books. In fact, every surface in the room had been cleared of its contents, the evidence scattered on the floor all around them. Lamps had been knocked over, coffee tables upturned, throw pillows slashed along with couch cushions. The place was a disaster.

Ash gave a low whistle. "Looks like the doc left in a hurry."

"I'm not so sure about that. It looks more like it's been ransacked. All right, I want this place searched inside out. I want to know who this guy is, if he's part of the Order, where he might be heading, does he have family, friends, everything, and I want it yesterday, so move your asses." Sloane stalked off into the next room, rounding the corner when he heard Letty's concerned voice.

"Damn, what's up with him?"

"He and Daley got into a lover's quarrel," Ash grumbled.

Dex's reply was a low, "Fuck you, Ash."

There was movement around the room before Rosa piped up. "You guys fighting?"

"It's nothing," Dex muttered, followed by more shuffling, before Dex let out a heavy sigh. Rosa was undoubtedly giving him "that look." "Okay, yes, we got into a fight."

Sloane told himself he shouldn't be eavesdropping, but then again if his team was going to carry on this conversation as if he couldn't hear it, then it wasn't his fault. Rosa spoke up in her usual no-nonsense tone.

"You need to make up."

Dex scoffed. "Says who?"

"Listen up, Rookie. You do *not* want to have him giving orders while he's pissed. He's an absolute miserable fuck. I love him, but it's the truth."

Thanks, Rosa.

"I didn't do anything wrong. He's the one who tore me a new one for doing my job. Yes, I went against orders, but I was right to. I'm not budging on this."

"*Carajo*, you two are so stubborn."

Sloane had heard enough. If Dex truly thought he hadn't done anything wrong then nothing Sloane said was going to change his mind. If anyone was being stubborn, it was Dex. He walked into the bedroom, which was in the same ransacked state as the living room. The queen-sized mattress had been pulled off the bed, its stuffing strewn everywhere. Drawers were open or upended, clothes, shoes, ties, scattered everywhere. However, what stood out the most was that there was nothing personal in the room. No photographs, artwork, nothing that could help him get a profile together of who lived here. He rummaged through the disorderly dresser, but found nothing except men's clothing. All he knew about this doctor was that he was a size "Medium."

On the opposite wall, a closet stretched from one end to the other, its wood louvered doors pulled wide open. He found a light switch, not surprised to find the closet had been searched as well. Inspecting the contents of the closet, he met with another dead end. Nothing but clothes, shoes, belts, and hats, most of it on the floor or dangling precariously off hangers. He checked pockets, but came up empty. Who the hell was this guy? And why was he so careful? Sloane was about to turn off the light, when he noticed something black and furry on the floor in the corner. It looked like it had fallen from somewhere. Picking it up, he found it was a toy. Wait....

"Oh my God." A lump formed in his throat as he stared at the stuffed toy of a black jaguar. It couldn't be. And yet.... He held the toy in his gloved hands, thinking about how much bigger it used to be. Then again, the last time he'd held it, he'd been smaller. It still had its white bandages around each paw, and Sloane swallowed hard. With a shaking hand, he turned it over, inhaling sharply at the white tag under its tail with the initials S.B. written in black marker. The letters were slightly faded and worn, but they were there, and they were his.

"Hey, you okay?"

Sloane held the toy behind him before Ash came into view. He nodded at his friend. "Yeah, um, see if you can find a photograph, or something we can use to physically identify this guy."

Ash cocked his head to one side, his expression one of concern. "You sure you're okay?"

"Yeah, fine."

As soon as Ash left, Sloane removed his backpack and stuffed the toy inside. He quickly zipped it up and clipped it back into place. He didn't know how the hell this had gotten here, or if it really was what he thought it was, but he needed to find out.

Letty's voice came in over his earpiece. "Sloane, we found something."

Sloane hurried through the house and into a large office where his team was gathered. It was in a worse state than the other rooms.

"Well, the guy definitely had something to do with the center, but...." Rosa held up a handful of invoices. "Tax write-offs. The guy donates to the center every month. Has been for years."

Dex shook his head, puzzled. "Why would he blow up a center he donates money to?"

"Not just money," Rosa said, shuffling through the paperwork in her hands. "Clothes, video games, gift cards. Hell, one year he donated six computers. His last donation was three weeks ago. Kids' furniture. Four bunk beds, two desks, beanbag chairs.... This guy was a saint. This makes no sense."

"It's starting to," Sloane said. "I'm thinking kidnapping. Someone was looking for something, something they thought this guy had."

Ash frowned. "I don't get it. Isaac plants the bomb then sets out to frame him? But he had to know we'd come looking for the guy. If he needs this doctor, wouldn't he want us *not* trying to track the guy down?"

Sloane was getting really tired of going in circles. "Whatever Isaac's reason, it undoubtedly figures into his plan. We need to find out why Isaac would want Dr. Freedman. Goddamn it, we need to know what Isaac found at the youth center. Either Morelli was the means to finding Dr. Freedman, or Freedman has information on Morelli that Isaac wants. Either way, the two are connected. Keep digging." He tapped his earpiece and had the switchboard patch him through to Maddock. "Sarge, we aren't going to get anywhere if we can't get access to the youth center files. Everything leads back to Morelli, and I have a suspicion this doctor knows something. The guy's gone. I'm willing to bet Isaac got his hands on him, and if that's the case, he led us here for a reason. Why are we being kept in the goddamn dark?"

"I'm working on it, but I keep getting the runaround from Lieutenant Sparks. I don't know what the hell is going on."

"Well someone better tell me something, because I've had about enough of this bullshit."

Maddock's voice was low, the warning subtle. "Take it easy, Sloane."

Damn, now he was getting pissy with his sergeant. "My apologies, Sarge. You know how I feel about red tape."

"The feeling's mutual. All I can do is keep working on it. See what else you can find."

"You mean other than the fact the guy seemed like a godsend for these kids?" Sloane let out a heavy sigh, pinching the bridge of his nose to ease the headache that was forming. "We'll keep looking."

"Copy that."

"Found something!" Letty waved a sheet of paper at him.

"What is it?"

"An elementary school newsletter." She showed it to Sloane and he gave it a quick read, stopping when he got to the captioned photograph.

"Shit. We need to go." He tapped his earpiece. "Agent Stone, Agent Taylor, keep searching the house. We're heading back to HQ to follow up on a lead. Let us know if you find anything." He received a confirmation from both Team Leaders, and Sloane didn't waste another second. He moved out with his team trailing quickly behind him.

"What's going om?" Ash asked, as he jogged toward the driver's side of the BearCat.

"I'm not sure, but I need to talk to Lieutenant Sparks." If his suspicions were right, things were a whole lot worse than they could have imagined.

SLOANE TOOK a deep, fortifying breath and knocked on Lieutenant Sparks's door. Her soft but firm voice asked him to enter. He pressed his hand to the panel on his left, entered his security pin and the door swished closed. There was no privacy mode setting for Lieutenant

Sparks's office because the whole office was created to be secure. It was spacious, but sparse with her desk in the center of the room across from the door, two chairs in front, a few filing cabinets, a digital board, and a personal bathroom off to the side. Sloane stood at attention with his hands clasped behind his back, waiting for permission to sit.

"One moment, Agent Brodie." Lieutenant Sparks tapped away at her keyboard with her bright red, manicured nails, the scarlet matching her lips in color. Lieutenant Sonya Sparks resembled a 1940s pinup girl with fiery hair falling in soft waves over her shoulders in Veronica Lake fashion, a pristine white pantsuit accentuating her ample curves, and white, three-inch heels that had her towering over a good deal of the agents, seeing as how she was already just under six feet tall without them. Pitch-black eyeliner and thick long lashes framed her deep-blue eyes. She was quiet, observant, and the government tattoo on her neck marked her Therian form as a cougar.

Anyone who underestimated Lieutenant Sparks was in for a real eye-opener. She was a hard ass, but a fair one. Sloane had no idea how old she was, only that she'd been with the THIRDS since he'd joined when he was sixteen, and she seemed to have barely aged since. It was no secret he held a certain amount of sway with her, though he had no idea what he'd done to earn such an honor, but she looked out for him and had offered invaluable advice over the years.

"My apologies. I needed to send off a report," she said, finally shifting her gaze to him. She motioned for him to take the seat in front of her desk and cocked her head to one side, studying him, her piercing-blue gaze intense. Sloane tried not to fidget in his seat. It was amazing how she was the only one around here who could make him feel like that uncertain teenager he'd been when he'd first joined. "What's on your mind?"

"I think we might have a problem," he replied, hating the rough way his voice sounded when he spoke.

"Dr. Shultzon."

The name made Sloane tense, and he sat forward, unwilling to believe she'd kept him in the dark. "It's true, then. And you knew?"

"That Dr. Freedman wasn't who you believed him to be? Yes. I was notified shortly after you and your team deployed. My orders were for Destructive Delta to carry on with their investigation. It was unlikely you would find anything, as the man has been in hiding for years." She smiled affectionately at him. "I knew if anyone would find something, it'd be you. I told them as much."

Sloane shook himself out of it. "So you know who he is, the information he has?"

"I know Dr. Shultzon was a First Gen doctor. Yours, Ash's, as well as dozens upon dozens of other First Gen Defense agents we employ. The Chief of Therian Defense is well aware of the danger Dr. Shultzon is in, and in turn, the danger the THIRDS is in. Isaac Pearce vowed he would destroy the THIRDS, and he's discovered a way to do that. Well, I don't know if it would destroy us, but it would certainly discredit us, and throw enough red tape to unleash chaos within our ranks. It seems that's why he kidnapped Morelli."

"What does…?" Suddenly it struck Sloane, and he couldn't believe he hadn't thought of it sooner. "Morelli was a First Gen recruit." Sloane ran a hand through his hair, trying not to let his anger get the better of him. "The Chief of Therian Defense knew, didn't he? That bastard knew from the beginning that Morelli was First Gen. And then they have the nerve to come down on us for not solving this thing fast enough when they're holding out on information?"

"You know how it works, Sloane. Morelli's file was doctored after his death, so as not to raise any questions on classified information, especially after learning Isaac had managed to get his hands on your file years ago. You told me so yourself, Isaac was obsessed, claiming the THIRDS was hiding information, and he was right. Isaac somehow discovered Morelli was First Gen. We know he forced Morelli to access his file in the hopes of finding something, and when he didn't, tried to get him to access Themis. Receiving no results, he killed Morelli and followed the one lead he did have—the CDC Therian registration office." She leaned forward, her gaze intense. "We cannot allow Isaac Pearce to get his hands on First Gen information."

"Okay, then help me. We know Morelli's file led Isaac to the CDC registration office, and from there, he followed the trail to the Therian Youth Center. Obviously, something there led him to Dr. Freed—I mean Dr. Shultzon. Why can't we get access to the youth center's files?" He watched Lieutenant Sparks rise to her feet. She paced behind her desk, her gaze on the floor, and her lips pursed. "Please, you gotta give me something, Lieutenant."

She nodded and turned to face him. "All right. Because it's you. That youth center is one of many belonging to the THIRDS. It's part of a recruitment program. It has been since the First Gens program was terminated. That's why your search for the founder has led you in circles. The THIRDS is the founder."

Sloane stared at her, unable to believe what he was hearing. The youth center had been a recruitment center? He had so many questions, he didn't know where to start.

"Sloane, think about the situation you found yourself in. Think about Ash and all the others like you. You needed a place to go, but at the time, there wasn't one. Dr. Shultzon went out personally to find those like you. He saw your potential and that of many others, so he devised the THIRDS First Gen Recruitment Program. Unfortunately, it meant your home became…." She cleared her throat and waved a hand in dismissal. "Well, anyway. After the THIRDS First Gen Recruitment Program ended, the THIRDS wanted to continue seeking out gifted Therian individuals, without all the media brouhaha and political meddling. If the Human military could recruit via high schools, why couldn't we recruit in a similar fashion?

"The THIRDS opened Therian Youth Centers all around the country. Those who don't qualify get what they need—education, food, shelter, and are soon found permanent housing. They're given the tools necessary to get out there and face the world. Those who show potential are introduced to a THIRDS Recruitment Specialist who discusses their future with them." She cocked her head to one side, studying him. "Do you need a moment?"

"No, I'm fine," he muttered, trying to take in all this new information. It wasn't as though he was surprised he'd been kept in the dark about all this. The THIRDS—for all its good intentions—was still a government organization, and no one loved secrets better than the U.S. government. What he wouldn't have given when he was younger to have somewhere like the youth center, somewhere colorful and bright, with other kids like him, toys and classrooms, the semblance of a normal life. A part of him was angry First Gens had suffered as they had, simply to be understood, to earn the right to be treated as citizens and not animals. He was glad the new recruits didn't have to go through what he did. He wouldn't wish that hell on anyone, but he still couldn't keep the bitterness from his voice when he spoke. "Must be nice, getting your pick of the best and brightest, knowing they're not a bunch of fucked up sociopaths."

The lieutenant's expression softened. "Sloane, it was a different time. The Humans didn't know what they were dealing with. Hell, even we didn't know what we were. Hundreds of Human and Therian citizens were losing their lives by the day. The riots were destroying everything, states, cities, families. The First Gens helped the THIRDS understand Therians and showed the world Therians were more than freaks of nature. Whatever you or anyone else thinks, without you, without the sacrifices you made, the THIRDS wouldn't be here, and equality for Therians would be nothing but a fanciful hope."

"I'm honored." The lieutenant was right, but that didn't mean he had to feel happy about. It wouldn't erase what had been done. "So how did Shultzon end up Dr. Freedman?"

"Like I said, the program was terminated after the THIRDS had finished recruiting First Gen agents. Anyone who had anything to do with the program was given a generous severance package. Most of them retired years ago. Shultzon continued to work for us. He wasn't ready to let go, and he had the right connections. They allowed him to work with the Therian Youth Center as a volunteer doctor under an alias. They gave him a new name, a new life, under the radar to protect him and the THIRDS."

"And now Isaac has him." Sloane shook his head. "This is a goddamn nightmare. What if Isaac tortures him for information?"

"Dr. Shultzon is trained to withstand torture."

Sloane shifted in his seat, hearing the crinkling of paper in his pocket. He cursed under his breath. Pulling out the folded newsletter, he opened it and swallowed hard before placing it on the lieutenant's desk and sliding it toward her. "What if he doesn't need torture?"

Lieutenant Sparks snatched up the piece of paper, her eyes going wide. "Shit. I wasn't told he had kids, much less grandchildren."

"Sucks being kept in the dark, doesn't it?"

She frowned at him, but didn't reply. After studying the photograph for a moment, she took a seat behind her desk. "I need to make a few phone calls. As soon as I have some answers, I'll hold a briefing. Tell your team you'll let them know as soon as you hear anything."

"Yes, ma'am." Great. More waiting. He stood and turned for the door when she stopped him.

"Sloane?"

He schooled his expression, making certain not to show any signs of his growing anxiety. "Yes?"

"We'll stop him, but I need to know you can handle this. If it's too much—"

"I can handle it," he stated firmly.

Her expression hardened, and her eyes met his. "I won't hesitate to pull you off this case."

"Understood." He gave her a curt nod, ready to leave, when something occurred to him. "What happened to the research facility?"

"It closed when the program terminated. All the archived files were being converted to digital files. There's not much left, and what is left is under heavy security. It's also in an undisclosed location. You don't even know where it is."

It was true, none of the First Gens knew where they'd been taken, where they'd lived, where they'd become what they were. "Shultzon knows."

"Like I said, it's in a secret location and heavily fortified. We would know the minute anyone unauthorized so much as attempted to step foot inside."

"For all our sakes, I hope you're right."

"Before you go. I need you and your partner to go to the hospital. I need to know when your teammates are ready to come in. Also, please remind Agent Summers he's due for briefing first thing tomorrow."

With a nod, Sloane walked out of her office, closing the door behind him, his thoughts on everything he'd learned. He had to watch his step. If he showed any signs of being unable to cope with the case, or God help him, a relapse, he'd become a hindrance, and possibly a danger to himself and his team. He couldn't allow that to happen. As much as he told himself he could cope, he couldn't say for certain what would happen the deeper they delved into this. For now, all he could do was his job, and pray Isaac didn't get his hands on any First Gen records. Now that he thought about it, it was probably a good thing Dex was keeping his distance.

Oh God, Dex. Sloane came to an abrupt halt outside his office. He hadn't even thought about Dex, about what he would think if he found out. Finding his office empty, Sloane quickly stepped inside and locked the room behind him, turning on privacy mode. He looked down at his hands, cursing under his breath at the sight of them trembling. What if Dex found out the truth about his past? This argument would be the least of their worries. How would Dex look him in the eye, much less work with him? Sloane sank into his chair behind his desk.

"Keep it together." This was exactly what Lieutenant Sparks was talking about. It would be fine. It had to be. The THIRDS wouldn't let that information get out. How many First Gen THIRDS agents would be pulled from duty if the public discovered where they'd come from or what they'd done? Who would look after his team while Sloane was…? *Damn it.* No. He stood and tapped his earpiece. "Daley, meet me at the car." As he headed out, he told himself he wasn't going to break. Now he had to make himself believe it.

CHAPTER 10

SILENCE.

Dex had never been exposed to so much of it as he had in the last few days since the youth center bombing. He hated it. It was becoming unbearable. Sloane ended up turning on the radio in the Suburban so they weren't driven crazy by it. For days, Dex had done his best to remain professional, speaking to Sloane when spoken to. He kept his head down, did his work. The worst part—aside from feeling like utter shit—was everyone constantly asking him if he was all right. Clearly, he wasn't, but what the hell was he supposed to do? Sloane had given him a verbal reprimand and for all the wrong reasons. Dex was sure of it. It had completely blindsided him, and he was having a hard time getting past it.

To make things worse, he hadn't received a Confirmation of Submission notice and that made him nervous.

As they walked through the hospital wing, Dex considered waving the white flag. Sloane was his superior. If he believed he was doing something for the right reasons, what could Dex do about it? How long could they carry on like this? It had only been a few days, but he hated this feeling. On top of that, his stupid head and heart were missing Sloane. Badly.

"Check on Calvin. He's barely left Hobbs's room since the incident. Lieutenant Sparks wants him in bright and early for briefing. I'll talk to your brother. You can find me there when you're done."

"Okay." Dex walked two doors down to Hobbs's room, smiling at Calvin talking to his partner who was sitting up, looking endearingly puzzled. A second later, Dex had an idea as to why Hobbs looked so confused. Calvin gently took hold of his best friend's face and kissed him. Not an "I'm so happy you're awake" kiss, or a drunken best friend kiss, but an "I want to know what your tonsils taste like" kiss. *Holy shit!* The large Therian had been stunned at first, but now he was eagerly returning Calvin's kiss, his fingers gripping his partner's arms. All Dex could do was stand there like an idiot. He needed to turn around, pretend he hadn't seen a thing, and run. *Run, Dex, run!*

"What the hell is going on in here?"

Dex spun around and threw a hand up. "It's my fault, Sarge. I made him do it."

"What?" Tony looked from Dex to the two agents behind him and back, not looking convinced. Dex turned, holding back a curse. Calvin was wide-eyed and breathless, his face as flushed as Hobbs's.

"Well, Hobbs was bitchin' about his ouchies, so I said Calvin would kiss it and make it better. Calvin said no, so I said the only alternative was for me to reenact *Romancing the Stone* scene for scene while singing Billy Ocean's "When the Going Gets Tough." And wouldn't you know it, Calvin puckered up. Absolutely no appreciation for the arts, these two." Dex shook his head in shame and started singing softly. Tony didn't hesitate. He shook his head and smacked Dex upside the head. "Ow!"

"Boy, what the hell's wrong with you? The poor guy got blown up and you're torturing him with your crappy-ass pop music?"

"Whoa, hey now. Don't you insult Billy. Billy's the man. But I understand what you're saying. I need to work on my selections." Dex thrust a finger at a startled looking Hobbs and started singing "Eye of the Tiger."

"No you don't." Tony grabbed Dex by the collar and dragged him out of the room. "You stay out here until you hit puberty." He disappeared inside, the door closing firmly behind him. Dex let out the deep breath he hadn't realized he'd been holding and dropped into the chair beside him. His phone buzzed and he smiled. It was a text from Calvin.

"Thank you."

Dex replied with a winking happy face and returned his phone to his pocket. That had been close, too close. Now that he thought about it, it sort of made sense. When Dex had first joined the team, those two had been off their game, even Rosa had said so. They'd been careless, and it had led to Calvin getting in over his head at Greenpoint when they'd been hunting for a Therian suspect.

The last few months, there'd been some tension between them, and now Dex understood why. The two had been best buds since they were kids, but clearly, those feelings had grown into something more for at least one of them. Thinking back to their behavior around each other, if Dex were to hazard a guess, he would say Calvin had been the one to fall first. Sounded familiar.

The door opened, snapping him out of his thoughts. He stood to greet his dad. "I was trying to cheer them up."

"Yeah, I know. You got a weird way of doing it."

Dex blinked at him. "I'm sorry, have we met?" He held out his hand. "Hi, I'm Dex. You've been watching me do weird shit since I was five. You have a drawer full of photographic evidence too."

Tony rolled his eyes at him. "I've been holding onto the hope that it's a phase. A really, really, really long phase."

"Ooh," Dex cringed. "I hate to be the one to crush your dreams, but you're better off giving up on that hope." Dex beamed up at him, laughing at the startled expression that crossed his dad's weary face.

"What did you do?"

Dex shrugged. "Nothing."

Tony gave him *that* look.

"I bought a karaoke machine for the break room."

"Oh hell no." Tony thrust a finger at him. "You're taking it back."

"But—"

"No. I'm putting my foot down on this."

"But we were going to have a sing-off. Destructive Delta versus Beta Ambush." He shook a fist at the air. "They're so damn cocky. They think they can out air guitar me? We'll see about that."

"No, we won't, because whatever's going through your head right now isn't happening. You want to do a sing-along—"

"Sing-off," Dex corrected.

"That machine enters the building and it's going back out via the nearest window. Be weird on your own time." Tony stormed off and Calvin stepped up to Dex, studying him.

"You didn't really buy a karaoke machine for the break room, did you?"

"What?" Dex laughed. "Don't be ridiculous. Of course I didn't. This whole case has him on edge."

Calvin appeared to give it some thought when it occurred to him. "And you were taking some of the edge off."

"When it seems like the world's burning down around you, a little sense of normality can go a long way." Dex resumed his seat, knowing Calvin had some 'splaining to do. "The sing-off is real, though. I'm going to crush those Beta bastards. Can you sing?" He waved a hand in dismissal. "Don't worry about it. We'll still beat them. So, you and Hobbs."

Calvin cleared his throat and took a seat, his cheeks going pink. "What about us?"

"Dude, I walked in on you two sucking face like a couple of college kids, come on. Whatever you say stays between us. If you can trust me with your life, you can trust me with this. Something's been up with you guys for months, and if you haven't noticed, the team's been worried."

Calvin's head shot up and he turned to Dex. "They don't suspect anything, do they?"

"Nah. Whatever they're thinking, it's nothing close to that, but if you don't sort it out soon, Sloane's going to get wind something's wrong, and you don't want him interrogating you. It's not fun. So?"

"You know Hobbs and I grew up together. We both came from a rough neighborhood. No segregated schools, at least not officially. Inside was a different matter. There were more Humans than Therians. We got shit for being friends. On top of that, Hobbs got bullied for his mutism. Those assholes knew he couldn't fight back. He was bigger than them, stronger, but he was so crippled by his anxiety, he didn't stand a chance.

"I don't think a day went by where I didn't end up in the principal's office for fighting, but I had to protect him. My mom wanted to put me in another school, one strictly Human, but I refused to leave Hobbs behind in that shithole to fend for himself. He needed me. I can count on one hand the number of times we weren't together. By college, Hobbs had gotten better with his mutism and the anxiety. We shared an apartment. Man, it was so much fun. We did some pretty stupid shit," Calvin said with a laugh. His expression grew somber, and he looked down at his fingers, lost in thought. "Anyway, things were good. After college, we got recruited by the THIRDS and moved into a bigger apartment together. We figured there was no point in spending a load of money on rent when we could save that money and help get our families out of the ghettos they were living in.

"Everything was cool between us. We'd never been closer. Then last year, we had this big Fourth of July party at our apartment, and both of us got shitfaced. We hooked up with these guys, the four of us in Hobbs's bedroom, and everything was fine until Hobbs started fucking this guy. He was blond, about my height and size. I bolted. I couldn't be in the same room while he screwed that guy."

"What did Hobbs do after you bolted?"

"He came after me. We had a huge fight, mostly because I was so pissed off at him and at myself. I didn't know what the hell I was feeling. All I knew was that I couldn't stand seeing him fuck another guy. It was selfish, I know. I told him I needed some space. You should have seen his face. It was like I'd stabbed him in the heart. For days I hid out in my room, making sure when I came out I didn't bump into him. He was so damn patient and good. He'd make me sandwiches and leave them in the fridge for me." Calvin's eyes grew glassy and he gave a sniff.

"He caught me one afternoon in the hall, and when he tried to apologize, as if he was the reason I was acting like such an asshole, I lost it. I told him I didn't want him fucking anyone else because… of how I felt about him. I couldn't say the words, mostly because until the explosion, I couldn't say exactly what it was I felt. I told him somewhere along the way, things had changed. The way I felt about him changed. I thought I was going to lose my mind waiting for him to say something. In the end, he hugged me and said we'd work it out." Calvin let out a heavy sigh. "He's scared we'll lose our friendship. I tried to tell him it would never happen. If things didn't work out, I'd never stop being his best friend."

"How's he feel about what just happened?" Dex asked, nodding to the closed door beside him.

Calvin shrugged, a small smile coming onto his hopeful face. "He kissed me back. That's a good sign, right?"

Dex threw an arm around Calvin and gave him a reassuring squeeze. "I think so. Give him time. It's a lot to take in. I'm betting Hobbs isn't the kind of guy crazy about change, especially when it concerns the possibility of losing his best friend."

"Thanks, Dex. I'm gonna head back in, say good-bye. Maddock and Sloane agree he needs more time to recuperate. I'll see you at HQ."

"No problem, buddy." Dex sat there long after Calvin had disappeared inside. He'd known his teammates were close, but he hadn't known they were *that* close. "Man, this team is incestuous." At least he had Rosa and Letty to keep the balance. Speaking of Rosa, she'd been right about Sloane. He was miserable to be around when he had something stuck in his craw, and he made everyone else around him miserable. Usually Dex kept Sloane from spending too much time grumping, finding ways to make him smile. Dex missed that smile.

With a groan, he let his head fall back against the chair. "Man, I am so screwed."

"YOU SURE you're ready to go back?"

Sloane sat on the blue couch beside Cael's bed, glad to see the young Therian looking like his old self. A pang of guilt hit him for the reprimand he'd intended to give Dex, and he chastised himself for being such a sentimental idiot. Now he was going to feel guilty about doing his job because of Cael?

"Yep." Cael patted his stomach with a laugh. "If I stay here any longer eating Rosa's cooking, I won't fit into my uniform." His smile faded. "Hey, you got a minute?"

"Sure. What's up?"

"I'm worried about Dex."

"Oh?" Sloane sat back, stretching his legs and meeting Cael's concerned gaze.

"He's acting like... I don't know. Like he's been dumped. Worse actually. When Lou dumped him, he got drunk, but after a few days was back to his old self. This... I can't remember the last time I saw him like this. Do you think he's been seeing someone?"

"Wouldn't he have told you?" Sloane laced his fingers over his stomach, his gaze unwavering. As much as he disliked lying to Cael concerning what was happening between him and Dex, Sloane had grown accustomed to hiding. His relationship, his vulnerabilities, the truth about himself, and what he was.

Cael cocked his head to one side. "I'm his brother. We've never kept secrets from each other. Unless he felt he didn't have a choice."

Something in Cael's eyes set off an alarm in Sloane's head. He'd learned a long time ago not to underestimate his young teammate. Cael's sweet disposition made those around him comfortable, enough for them to let their guard down, and the cheetah Therian knew how to use that to his advantage. The kid wasn't just quick on his feet. "What do you mean?"

"Like you and Gabe."

Sloane's heart slammed and he forced himself to remain stoic. "What are you talking about?"

"Don't worry, no one else knows, and they won't, at least they won't find out from me." Sloane didn't say a word, and Cael let out a heavy sigh. "I was the one assigned to clear out his interface and send his files to the lieutenant's office. You know when an agent leaves, gets dismissed, or is killed in action, Recon is assigned to remove them from Themis, do a sweep of their systems and report all our findings."

Sloane shrugged. "It's a routine sweep, to make sure no case files or sensitive information is left behind for the subsequent agent." He congratulated himself on not freaking out. Cael knew something, but until Sloane knew exactly what that was, he wasn't about to take any chances.

"We do an in-depth sweep as well, to search for any possible theft or misuse of information. It's the government, Sloane. We don't trust ourselves."

"Cael, if you have something you want to say, say it."

"I found a hidden folder with heavy protection on it in Gabe's hard drive. It had a confirmation e-mail from a cruise company."

"And?" Sloane arched an eyebrow at the young agent. He watched Cael intently, noticing his slight fidget and the way he suddenly moved his gaze away.

"I don't think—"

"Say it."

"It was an e-mail requesting to extend the cruise by one night, a stop at the Bahamas for a romantic dinner for two. He also paid for champagne and a photographer. Your name was down as his partner, and I don't mean work partner, so please, Sloane, don't lie to me. I'm young, not stupid. I deleted anything that pertained to Gabe's personal life which had a connection to you."

The room fell silent. All this time, and now, after everything, he was finding this out? What was he supposed to do with this information other than feel shitty about it? He didn't blame Cael. The young Therian was doing his job, and Sloane appreciated his honesty. Things would have turned out a whole lot different if Cael had simply handed everything over to the lieutenant blindly, not bothering to check it out. Still, the knowledge of Gabe's gesture picked at the scab of Sloane's wounded heart. He was so exhausted and tired of feeling the ache there, but too afraid to let it go. "Thank you," Sloane replied when he managed to find his voice. "So now what?"

"Now nothing. I've kept your secret this long. Do you really think I'm going to say something now? I hope you don't think that little of me."

It was amazing how much Cael reminded Sloane of Dex, despite the two not being related by blood. They were so different, yet shared many of the same mannerisms, had similar patterns of speech, and a similar sense of humor. "You're right. Is that all you wanted to say?"

"No. When Dex cares about something, he puts his whole heart and soul into it. He's the best guy I know, and not because he's my brother. He'll never let you down, never betray you. But he's not so good at doing the same for himself. He'll let you keep hurting him, Sloane, and he deserves better than that."

Sloane nodded. "You're right, he does."

"May I speak freely?"

"Always."

Cael rounded his shoulders, his silver-gray eyes penetrating. "You're scared, I get that. I know it must be hard for you, and I have no right to dismiss what you're going through, but if you're willing to walk away from my brother because you're too much of a chickenshit to take a risk, well, he's better off without you."

Sloane stared at him. Wow. The kid really didn't mince words when it came to his family. Cael's expression softened, but he remained firm on his position. Sloane couldn't blame Cael for being protective of his big brother. A part of Sloane believed Dex was indeed better off without him, but the other half of him didn't want to let go.

"I respect you, Sloane, and that won't go away no matter what you decide. I'm asking you to really think about things. Don't let him get caught up in a future with you if you have no intention of ever letting it get that far."

Sloane mulled over Cael's words and decided to take a chance. "And if I don't walk away? If things do work out?"

"If he's happy, I'm happy. As long as no one finds out." Cael smiled a wide dopey grin. "I like having him on our team."

The door opened and Dex came strolling in with a cheerful smile. "Hey, Chirpy, you ready to…."

"Oh my God, Dex!" Cael wailed, his eyes going huge, and his face turning a bright crimson.

Dex saw Sloane and cringed. "Woops."

"Chirpy?" Sloane arched an eyebrow at Cael, holding back a laugh.

"You dick!" Cael's murderous glare was at full strength, and Sloane was relieved it wasn't aimed at him. For all his timidness, Cael could be pretty scary at times. "You swore you'd never call me that in public! I can't believe you."

"I didn't know anyone was here!" Dex replied in a panic. "I'm sorry!"

Cael declared loudly, "When Dex was fourteen, we walked in on him with his penis in the vacuum cleaner hose!"

Dex let out a dramatic gasp. "Judas! How could you?" He turned to Sloane, who was desperately trying not to laugh. "It's not what you think."

"It's exactly what you think," Cael said with a smug grin. "He tried to fuck the vacuum."

"It was an accident," Dex insisted.

Cael rolled his eyes. "Really? You were vacuuming your room, slipped, and 'oh, look at that. Vacuum fell on my penis.' Please."

Sloane burst into laughter. He doubled over, covered his face with his hands, his shoulders shaking as he tried to control himself. *Oh, fuck.* He didn't have words. The brothers continued to argue, until Cael gave in, apologized, and they made up. On the ride back to HQ, Sloane had to bite the inside of his cheeks to keep himself from breaking out into spontaneous laughter, especially since Dex sulked the entire way. That had been hours ago.

Now, he lay sprawled on his bed in his sleeper bay, staring at the ceiling. With Unit Alpha working overtime to find Isaac, squads were taking turns catching a few hours of sleep in the bays. It was easier to spend the night here than waste time going home, not to mention less dangerous. The THIRDS didn't want any of their agents falling asleep behind the wheel. Not that Sloane's apartment was far, and he could always take a cab. Unlike many other agents, Sloane really had no need to sleep here, but he found it comforting.

Since Gabe had died, he'd spent a lot of rough nights here at HQ. He'd made countless excuses to himself as to why that was, but now he knew the truth. He didn't want to go home to his big empty apartment. He wasn't one of those guys who always needed to have someone in his bed, but he'd be fooling no one if he said he didn't like having a certain someone in his bed. It was his own fault. He'd been spending too much time with Dex, either sleeping in Dex's bed or having Dex in his own, but there was something about the guy that made it hard for Sloane to stay away. The last few days had been fucking miserable.

Sloane rolled onto his side with a huff. God, look at him, sulking like some teenager infected with puppy love. So he liked having Dex around. So what? Who the hell *didn't* like having Dex around? Ash of course, but well, it was Ash. Eight months, and his team had accepted Dex as one of their own, as if he'd always been there. Rosa fussed over him as much as she did Cael, acting like a mother hen despite being a couple of years older than Dex. Letty teased and roughhoused with him as if they were siblings, jumping on him, hugging him, asking him for advice on whatever hot guy she had her eye on, while Calvin and Hobbs followed Dex around like a couple of groupies.

Dex walked around with a smile on his face, giving his undivided attention to whoever approached him, going out of his way to help however he could. He wasn't arrogant or cocky, but playful. At times, he was shy, hiding behind his humor or that dopey grin of his. He was weird, no doubt about it, what with his bizarre fixation on music released before 1989, his unhealthy obsession with cheese snacks, and his inability to shut up at times, but somehow, that made him more attractive in Sloane's eyes.

"What the hell is wrong with you?" Sloane groaned at himself, rubbing his hands over his face. He should have been sleeping, instead he was thinking about how great Dex was. If the guy was so goddamn great, what the hell was Sloane doing alone? He kept telling himself he wasn't ready to label whatever he had with Dex, especially since it was strictly between them, so what was the point, but what else was Dex if not his boyfriend? They weren't sleeping around. Hell, the thought of Dex being fucked by someone else made him want to punch something.

Dex was a good guy, faithful, smart, funny, sexy, and he was crazy about Sloane. What more could Sloane want? He should be counting his lucky stars that a guy like Dex wanted anything to do with his miserable ass, and what was he doing? Disciplining him, and beating the shit out of him for saving a teammate's life. Cael's words kept coming back to him. The kid had really called him out on his behavior. And he was right. Sloane was being a complete chickenshit.

He was such an asshole. If he wasn't with Dex, he had no one to blame but himself. No matter how many times he told himself Dex had disobeyed orders, deep down, he knew that wasn't it. Had anyone else on the team done what Dex did, Sloane would have been royally pissed off at first, but then he would have been proud of them. He sure as hell wouldn't have taken disciplinary measures.

It had been easy to let his anger get out of hand and turn into something else. Was he taking it out on Dex because he was too scared of where things were heading? This was their first real fight. Sure, they'd argued plenty of times before, but it never resulted in this... this horrible feeling in his chest. He sat up and shifted to the edge of the bed with a frown. Getting up, he pulled back the covers, determined to get some sleep, when he heard faint music. It was coming from the room next door.

The rooms were heavily insulated so occupants could go about their business without disturbing their fellow agents. He doubted his Human teammates could hear the tune, and if Sloane's room hadn't been silent, he wouldn't have either. Curious, he pressed his ear to the wall, his heart lurching when he heard the familiar power ballad. He closed his eyes as he listened to the faint lyrics of Journey's "Faithfully."

Straightening, he left his room, closing the door behind him, and with a deep breath, he knocked on the door next to his. He ran his fingers through his hair in a feeble attempt to comb it back then told himself to stop being such an ass. The door opened, and a tired, disheveled-looking Dex sporting a distressed *Back to the Future* T-shirt and gray sweats stood on the other side.

"Hi. I heard the music."

"Oh." Dex walked over to the desk and tapped his tablet, turning it down. "Sorry."

"No, I didn't mean it was bothering me. When I heard it, I figured it was you."

Dex nodded.

"Can I come in?"

"You're the Team Leader. You can do what you want." Dex took a seat on the edge of his bed, his gaze going to his bare feet.

"I didn't come here to fight," Sloane said with a sigh, closing the door behind him and locking it. He joined Dex on the edge of the bed.

Again, Dex nodded, but didn't say anything. Sloane watched him worry his bottom lip, close his eyes, and release a heavy sigh. "You have a job to do, I get it. I've been a THIRDS agent a few months.

You've been one for years. Who the hell am I to question your judgment?"

"I deleted the reprimand."

Dex stared at him. "Why?"

"Because it wasn't right. Hell, even Ash was pissed off at me for it."

"Ash?" Dex's expression would have made Sloane laugh if he wasn't feeling so shitty about what he'd done, not to mention how far he'd let it go. What kind of a partner was he?

"Yeah, he said if it had been anyone else on the team, I wouldn't have done it, and he's right. What you did was brave, kinda stupid too, but brave."

"So why did you do it?"

"I've been asking myself the same question since the day of the bombing. I think a part of me wondered if you thought the rules didn't apply to you because we're sleeping together." He wanted to tell Dex about the other part, the part that was scared shitless of a relationship.

"I'd never take advantage like that. I disobeyed the order because it wasn't right. Not to me."

"Dex, I understand that, I do, but sometimes we have to make decisions we don't want to make or that don't seem to make sense. Our objective and how we feel about it won't always add up. The team is our family, and we do what we have to in order to protect it, but there are priorities. That's the job." It hurt to say it, but he had to, because it was the truth. "I have to do everything in my power to preserve civilian life, even if it means losing one of my own. Even if it means… losing you."

"Still, it doesn't make it any easier when it's staring you in the face," Dex murmured, his gaze everywhere else but on Sloane.

"No."

"I didn't mean to make your job harder than it is."

Sloane shook his head. "This is on me. You said the structure was sound, I should have trusted you. That's part of my job too." He needed to make some changes, to take more chances. Now was as good a time as any to start. "I did learn something else from all this."

"Oh?" Dex did look at him then.

Sloane was pouting, but he couldn't help it. Thinking back to the last few days and how it had felt without Dex. It sucked. "Yeah, I don't like how it feels."

"How what feels?"

"Fighting like this."

Dex looked surprised by his admission. "So… what you're saying is you like having me around?"

"You know I do." He studied Dex's guarded expression. The guy was crap at trying to hide his feelings. "Don't you?"

Dex gave him a warm smile, but it didn't reach his eyes. "Yeah."

"Cael's right. You're a shitty liar." Sloane shifted closer to him and slipped an arm around him, tentatively pulling him closer, relieved when Dex went along with it. "It's okay. You're right. I could do a better job of showing you. It's not just about the sex. I apologize if I gave you that impression."

"Don't get me wrong, I'm not complaining about the sex," Dex said, holding back a smile.

"Me neither."

Dex smiled, and this time it reached his sparkling-blue eyes. He gave Sloane's shoulder a playful bump, his voice teasing. "Did you miss me?"

God, the guy had no idea. "I couldn't sleep." He frowned knowing he probably looked and sounded pathetic. "And yeah, I did miss you."

"You've ruined Journey for me, you know that? Anytime I hear it, all I can see is you."

Sloane was taken aback. He knew exactly what that meant for Dex. He cupped Dex's cheek, using his thumb to stroke the stubble growing in. Now that he looked closer, he could see the bags under Dex's eyes, and he had a feeling it wasn't just from the case. It looked like Sloane wasn't the only one who'd had trouble sleeping since the day of the bombing. He leaned in hesitantly, allowing Dex time to pull away, or tell him to get the hell out if he wanted. Instead, Dex leaned into him so their lips pressed together.

Dex's scent reminded Sloane how crazy Dex made him feel. He slipped his hand around the back of Dex's neck, pulling him harder against him, their kiss quickly turning heated. He tried to slow down—for fuck's sake, it had been a few days—but he couldn't. Dex's scent, his taste, the feel of his body pressed against Sloane's was hitting all the right buttons, and Sloane wanted more. He pulled off Dex's shirt. "How about a little Journey?"

"You're asking for Journey?" Dex breathed, his fingers digging into Sloane's arms. "Wow, you really did miss my sexing you up."

"You have no idea," Sloane replied with a chuckle, his eyes glued to Dex as he tapped the tablet and raised the volume. When Dex turned to him, his smile stole Sloane's breath away.

"I think maybe I do."

Their bodies crashed together in a frenzy of desperate kisses, painful rutting, and scorching touches. By the way they assaulted each other's lips, it was as if they'd been apart for years rather than days. Sloane lay over Dex, his fingers curled around fistfuls of Dex's hair, his mouth hungrily plundering, reveling in the taste of his lover. Beneath him, Dex writhed and arched his back, gasping for air after Sloane released his mouth. Dex's fingers dug into Sloane's ass, their cocks painfully hard.

"Sloane, I need you to fuck me. Please."

"Supplies?"

Dex motioned to his backpack on the desk's chair, and Sloane reached out, snatching one of the straps and yanking it over. He sat back on his heels, rummaged through one of the zipper pockets, pulling out a condom and a small packet of lube. Beneath him, Dex broke speed records undressing. He threw his clothes to the floor, and Sloane's clothes soon joined them, along with Dex's backpack.

Dex lay on his back, running his hand up Sloane's inner thigh, making him shiver. "I'm sorry. I'm so sorry for being stupid. We could have been doing this days ago."

Sloane shook his head and leaned in to kiss Dex. "No. I was the one being stupid and stubborn." God, how he'd missed this. The feel of Dex's skin, the taste of him, his scent mixed in with the smell of his shampoo and shower gel, his firm body beneath Sloane's touch. Sloane doubted he would last long, but he was practically vibrating with anticipation. He quickly lubed himself up, as well as his fingers before prepping Dex, watching enthralled as Dex threw his head back with a low groan, sweat beading his brow and his tongue poking out to lick his bottom lip. "Fuck, you're beautiful."

Dex's eyes met his, a stunning smile coming onto his face, and his cheeks flushed. The affection in his eyes squeezed Sloane's heart, and he brought their lips together again, doing his best to show Dex how he made Sloane feel through his kiss, even if he had trouble finding the words to go with it. He lined himself up with one hand and lifted Dex's leg with the other before he tenderly pushed himself inside. His lover inhaled sharply and Sloane paused, allowing Dex to adjust around him. A heartbeat later, Dex nodded, and Sloane pushed through until he was buried deep, the tight heat both excruciating and exhilarating.

Sloane rocked against Dex, his muscles pulled and tensed as he moved, drawing out, and then pushing in. He kept a steady pace, his eyes never leaving Dex's as he moved. Dex reached down between them to stroke his cock, and Sloane bucked his hips at the sight, making Dex gasp. With a wicked grin, Sloane pulled out, grabbed a pillow from beside Dex's head and tapped Dex's flank, receiving a naughty smile when Sloane slipped the pillow underneath Dex's lower back.

"Hold on tight?" Dex asked with a knowing grin.

"Hold on tight," Sloane growled playfully. He lined his cock up against Dex's hole once again, thrusting inside him, and Dex clamped a hand over his mouth to stifle his cry, his other hand thrown up against the headboard. Sloane snapped his hips, thrusting hard inside Dex. He held Dex's legs up against him, his arms around them as he fucked him, his breath ragged, and his pulse soaring.

"Oh God," Dex moaned, arching his back. He took himself in hand, jerking himself off as Sloane snapped his hips and rotated them, hitting Dex's prostate. Dex threw a hand out to his side, gripping a fistful of the sheets as the bed moved beneath them. Sloane closed his eyes for a moment, the feel of fucking Dex incredible. His abdomen tightened, and he let out a low warning growl. Dex shook his head. "In my mouth. I want to taste you."

The thought almost had Sloane coming. He swiftly pulled out, rolled off the condom, and cursed under his breath when Dex got on his hands and knees in front of him, that gorgeous mouth swallowing Sloane's cock to the root, sucking, licking, moaning with need.

"Oh God, Dex." He put his hands to Dex's head, thrusting his hips, a shiver going up his spine as Dex allowed him to fuck his mouth. "I'm gonna come."

Dex hummed, and Sloane gritted his teeth to keep himself from crying out as he shot into Dex's hot mouth, feeling Dex's throat swallowing around him. He doubled over, his arms wrapped around Dex's head as he let himself go completely, his body trembling. When Dex pulled off, Sloane pushed him onto his back to return the favor, loving the taste of Dex as he sucked his beautiful cock. He bobbed his head, licking and circling the head with his tongue, pressing the tip into Dex's slit, enjoying the way Dex bucked his hips beneath him. He continued to suck Dex off, sliding his free hand up Dex's chest to tweak one pebbled nipple.

"Sloane," Dex warned, arching his back. Just as he finished saying Sloane's name, Dex came, his muscles stiffening under Sloane's touch. Around them, there was only the music coming from Dex's tablet, and for a moment, everything was right with the world. He could close his eyes and pretend they were in Dex's house, the last week having never happened.

Sloane laid his head on Dex's flat stomach, smiling to himself as Dex stroked his hair, his breath steadying. "Can you stay?"

"Yes."

As he lay there, enjoying Dex's ministrations, feeling wanted, needed, and cared for, Sloane had a desperate urge to say "yes" to anything Dex wanted. But he knew he couldn't, not while his past loomed over him, threatening to shatter everything. Now, more than ever, he wanted this. He wanted to experience what it would be like to truly *be* with Dex. What the hell was he supposed to do?

THE NEXT morning, Dex wasn't surprised when he found his bed empty. Sloane's side was cold, meaning he'd left some time ago. He hoped it was just his partner being cautious, but his heart was telling him he was kidding himself. With a sigh, Dex sat up and ran a hand through his hair. Coffee. Coffee would help his brain function. He stood and switched on the personal one-cup coffee maker the THIRDS equipped all the rooms with. He thanked his lucky stars he worked for an organization that appreciated java as much as he did.

While his coffee brewed, he dressed in his uniform, dragging his thigh rig off the desk and tossing it onto the bed. To his coffee he added sugar and milk from the small fridge tucked underneath the desk and sat on the edge of his bed to think as he sipped the heavenly nectar, hoping it might make him feel remotely not like crap. For a moment, he'd actually thought everything might go back to normal. Idiot. He might be a shitty liar, but he'd perfected the art of playing dumb. Sloane was getting scared. The reprimand, the fight, the fear at the mere mention of the word "boyfriend." Although Dex believed Sloane when he said there was more between them than sex, that didn't mean Sloane was ready to turn that something more into a relationship, and part of him wondered if the guy ever would be.

Securing his thigh rig to his belt and the straps around his leg, he left his room to head for the bullpen. Ash was standing outside his office chatting to Cael. "Hey. Have you seen Sloane?" Dex asked him, after giving his brother a welcome back pat on his ass.

"No. You look like shit."

"I had a feeling I might, considering I feel like shit," Dex muttered. "Thanks for confirming it, though."

Ash held his arms out, his bottom lip jutted out. "Do you need a cuddle?"

"I'm too tired right now to come up with an appropriate response, so I'm going to pencil you in for later in the week. How's Thursday work for you? I can tell you to fuck off properly then." He let out a yawn and Ash chuckled.

"My week's kind of full, but since it's you, I'll move some things around."

"I appreciate it. Now if you'll excuse me, I have some more moping to do. Tell Taylor I know he's the one who ate my maple donut, and if he does it again, I'm going to shank him with a spork."

"Whoa, that time of the month, Daley?"

Just his luck, Rosa and Letty were walking past. "Rosa, Ash is calling me a woman on my period. Crush him." He strolled away to the sound of Rosa cursing Ash out in two languages. Then Ash made the mistake of accusing her of having PMS, and Dex felt marginally better, knowing the guy would soon find himself in physical pain.

Dex closed the office door behind him, tapping his security code into the panel, and setting the room to privacy mode. Might as well get some work done between moping and waiting to hear from Lieutenant Sparks. He initiated his desk's interface and dropped down into his chair. "This sucks." His cell phone buzzed in his pocket, and he pulled it out, his heart in his throat at the sight of Sloane's grumpy face appearing on his caller ID screen. "Hey."

"Hi. About this morning... I needed time to think."

Wow. Straight and to the point. "Sure."

"I know you're probably wondering what the hell's going on, and you deserve better than some vague answers and pathetic excuses. I shouldn't have done what I did last night."

"Oh." Dex tried not to let the words sting, but they did. A horn honked somewhere in the distance, and Dex realized Sloane was offsite.

"Shit, that came out wrong. I don't regret it. I don't regret you. I'm not in the right frame of mind right now, and I shouldn't have done what I did if I was going to be an asshole this morning."

"You're not an asshole. Most of the time."

There was a chuckle on the other end before the line went quiet.

"You still there?" Dex asked, closing his eyes, inhaling deeply and releasing it slowly. He knew this feeling. This sense of impending doom.

"Yeah."

"Are you... I mean, is this *the* phone call?" *Over before it began.* Was he really that surprised? A part of him was. Things weren't great between them, not by far, but he'd expected the chance to work things out, to at least try to make something of whatever was between them. Had he been hoping for too much? Maybe Sloane wasn't a relationship kind of guy. Maybe Dex was trying to make Sloane into something he wasn't. He didn't want that.

"I'm not that much of an asshole, Dex. I would never end things over the phone."

"Good to know," Dex muttered. Not that it made him feel any better. Something was up with Sloane, and it was more than the usual relationship insecurities.

"No, it's not *the* phone call. I was calling to apologize. Again. And to tell you I'm taking a couple of days off. I know it's going to sound cliché, but it's not you, it's me."

"Is there something worse than cliché? Because if there is, that was it." Were they really having this conversation? Why couldn't Sloane come out and tell him what the hell was going on. "You know, if it's not working for you, say so. I understand. We said we'd take things as they came, and I meant it."

"No, Dex. I—I'm fucked up right now, so please, when I say it's not you, believe me. It's not you. It has nothing to do with you, or us."

Sloane's tone had Dex sitting up. Shit, something really was wrong. "What's going on?"

"I can't talk about it. Not right now. I feel like a dick for asking, but you and Ash are the only ones I can turn to. Can you not tell anyone I'm off sick? I told your dad I was out chasing leads. I need a couple of days. If Lieutenant Sparks finds out, she'll start asking questions, and—"

"Done. And if you need me, you know where to find me. Is there anything else I can do to help?"

There was another long pause. "Wait for me?"

Dex's heart fluttered. "You bet."

"Thank you."

Sloane hung up, and Dex returned his phone to his pocket, his mind racing. He was worried about his partner. It wasn't like him to go off the grid like this. Whatever it was, it was serious, and Dex was sure it had something to do with the case. He hoped Sloane didn't do anything rash, or attempt anything on his own. Lord knew the guy was pigheaded, worse when it came to asking for help. Dex would give Sloane the time he needed, but after that, he was going to make it clear to Sloane that he was no longer alone, and it was time he realized it.

CHAPTER 11

WHAT A nightmare.

Dex dropped down onto his couch with a groan. He'd had one hell of a day juggling his workload, along with the dozens of coworkers who came to him asking for Sloane. And to make things worse, before noon the switchboards lit up and emergency calls started flooding in.

All over the city, violence was erupting between Humans and Therians. At first, they believed it was random, until they watched surveillance footage from several businesses. In all the videos, the Therians fighting the Humans wore black masks and were dressed in military camouflage with military grade weapons. News stations hounded the THIRDS, demanding to know if the Therians were agents. It was a PR nightmare. Themis analyzed the footage and identified several of the Humans as being members of one of the Humans 4 Dominance forum. That's when the theories started.

It soon became shockingly clear this new Therian group was drawing Isaac's followers out of the woodworks, which was awesome, but they were doing it through violence, which was a nightmare for everyone involved. The last thing the city needed was a trigger-happy group of vigilantes. Unit Alpha was being stretched thin despite passing on some of their cases to other units.

He'd settled down for some vegetating in front of the TV when someone pounded on his door, giving him a start. What the hell? Dex got to his feet, edging cautiously to his front door, his gaze shifting momentarily to the baseball bat propped up in the corner beside it. It was well past midnight and he hadn't been expecting anyone. He unlocked the door and cautiously opened it, his jaw dropping. Swinging the door open, he stared at his partner.

"Sloane? What the hell happened to you?"

The corner of Sloane's lips lifted in a halfhearted smile, before it faltered and trembled, a laugh that was half a sob escaping him and breaking Dex's heart. "You should see the other guys."

"You got in a fight?"

Sloane's smile faded. "Yeah. I don't feel so well, Dex. Can I come in? You can say no. I deserve a 'no.'"

Dex had no idea what was going on, but he couldn't leave Sloane like this. He took hold of his arm and gently pulled him inside, closing the door behind him. "You feeling sick?"

Sloane nodded and Dex didn't give it another thought. He laced his fingers with Sloane's and led him to the stairs. Wrapping an arm around him, he helped Sloane upstairs. The guy looked like he was ready to pass out. As soon as Dex switched on the bathroom lights, Sloane made a dash to the toilet. He dropped to his knees and hurled into the bowl. Well, this was nothing he hadn't done for his brother and vice versa. He knelt down beside Sloane and rubbed a hand soothingly over his back.

"It's okay, buddy. Let it all out." After giving Sloane's back a pat, he rose and went to the cabinet underneath the sink. He grabbed a small plastic cup, a couple of paper towels from the roll he kept down there, and a bottle of mouthwash, then took a seat on the floor beside Sloane. When the guy was finally done, Dex handed him a paper towel, followed by some mouthwash. "Here."

"Thanks," Sloane grumbled, before spitting out a mouthful of the minty blue liquid into the bowl. "I must reek."

"You do, but you left behind a couple of T-shirts and a pair of sweatpants. I'll get them for you."

"You ever wish you were anyone else but you?"

Dex paused. He opened his mouth, but Sloane waved a hand in his face. "Don't answer that. You don't. I know you don't. Why would you? You're so good." Dex's confusion must have shown, because

Sloane cupped Dex's face in his big hands. "Being around you… I don't hate myself so much."

"Why would you hate yourself? Hey, look at me." Dex ran a hand over Sloane's head. "Whatever happened, it doesn't change the fact you're a good guy."

Sloane shook his head, the tears in his eyes catching Dex by surprise. Jesus, what the hell had happened? This was the first he'd seen Sloane like this.

"I keep telling myself I should walk away from you, that it would hurt less than you walking out on me, but I'm too much of a coward. Can't walk away, can't stay. I don't know what the hell to do anymore."

"Why would I walk out on you when all I've been trying to do for months is convince you how much I want to be with you?"

Sloane shook his head, his hands falling to his sides in defeat. "You don't want to be with me, Dex. You shouldn't be."

"Stop. I don't know what's happened, but nothing's changed."

Sloane let out a harsh laugh. "It will."

"I'm not going to walk away."

"You have to," Sloane insisted, his words slightly slurred. "For your own good."

"Damn it, Sloane, what the hell is going on?"

"I need to go." Sloane moved to get up, and Dex put a stop to that, his hands on Sloane's shoulders. He gave them a squeeze.

"You think I'm letting you out of my sight while you're like this? I'm getting you a change of clothes, and you're crashing here."

"Leave me alone." Sloane pushed himself to his feet, wavering and grabbing onto the sink to steady himself.

"Not a chance." If Sloane thought Dex was going to back off that easy, he had another think coming. There was no way Dex was letting Sloane leave this house, even if he had to knock the guy out himself to keep him there.

"Fuck off!" Sloane spat out.

"I'm not going anywhere, and neither are you."

Sloane turned, looking distraught. "You don't understand."

"Then help me understand."

Sloane pushed past Dex, stumbling through the bedroom. Before he reached the stairs, Dex grabbed him by the shirt and jerked him back. The last thing he wanted was for Sloane to break his neck on the stairs, or bring them both crashing down. Sober, Dex wouldn't have been able to budge him, but shitfaced was another matter. Sloane flailed and hit the hall carpet with a loud thud. He rolled onto his side, making a low growling noise. Ignoring him, Dex reached down to help, only to have Sloane grab his ankle and pull it out from under him. With a groan, Dex found himself on his back with Sloane leaning over him, a fist hovering over Dex's face. Making sure not to make too sudden a movement, Dex reached out and wrapped his hand around Sloane's fist. He remained silent, his eyes not moving from his partner's.

The fist in Dex's hand started to shake. Pulling it away, Sloane fell back onto his ass, his knees drawn up and apart as he hung his head in his hands. Not knowing what to expect, Dex carefully sat up and nudged closer inch by inch, when Sloane grabbed his arm and dragged him onto his lap. Dex shifted his position so he could face Sloane, slipping his arms around him and feeling a sense of relief when Sloane held him tightly to him, his face buried against Dex's neck, whispering, "I'm not a monster."

Dex ran a soothing hand over Sloane's head. "I know that." Sloane shook his head, a shuddered sigh escaping him, moisture against Dex's neck.

"Whatever you hear, whatever they say, please... don't believe it." Dex opened his mouth to reassure him, when Sloane's choked voice whispered in his ear. "I never meant to hurt her. I'm not a monster."

Dex held Sloane, whispering soothing words and rubbing a hand over his back. When Sloane had stopped sniffing and let out a shuddered breath, Dex gently urged him to stand. With great effort, Dex helped his sluggish partner to his feet and into the bedroom. He guided Sloane to what he considered his side of the bed and sat him down. Sloane lay on his side, his eyes bloodshot, dark circles around them. Dex kissed him, brushed his hair away from his face, and went about undressing him. Sloane was out for the count by the time Dex had him dressed in the spare T-shirt and loose sweatpants. He emptied out Sloane's pockets before collecting the clothes and carrying them downstairs to the basement to chuck them in the washing machine. Once back upstairs, he turned off everything as he made his way back to the bedroom, feeling numb.

Tonight had been a strange and disturbing night. He didn't know what had brought all this about, but he sure as hell was going to ask his partner about it in the morning. Once he'd brushed his teeth and changed, he climbed into bed beside Sloane who'd rolled himself onto his back. There was so much Dex didn't know about his partner, about his past, and he tried not to dwell on it. Sloane was a good guy, he knew that much. Dex trusted him, though at times he thought he was crazy for doing so. His eyes landed on Sloane's hands, and Dex took one gently in his. He gave the back of it a kiss before turning it over, his thumb brushing over the faint line on his wrist. Sloane had suffered in his youth. So much so, he'd been desperate to escape any way he could. That much he'd told Dex.

"Why won't you let me help you?" He held onto Sloane's hand and closed his eyes, hoping Sloane might explain tomorrow, though he wouldn't hold his breath. He had to try to get through to his partner for both their sakes.

THE NEXT morning, Dex had gotten up before Sloane for the first time ever. Most likely due to the fact he'd barely slept. He dragged himself out of bed and made coffee, and breakfast. After he'd eaten, he sat at the counter wondering if he should wake Sloane up before Dex headed out, when he heard Sloane coming down the stairs. His heart squeezed at the sight of Sloane standing in his pajamas and unlaced biker boots, looking disheveled and fragile.

"Hi," Sloane croaked. He cleared his throat and rubbed his arm, trying again. "Hi."

"Hey, how are you feeling?"

"As shitty as I probably look." His voice was hoarse, and he shifted uncomfortably, but he didn't move from where he stood.

Dex waved a hand in dismissal. "Nah, you look fine." Sloane narrowed his eyes at him, and Dex cringed. "Yeah, okay, you look pretty shitty."

"I appreciate your honesty."

"Coffee?"

"No, thanks. I'm uh, gonna go. Thank you for not slamming the door in my face."

"You're my partner." Dex got up, but didn't move from his spot, afraid if he did, Sloane would leave. So far, he'd said he was going to, but hadn't. Dex took that as a good sign. However, Sloane's inability to look him in the eye, wasn't such a good sign.

"How can you keep being so good to me? I don't deserve it."

"I'm worried about you."

"I'm worried too."

Dex couldn't hold back anymore. He walked around the counter and approached his partner. "Sloane? What's going on? You're really freaking me out here."

"I gotta go." Sloane turned, but Dex caught his arm. He couldn't let him leave, not like this, not without giving him *something*.

"Goddamn it, Sloane. Last night you were so shitfaced, I'm amazed you managed to stay on your feet, yet out of everywhere you could have gone, you came here. You came to me. Why can't you let yourself trust me? Forget what is or isn't going on between us. Trust me."

"I'm scared."

Sloane's confession startled Dex. "Of what?"

"Of going back there. Of not being strong enough. I can't drag you down with me." Again, Sloane tried to walk off, when Dex called out after him.

"What happened to her?"

Sloane stopped in his tracks. "What?"

"Last night. Before you passed out, you told me you never meant to hurt her. That you weren't a monster." He watched Sloane rub his hands over his face in frustration, before he cursed under his breath. "Yeah, I figured you probably never meant for me to hear that. When's the right time for me to hear it, Sloane? When you're gone? When I'm helpless to do anything to help you?"

Sloane stood, and just when Dex thought the guy was going to make a break for it, he spoke up, his back still to Dex. "Dr. Freedman isn't his real name. His name is Dr. Abraham Shultzon. He saved my life. Twice. The second time, you sort of know about." He turned to face Dex, and the expression in his partner's amber eyes crushed Dex's heart. It was fear mixed with desperation, self-loathing, and God knew what else. "All you need to know is if the public finds out what he knows.... They'll demand more than my resignation. They'll want to see me put in a cage. The THIRDS will lose credibility. They'll demand to know about all the other First Gen agents. Ash...." Sloane put a hand to his head, and Dex crossed the distance between them, leading Sloane to the couch to sit.

"Take it easy. We won't let that happen. Come on, Sloane. We can do this. Destructive Delta hasn't left a case unsolved. I'll be damned if this becomes the first. We'll find Dr. Shultzon, and we'll stop Isaac. But we can't do it without our Team Leader." Dex knelt before him, meeting his lover's reddened gaze. "Shultzon believed in you. He might have helped you become the agent you are today, but that never would have happened if it wasn't in you. I don't know what hell you suffered, but the important thing is, you made it out, and you're stronger for it."

"Why do you do it?" The words were spoken so softly, Dex barely heard them.

"Do what?"

"Believe in me like that. You don't know any more about me than what I choose to show you, yet no matter what, you never lose faith in me."

Dex smiled at him, his hand stroking Sloane's arm. "You're my partner, and because I care about you."

"I... I need to go. Please."

"Okay." Dex nodded and stood, taking a step to one side, his hands shoved into his pockets. It hurt. It shouldn't. Not this soon. Dex was screwed and he knew it. He watched Sloane head for the door and something in him broke. "Don't go."

Sloane stopped in his tracks, but didn't turn around, didn't speak.

"I know I should let you do whatever you need to do, whatever you've always done, but things are different now. You're not alone anymore, Sloane. It's not just about you. I know it sounds selfish, with everything you're going through, and maybe it is, but I want to be there for you. I want to do whatever I can. I'm your partner, but... I'm also more than that, aren't I? You don't have to tell me everything. I won't push you for answers. But please, stay. Don't make me stand on the sidelines with everyone else." Dex was exceptionally still, afraid if he made any movement at all, Sloane would disappear. He didn't want to be on the outside looking in.

Dex held his breath, his teeth worrying his bottom lip. In his head, he prepared himself for disappointment. Months ago, when they'd been doing their dance around each other, Sloane had told him he'd grown up leaning on others, until they all left him and there was no one left to lean on except Ash. Sloane had grown accustomed to not needing anyone for anything until Gabe, and then Gabe was ripped from his life.

"You said it yourself. No matter what, I don't lose faith in you. Well, maybe it's time you have some faith in me. You *know* me. Whatever happens between us, you know I wouldn't walk away from you, so please, don't walk away from me."

Sloane let out a shuddered breath and ran a hand over his face. He carried on to the door, and Dex's heart plummeted. Not wanting to see him disappear, Dex went upstairs, his chest constricted. If Sloane couldn't stay now, what possible future could they have together? Dex sat on the edge of his bed, trying not to give in to the sense of loss. Maybe that was the point. Maybe they had no future together. Was he really surprised?

The door closed downstairs, the sound reverberating through the silent house, and Dex cursed himself for being such an idiot, for ignoring the warnings in his head over and over. He leaned his elbows on his legs and let his head fall into his hands. Well, what else could he do but get on with it? He still had a job to do, and regardless of how Sloane felt about them, Dex wouldn't give up on helping his partner through whatever hell storm awaited them. He got to his feet and froze.

"Sorry," Sloane said quietly. "I was trying to think of something to say that wouldn't result in you punching me in the face."

"What makes you think I'd punch you?" Sloane wasn't wrong. It was exactly what Dex wanted to do, but his stupid heart kept him from carrying through with it.

"No matter how hard I try to stay away, I keep coming back, and you let me."

If the guy wanted an answer to his unspoken question of why Dex was allowing it, he wouldn't be getting one, mostly because Dex didn't have one. "Misery loves company, right?"

Sloane shook his head. "I don't want you to be miserable, Dex. That's why I keep pushing you away."

For all his Team Leader's smarts, sometimes he could be pretty damn thick. "If you haven't noticed, that has the exact opposite effect."

"I wish I could think of something better to say than 'I'm sorry.' I wonder how many times it'll take before you stop believing me."

"That won't happen. I might tell you to take your sorry and shove it, but I won't stop believing you mean it."

Sloane chuckled, his smile the best thing Dex had seen in a long time. "Gotcha."

Dare he ask? "So?"

"This is going to sound shitty, but I won't lie to you. I can't make any promises."

"I don't want promises. I want you to trust me and try. When that little voice in your head tells you to get out, you tell it to shut up, and instead of heading to the door, you turn your ass around, and you come to me. No more lone-wolf bullshit, or uh, lone jaguar."

"Jaguars are loners by nature." Despite his somber tone, Dex could see the smile in Sloane's eyes, and it warmed his heart.

"Yeah, well, if you don't change those spots, I'll rearrange them for you."

Sloane's smile stole Dex's breath away. He shoved his hands in his pockets and lowered his gaze to the floor, his cheeks somewhat flushed. His partner was looking like his old self more and more.

"Hey." Dex held his hand out. "How about we get rid of some of this space between us?" He watched Sloane's eyes shift to Dex's hand before moving up to his face. A moment of hesitation, and in two strides, he had his hand in Dex's.

"You really are amazing," Sloane said, bending his head to Dex's and kissing his lips. His mouth tasted of minty toothpaste, and Dex couldn't help but melt into him, until he caught a whiff of his partner. He pulled back, scrunching up his nose. "I think maybe we should continue this in the shower. What do you say?"

"Deal," Sloane laughed. He pulled Dex with him, when Dex's cell phone buzzed.

Dashing over to the nightstand, he checked his phone. "Looks like we're going to have to make this a quickie. Lieutenant Sparks is holding a briefing at eight sharp." He put his phone down and turned to Sloane, noticing his partner's unease. "Okay?"

Sloane smiled warmly and held his hand out to Dex. "I am now."

With a skip in his step, Dex joined Sloane. Although they still had to work things out, for the first time in a while, Dex had hope. Sloane had stayed when everything in him had been pushing him to leave, he'd come back to Dex. *One day at a time.*

SLOANE SAT behind Dex in the briefing room, his chair closer than necessary and his leg discreetly pressed against Dex's. The tiny gesture was enough to help him settle his nerves. His team—with the exception of Hobbes—along with Beta Ambush and Beta Pride, sat waiting for Lieutenant Sparks to begin her briefing. She finished consulting with Maddock before approaching the podium, the large screen behind her coming to life with an image of Dr. Shultzon. Dex's leg shifted gently beside Sloane, offering comfort.

"The information I'm about to disclose is classified, with only the members of the teams in this room receiving security clearance to discuss it. This is Dr. Shultzon. You know him as Dr. Freedman. We believe Isaac Pearce has kidnapped him in order to gain access to classified THIRDS information regarding First Gen recruits.

"When the THIRDS was being structured, the Therian Department of Defense decided the best place to find recruits would be within the population of First Generation Therians. They were, after all, scientifically proven to be the first Therians with both stable DNA and the finalized version of the modifications initiated by Eppione.8. There isn't much I can share about the THIRDS First Gen Recruitment Program, other than it, along with a secure facility, closed when the THIRDS had their agents, and the research into Therians was completed. Dr. Shultzon was one of a handful of doctors to hand select candidates and help them achieve their potential.

"There are files concerning the First Gen Recruitment Program that we cannot allow to fall into public view. It would be catastrophic for the THIRDS, damaging our reputation and the careers of all your First Gen fellow agents. We believe it's this information Isaac has been after, and why he abducted Agent Morelli."

Agent Taylor raised his hand.

"Yes?"

"Was Morelli a First Gen Therian?"

"He was. Isaac Pearce abducted Agent Morelli in the hopes of being led to this information. As you all know, Morelli's file included the CDC registration office where he was registered. Gaining access to Morelli's file at the registration office led him to the Therian Youth Center where Morelli spent time before Dr. Shultzon found him and picked him up for recruitment. For security reasons, once the program ended, Dr. Shultzon was given a new identity. The youth center's files were altered to reflect this change in identity, including Morelli's file. It didn't take long for Isaac to track down the doctor." Lieutenant Sparks tapped the tablet before her, and the screen split into three, showing photographs and personal information on three Humans.

"Although Dr. Shultzon would have been trained to withstand torture, it's come to our attention that he may have been compromised. He has a daughter and two grandchildren who we can confirm have been placed under twenty-four hour surveillance by Isaac Pearce. My guess is Isaac has threatened to harm them if he doesn't get the First Gen files. Considering we haven't heard anything in the news, it's safe to say Isaac has yet to get his hands on the information. However, we must act quickly."

Again, Taylor held his hand up, receiving a nod from the lieutenant. "Do we know who's performing the surveillance?"

"Yes. These three Humans: Ennio Mortiz, Reggie Long, and Ian Sanders. I expect you to bring them in for questioning. They must have some way of communicating with Isaac. I can't stress enough how imperative it is we recover Dr. Shultzon and stop Isaac Pearce from gaining access to the First Gen information. The research facility where what's left of the information is stored is in a secure location and has been placed under lockdown. If anyone goes near it, we'll hear about it. Agent Taylor, you and your team will be providing backup to Destructive Delta. Now move out."

Finally, they were getting somewhere. Maddock joined Sloane who'd gathered their team, the rest of their backup around them waiting for orders.

"Cael, you're our eyes in the BearCat with Maddock. Letty, Ash, you're team one, you take Mortiz. Rosa, Calvin, you're team two, you take Long. Dex and I will take Sanders. Agent Stone, Agent Taylor, I want you to divide your teams up into four groups, one to ride with Sergeant Maddock and Cael, the other three groups pick one of my teams and stay close. These guys aren't going to go down without a fight. Watch your backs. Anyone runs into any trouble, call for backup. Let's go."

Once they got to the armory, they geared up and grabbed what they needed, the rest of their weapons locked securely in the back of their individual Suburban vehicles. Sloane climbed behind the wheel with Dex settling in beside him. They were close. Sloane could feel it. One of these Humans had to have a way of contacting Isaac. The doctor was too important for Isaac to leave the surveillance of the man's family to any idiot. They had to be trusted.

Sloane drove through the wide tunnel leading out of THIRDS headquarters and out to the street, a convoy of black vehicles like theirs, along with the BearCat transporting Cael and Maddock bringing up the rear. As soon as they reached Second Avenue, the cars split up into two groups.

"Do we know where Sanders is?" Dex asked, logging into the Suburban's console.

"See what Themis has on file for him."

Dex tapped through the glowing blue tabs, bringing up Sanders's file, personal information, and tabs to any relevant information associated with Sanders.

"Hells yeah. Themis has a GPS location. Looks like he's parked on Eleventh Street, just off Second Avenue. Shit."

"What?"

"He's parked across from a music school. The same one Dr. Shultzon's grandson has piano lessons in." Dex tapped away at the screen, cross-referencing the information with Shultzon's family file. "The kid's scheduled for a lesson right now."

"Son of a bitch. Okay, hang on." Sloane flipped on the lights and sounded the sirens. Taylor and the members of his team in the Suburban behind Sloane followed his lead. They were less than three minutes away.

The moment they turned onto Eleventh Street, Sanders's Gray Corolla burned rubber. Sloane tapped his earpiece as he gave chase. "Sarge, we're on Ian Sanders's tail. He's heading down Third Avenue. Taylor, you and your team secure Shultzon's grandson. He's inside the music school having lessons."

"Copy that." Taylor's Suburban pulled back, as Sloane turned onto Third Avenue, maneuvering through heavy traffic after Sanders.

"Sarge?"

"We're heading your way."

Sloane turned onto East Ninth Street, honking at cars to get out of his way, and praying Sanders's car didn't cause a pileup as he fled. The closer they got to Broadway, the more traffic they came across.

"Goddamn construction! Son of a bitch! Move your ass!" Sloane yelled at no one in particular, slamming his gloved hand down against the horn, and having to swerve around the cars stopped at the red light at the intersection. Oncoming traffic slowed and stopped, some skidding to a screeching halt as Sanders turned left on Broadway. Sloane hit the gas on the Fire Lane, yellow cabs and cyclists darting out of their way. He had no idea where the hell Sanders thought he was going. The guy was driving fast, but he never got far from Sloane. Something in his gut twisted, but he ignored it. He was getting close. He could feel it.

CHAPTER 12

"WHAT'S YOUR twenty, Sloane?"

Maddock's voice came in over Sloane's earpiece, and he hoped his team got there soon. The longer they followed Sanders, the more uneasy Sloane felt. "We're following him up West Houston Street. Looks like he's making a right on Hudson Street. I don't know what the hell he's got up his sleeve, but he's slowed down." As Sloane said the words, the car jolted forward. "Strike that. He's on the move." Sloane slammed down on the accelerator, making a left on Leroy Street, and another left onto Washington Street, speeding past an open parking garage on the left, and a large building—a mix of condominiums and businesses—on the right.

"He's turning right on West Houston Street and the underpass." Sloane made a sharp turn and slammed the breaks. "What the hell?"

"What's going on?"

"He…. He disappeared," Dex replied, turning in his seat to look around them.

"We're heading your way. Watch your backs."

"Copy that." Sloane put the Suburban into reverse and backed up, turning onto Washington Street where they'd come from. He parked a few feet from the corner and turned off the engine, a deep frown on his face. "I don't like this."

"Me neither, but we can't let this asshole get away. Come on." Dex jumped out of the car and headed for the back with Sloane a few steps behind. He unlocked the back double doors, followed by the deadbolts on the heavy-duty weapons drawers. Dex grabbed his ballistic helmet from the side hook and put it on, securing the straps. Sloane did the same and tested his earpiece.

"Can you hear me?"

"Loud and clear, partner."

Sloane lifted his AR15 from its foam padding, and Dex stared at him wide-eyed. "You know something I don't?"

"I don't trust Isaac or anyone who's with him. This guy led us here. For all we know, he'll come at us with a fucking tank." Sloane checked his rifle's magazine before grabbing an extra three and securing them to his utility belt. "Hope for the best, prepare for the worst, right?"

Dex smiled at him. "Right."

They finished gathering what equipment they needed, and Sloane secured the Suburban. As Dex turned, Sloane grabbed him by the vest and pulled him over. Dex gave him a questioning smile.

"You be careful. You got me?" Dex nodded, and Sloane knocked his helmet gently against Dex's, his chest feeling tight at his partner's affectionate smile. "Okay. Let's kick some ass." Sloane went ahead of Dex, his rifle at the ready as he stayed close to the building and rounded the corner on Washington Street. Someone screamed and pedestrians started running, but Sloane ignored the commotion. He headed through the underpass with Dex close on his heels. It was dark, the only light coming from the red LED lights positioned above the garage doors. On the left hand side were three windows with burglar bars and the doors were all labeled. From the looks of it, some were warehouses while others were storage units. On the right hand side of the street, there was a solitary white van parked in front of a closed garage door. There was nothing but deathly silence around them.

Sloane was about to cross the street to what looked like a side entrance when the thundering sound of clanking metal echoed through the underpass, stopping him in his tracks. One by one, the garage doors across from them opened, and armed men in bulletproof vests emerged from the shadows.

"Take cover!" Sloane ordered, grabbing Dex and pulling him behind the van as shots rang out. Bullets sprayed the van, windows bursting, and tiny shards of glass raining down in all directions. Small chunks of brick from the building next to them flew off and crumbled to dust. Sloane hit the small communicator button on his vest's radio. "Destructive Delta, come in."

Maddock's gruff tone did little to mask the concern in his voice as it came on the line. "What's your position?"

"It's a trap. They were waiting for us. I make over a dozen heavily armed men, but there could be more. We're under heavy fire. Where the hell are you guys?"

"Less than ten minutes away."

"Okay. We'll try and hold them off."

"Copy that."

Sloane edged toward the front wheel of the van, peeking around the front fender. A bullet ricocheted right by his helmet and he jerked back. He prepared to fire when the garage door on their right just ahead rolled open. He aimed his rifle, Dex at his back, but no one came out. "That can't be good."

"What's our next move?"

"If we stay out here, we're dead. I'll cover you. Ready?"

"Ready."

"Now!" Sloane popped up from behind the van, firing at the gunmen, who took cover, but not before Sloane clipped two of them in the leg, sending them to the floor with cries of pain. Sloane took off after Dex, firing as he went until he was inside the garage, or at least that's what he thought it was. It was actually a huge storage unit that stretched down the length of the building, sectioned off into smaller units, and supported by several concrete columns. There was everything from wooden pallets to metal racking, department store mannequins, holiday displays, old signage, and cleaning equipment.

"Come on, we can take cover behind that racking." Dex motioned ahead of them, and Sloane followed, shots ringing out behind them. They ran further into the storage unit, a set of red wires catching his attention. He came to a halt, his eyes widening at the C4 strapped to one of the concrete columns.

"Run!"

They raced back toward the entrance when the explosion knocked Sloane off his feet. He hit something solid and bounced off before hitting the ground hard, the wind knocked out of him from the impact. His ears rang, and his vision was blurry. He sucked in a sharp breath and winced. His lungs burned, his throat was raw, and breathing in deep resulted in a mouthful of dust. Coughing and sputtering, he turned his head, his blurry vision focusing on a dirt-smudged face.

"Dex," Sloane wheezed, trying to push himself up, but his body wasn't cooperating. A look over his shoulder revealed the reason why. A large chunk of a concrete column had him pinned. A shot hit the dirt beside his head, and Sloane jerked out of the way as much as the slab of concrete would allow, a harsh voice echoing from somewhere in the distance.

"Don't shoot him you idiots! I want him alive. Grab the blond."

The blond? Oh God, they were going to take Dex. He had to do something. "Dex," Sloane rasped, "wake up. Please. Dex. Wake up."

Dex groaned, his eyelids slowly opening. "Wh—what happened?"

"Get up. You have to get up right now. Run."

Despite his confusion, Dex reacted to the urgency in Sloane's voice, rolling onto his side and shakily pushing himself to his feet. Sloane opened his mouth when a series of shots rang out, two hitting Dex in the vest, throwing him off his feet. But it was the dart in Dex's arm that frightened Sloane the most.

"No!" Something in Sloane's brain snapped, and his vision cleared. He pushed as hard as he could against the ground. "You son of a bitch!"

Dex coughed and gasped, sucking in as much oxygen as he could after being winded, his face a deep red, his eyes bloodshot and teary from whatever was going through his system. Sloane could see his partner trying to push through the pain caused by the impact of the bullets hitting his vest, through whatever was making Dex writhe. "Sloane," Dex breathed, shutting his eyes tight.

"No, please. Dex!" Sloane reached out again, stretching his arm as far as his protesting muscles would allow. The back of his eyes stung as Dex's head lolled toward him, and he attempted a reassuring smile. The bastard. How could he think about Sloane at a time like this? "Dex!"

With whatever strength Dex seemed to have left, he dragged his arm up, and his fingers crawled to Sloane's until they could touch. Sloane took Dex's fingers in his. Seconds later two men arrived, grabbing Dex by his vest.

"Don't you dare hurt him! Dex!"

Dex was out cold, lying limp as the two men carried him away. Teeth gritted, Sloane desperately tried to pull himself free. He was going to tear them apart. A boot pounded down against his back, forcing him against the concrete floor.

"My, how the mighty have fallen." Isaac chuckled. "And have still to fall."

"What do you want with Dex?" Sloane growled, trying to grab Isaac, only to have the man stomp on his arm. He let out a hoarse cry, his face growing hot and red as he seethed.

"I want from him the same thing you do. His loyalty, his friendship, devotion, everything you don't deserve. How do you do it? How do you take good, honest men like Dex, like my brother, and turn them into your filthy toys? Is it through loyalty? Do you lure them with the illusion of happiness? A happiness you can never give them?" He leaned in, his voice quiet, but his words shaking Sloane down to his core. "Do you honestly believe a man like Dex will want you when he finds out what you are? What you've done?"

Sloane went still.

"That's right. I know everything. My brother was blinded by your lies, and I've watched as you've woven your web of deception around Dex, but I can still save him. When he finds out the truth, he'll see you for the animal you are."

"Maybe, but he'll never be loyal to you."

"Oh, he will. Believe me, he will, and then we'll crush the THIRDS under our thumbs, and rule this city the way it was meant to be ruled. Without your filthy kind."

Isaac's words sent dread through Sloane. "What have you done?"

"You'll just have to wait and see."

"Why don't we get this over with, Isaac? You and me, without these games."

"And miss out on making your life miserable? I'll be waiting for you, Sloane. Right where it all began for you and your feral friends."

Isaac disappeared, and Sloane pushed against the floor, desperate. He had to stop them.

"Sloane? Dex? Where are you?"

"Maddock! In the storage garage!" Sloane called out as loud as he could. Within seconds, his team was racing in, Ash and Calvin rushing to his side to lift the slab. "Dex! They have Dex!" Sloane thrust his finger in the direction Isaac had run off to, and Maddock darted off with Rosa, Letty, and Cael.

His legs free, Sloane pulled himself out, and with Ash's help, got to his feet. "Isaac took Dex," Sloane ground out, trying to push away from Ash. To his horror, his team ran back, the pain in Maddock's face telling him all he needed to know. "No." Sloane shook his head. He refused. "I have to go." Sloane tried to push against his friend, furious when Ash wouldn't let him go. "Get the fuck off me! I need to get him back."

"Sloane, they're gone," Rosa said. "They had a plan. This whole thing was planned."

"I can't…." Sloane shook his head. What did he want to say? He couldn't lose Dex the way he lost Gabe. He couldn't. "I have to save my partner." His rough words sounded more like a plea, but he didn't care.

"And we will," Maddock assured him. "What did Isaac say to you? Did he give any clue to where he might be taking Dex?"

Isaac's words echoed in his head, and then it all came crashing down.

"I know where he is."

SLOANE STORMED into Lieutenant Sparks's office, his fingers flexing at his sides. "Where is it?" he demanded.

"I beg your pardon?"

"Where the hell is the facility?"

Lieutenant Sparks stared at him, her hand covering the receiver of her phone. "Agent Brodie, I have the Chief of Therian Defense on the line."

"Good." Sloane marched over and snatched the phone from her. "This is Agent Sloane Brodie. I need to know where the First Gen Research Facility is." He listened as the Chief of Defense huffed and spewed a bunch of bureaucratic bullshit and threats, none of which Sloane gave two flying fucks about. "Now you listen to me, you paper-pushing son of a bitch, Isaac Pearce has my partner. He has Dr. Shultzon, and most likely the First Gen files. If you want to suspend me, you do that, but after I save my partner, and your sorry ass from a media shit storm. Now where is the goddamn facility?"

There was a long pause, and as Sloane was about to give the Therian a piece of his mind, he rattled off the address. Sloane thought maybe he'd heard wrong, but he knew he hadn't. *You've got to be kidding me.*

"*That's* the secure location? In the middle of fucking Manhattan? No offense, sir, but you need to revisit the meaning of 'secure,' because that sure as hell isn't it." He thrust the phone at his lieutenant and stormed off, calling out over his shoulder. "I'll sign my suspension papers when I get back!" He headed for the briefing room, rounding up his team, along with Beta Ambush and Beta Pride. Inside, he addressed the room, aware of Maddock hovering by the door, his expression grave.

"All right, listen up. This is an extraction. Our priority is to preserve life. Get Agent Daley and Dr. Shultzon out of there alive. Destructive Delta, you know what you have to do. Everyone else, I don't think I need to paint you a picture of the extreme danger this group poses to our city and our organization. Approach the facility with extreme caution. Whatever happens, Isaac Pearce does not leave that building unless it's in cuffs or a body bag. Understood?"

"Understood, sir!"

"Then let's move out."

Moments later, they were all sitting in brooding silence, strapped in their seats inside the BearCat as it drove through Manhattan. Sloane couldn't stop himself from thinking the worst. What if they were too late? What if he lost Dex like he'd lost Gabe? Would he be able to handle it? What the hell did Isaac want with Dex? There was no way the guy believed Dex would join him. Sloane quickly pushed all those thoughts out of his head. Dex needed him. He needed to keep it together. As the BearCat sped through the city, Ash spoke up beside him.

"I can't believe the facility's been there all this time."

Rose checked the magazine of her Remington rifle, before moving onto her next weapon. His team wasn't leaving anything to chance, considering what was at stake. "You think they were trying to hide it in plain sight?"

"I don't know what they were thinking, probably that it was secure, and no one would be able to breach it," Ash muttered. "Same shit they believe about every secure location until someone infiltrates it. Secure, my ass."

As soon as they'd boarded the BearCat, they'd received word from Lieutenant Sparks. The facility had been breached. From the inside. Which was why they hadn't been alerted. The reason they knew anything about it now was because Isaac himself had sounded the alert. Sloane wasn't surprised. If Isaac had managed to get Dr. Shultzon to cooperate using his family, Sloane had no doubts the guy had used similar tactics to infiltrate security. Themis had confirmed several guards with high levels of clearance at the facility had families, including young children. Isaac wasn't the sort to go in guns blazing, hoping everything would sort itself out. He meticulously planned, went in under the radar, and exposed the weaknesses. Then he made himself known.

The First Gen Therian Research Facility was located on East Seventy-First Street, past an antique shop, Sokol, and Cornell University Medical Center. It was a light gray building with dark gray accents, eight floors containing seven large mirrored windows per floor (except for the highest two floors, which had three windows), a parking garage, and a set of large glass doors. No numbers, no signs, or information. It was frightening knowing how in this innocent looking neighborhood, all manner of tests and experiments had been performed on young Therians. How countless lives had been altered, destroyed, and saved. Looking at it made him want to be sick. After years of trying to put this place behind him, there it was staring back at him, larger than life.

"Hey, you okay?"

Sloane heard Cael's soft words, and was about to answer, believing his teammate had been addressing him, but when he turned, he found Cael had actually been talking to Ash. His friend had gone pale, his eyes on the building across from them.

"Yeah, I uh…." Ash shook his head, his words trailing off into nothing. Shit, Sloane hadn't thought of how being back might affect Ash. He gave Cael a reassuring smile and pulled his friend behind the truck, away from prying eyes.

"Hey, look at me," He took Ash's face in his hands, turning his face so he could look his friend in the eye. "It's okay. They can't hurt us. Things are different now. We're not those scared kids anymore." Ash nodded, though Sloane could still see the uncertainty and fear in his friend's eyes. "Ash, you can do this. I need you, buddy. I need you to help me get Dex back. I wouldn't be here if it wasn't for you. Please."

Ash looked at him then, truly looked at him, his expression turning hard. He took a deep breath and nodded. "Let's go get that partner of yours out of there."

With a grin, Sloane grabbed Ash's head, and Ash did the same to Sloane. They pressed their heads together like they used to do when they were kids, pretending to be tough soldiers, brothers-in-arms. Now they were.

"Let's do this," Ash declared, moving away. He jumped into the van, helping Cael up. "Show me the building's layout."

Cael brought up a digital 3D rendering of the facility's schematics. At least the Chief of Defense was finally cooperating.

"Can you get into the security feed?" Ash asked, cursing under his breath when Cael shook his head.

"This is military grade encryption and Isaac's locked us out. It'd take far longer than we have time for in order to gain access. I brought up the facility network, and there's a load of failed login attempts. At least Isaac hasn't been able to connect so far. It might be the only thing keeping those files from going public."

"Okay." Ash studied the floor plans. "We have no idea how many guys Isaac has in there. Our best bet is to have teams go in aggressive on the ground floor, disable and distract, while our team goes in through the roof. Ground floor teams use a shitload of nonlethals to confuse and incapacitate them: flash bangs, smoke bombs, grenade launcher. Have the other teams go in after and start taking the floors one at a time. Destructive Delta enters the building though here." Ash pointed to the building next to the facility. "The ninth floor window of this building opens right onto the roof of the facility. There's a door and a vent, leading inside. If we're lucky, we can catch that bastard by surprise."

"Okay, team. Let's move out." Sloane tapped his earpiece. "Sarge?"

"Heard you loud and clear. Beta Ambush and Beta Pride are getting into position to go in through the front. They'll wait for your signal."

"Copy that." Sloane grabbed his helmet and jumped from the truck, his team falling into formation behind him, except for Cael who remained to keep surveillance and provide technical backup. They went around the back to the BearCat, using the cars parked along the street to give them cover until they crossed to the building beside the facility. Inside, agents from a backup squad were evacuating the building.

Taking the stairwell, Sloane rushed up with Ash, Rosa, Letty, and Calvin behind him. They had nine floors to climb. By the time they got to the ninth floor and out into the offices, Sloane's breath was heavy in his ears. He tapped his earpiece. "Cael, we're outside the emergency exit on the ninth floor. Which way?"

"Make a right, straight down, last set of offices on the right. It's the middle one, belonging to a Mr. Trine."

"Copy that." They rushed past rows and rows of cubicles until they reached the end of the floor and the many rows of closed doors. They found the one they needed and Sloane stepped aside. Ash slammed his shoulder into the door and it splintered open. The window was big, enough for all of them to get through. Lucky for them it opened and they didn't have to blast it. It took mere seconds to get onto the roof and they headed straight for the door. Unsurprisingly, he found it locked.

"Calvin. Get this open."

Sloane tapped his earpiece. "Sarge, we're going in. Send in the teams."

"Copy that. All teams move in!"

Leaving his sergeant and the rest of Unit Alpha's teams to take care of business downstairs, Sloane gave Calvin the go ahead. He stood back as Calvin swiftly unclasped his backpack and removed two pieces of det cord before securing them to the door's hinges. They all darted away, ducking behind the concrete wall, hearing Calvin's warning.

"Fire in the hole!"

There was a loud boom, followed by the clanking and screeching of metal sliding across the roof floor. Sloane rushed out, checking they were clear before going in through the doorway. He led his teammates into the darkness, hoping he'd find his partner at the other end of it, alive and in one piece.

Hang on for me, Dex. Please, hang on.

HIS CHEST hurt.

With a groan, Dex rolled forward. His throat was dry, his tongue felt gross and furry, and his whole body ached as if someone had gone at him with a baseball bat, though nothing hurt more than his chest. Breathing hurt. His arms hurt. Why did his arms hurt? He went to rub his face when he discovered the reason. His arms were tied behind his back. Opening his eyes, he blinked a few times to clear the fuzziness. He was nauseous, groggy, and felt like utter crap. Scanning his surroundings, he was stunned to find himself in a white room with nothing but a wide hospital bed. Where the hell was he? He wracked his brain. Last thing he remembered, he'd been with Sloane who'd been trapped under something next to him, telling him to run.

"What the hell?" He sat upright with a hiss, his throat thick as his memory filled in the blanks. Shit, he'd been shot in the vest like three times. No wonder his chest was killing him. He recalled something else. Drugs. He'd been drugged. Someone shot his arm with some kind of tranquilizer.

Isaac.

That son of a bitch. He was behind this. Looking down at himself, he cursed the guy out some more. The bastard had taken his equipment. Everything from his utility belt, to his backup weapon, thigh rig, and his uniform shirt, leaving him in his tac pants and black undershirt. They'd taken his watch too. Tony had given him that watch. Assholes.

Dex had no idea where he was. All he knew was that he couldn't stay here, waiting for Isaac to come back for him. If he were going to move, he'd have to do it fast. There was no telling if he was being monitored. With his head slightly lowered, he discreetly took in the room, spotting his way out, considering the front door was likely not an option. He tested the restraint on his wrist and held back a smile. Zip tie. They'd used tape for his ankles. Fucking aces. Closing his eyes, he gave himself a pep talk. He could do this. It was going to hurt like hell, but it was do or die.

Pushing himself to his feet, he bent over and thrust his arms down. It took him a few tries, but on the third, the tie snapped. He swiftly went about untying his ankles. As soon as he'd pulled all the tape off, he ran to the door. Locked. Okay, Plan B.

He dashed over to the bed, wobbling for a minute when a wave of dizziness and nausea hit him. Breathing in deep, he straightened and pushed the bed against the wall. He gritted his teeth and lifted the bed, turning it so it stood on its large steel footboard. He hoped he didn't end up breaking his neck. Sliding the bed against the wall until the legs hit, he reached up, grabbed two of the headboard's steel bars, and pulled himself up.

His muscles strained, a headache exploded inside his skull, and his face grew hot as he pulled his weight up. Once up, he carefully balanced on the headboard on his knees and reached up, removing the medium sized silver vent. It was a good thing none of his Therian teammates had been taken with him, because there was no way in hell they'd fit through there. It was going to be a tight squeeze for Dex as it was.

Doing his best not to jar the bed too much, he rose to his feet, holding his arms out to keep his balance. The bed wobbled and Dex let out a steady breath. "Easy there." Soon as it stilled, he reached up and stuck his head through. The ventilation shaft stretched down in two directions. It was hot, cramped, and dark, with the faintest hints of light far in the distance to his right. Dex grinned to himself. "And Sloane says I watch too many movies." He pulled himself up into the shaft, his ass dangling below as he struggled to drag himself fully inside, his chest feeling as if it was in a vise as it pressed against the metal surface. He threw one hand out and pulled, muscles stretching and burning. Finally, after an excruciating amount of time, his whole body was inside. He was out of breath already, thanks to the remnants of whatever Isaac had given him.

"Move your ass, Daley," Dex growled, thinking of Sloane. He had to get to his partner. Whatever Isaac had planned, Dex was certain it would somehow involve Sloane. He crawled through the tight space, moving forward despite being unable to see anything. Up ahead there was a soft glow, and he picked up his pace, trying to keep himself from making too much noise. The glow was coming from a room below, and Dex cautiously slid his body up to the vent and peered down through the slats. It was a white room, but unlike the one he'd escaped, this one was filled with lab equipment. There were tables filled with electronic meters, filtration systems, centrifuges, glassware, incubators, microscopes, mixers, and a load of other stuff Dex didn't recognize.

Oh, shit. He was at the research facility. So much for it being secure. There was one thing he didn't understand. If the facility was closed and no longer in use, why was all this equipment still here? It sure as hell didn't look abandoned. Everything looked shiny and new. He listened for any signs that someone might be in the room, and when he heard none, he carefully pushed the vent down on one side, catching it before it could clatter to the floor. He gently placed it inside the shaft ahead of him and gingerly stuck his head out. The room was empty.

Sliding over the vent, he went down feet first, dangling from his waist again, before lowering himself. Gripping the edge of the vent, he let go, hitting he floor hard and falling back on his ass. Quickly he got to his feet, ignoring the sick feeling in the pit of his stomach. The room was cold, and it sure as hell had been used recently. Did the THIRDS know it was in use? They had to. Someone was ordering this stuff.

Dex went to one of the incubators and opened the glass door to find scores of tiny vials and glass bottles sporting names of chemicals and drugs he'd never heard of. What he did know was that they had a shelf life, and these liquids all had expiration dates for the following year. What disturbed him as much as the knowledge the lab was in use, was the mobile stretcher chair with straps parked on one side of the room. He needed to get out of here, and maybe find the First Gen files. They had to be somewhere close. As the thought crossed his mind, he spotted a tablet on one of the tables in the corner of the room. Dashing over, he found an external hard drive was connected to it. He tapped the screen and stifled a gasp.

The sleek screen was littered with rows and rows of personnel files. One name jumped out at him. Sloane Brodie. It was the First Gen files. Inspecting the drive, he discovered it was empty, but the serial number, along with the information on the plate indicated it was property of the THIRDS. It looked like Isaac had transferred the files to his device. A small padded protective case sat beside the tablet, and Dex snatched it up. On the bottom several tabs were open, and he clicked them, his heart leaping in his throat. They were network connections and news sites. To his relief, there was a nice big, red "X." Looked like Isaac was having trouble logging on, which meant he hadn't transferred any files. Unhooking the hard drive, he powered off the tablet and stuck it in the protective case, before sliding it into the zip pocket in his tac pants made to hold a ballistic plate. Then he tucked the portable drive into another pocket. Now he really had to get the hell out. If the tablet was here, it meant Isaac couldn't be far.

Dex snuck over to the lab's closed door and peeked through the window. His view of the brightly lit hall was restricted. He listened but couldn't hear anything. Quietly, he turned the doorknob and slowly pushed the door open. When nothing happened, he slipped outside. He turned and was struck across the jaw, sending him reeling against the corridor wall. Shaking himself out of it, he pushed away from the wall and backed up, barely having enough time to block the punch looking to land against his ribs. He pulled his arms in, blocking the fist, digging deep to push away all the pain and sickness he was feeling as a result of the drugs, and he threw a punch at his attacker, a huge, musclebound asshole the size of Ash, and just as mean looking, though admittedly far uglier.

Dex landed a right hook against the guy's jaw, but he shook it off like a pesky fly. With a growl, Dex moved in with a jab to the ribs when the beady-eyed bastard clamped an arm down, trapping Dex's wrist. He snatched Dex's other arm and head-butted him. It was like smacking into a concrete wall. Dex crumpled to the ground, the larger man on top of him, landing a hit to Dex's nose and bloodying it. Dizzy and gasping for breath, Dex refused to go down without a fight, punching the guy square in the balls. The guy doubled over with a fierce whine, and Dex put all his strength behind his fist, knocking him across the jaw. The guy fell limp to his side, and Dex scrambled to his feet, his knees buckling and almost giving way under him. He stumbled, but righted himself, leaning against the wall to catch his breath. With a wince, he swiped the blood from his nose.

"Dex, what on earth are you doing?"

He stiffened, turning to find Isaac observing him in amusement, three larger men with him. Shit. Dex pushed himself away from the wall and held his fists up.

"If you think I'm gonna go give in, you're crazier than I thought you were."

Isaac shook his head with a "tsk." "Dex, I don't want to fight you. Believe it or not, seeing you get hurt doesn't make me happy."

Dex let out a snort, cringed, and spit out a mouthful of blood. "You'll have to forgive me if I don't believe you. You know, what with shooting me, drugging me, and sending your Gollum here to beat the shit out of me."

"Gill was only doing his job," Isaac replied with a shrug. "Gentlemen, if you'll please restrain Agent Daley before he hurts himself any further."

Shit. Dex turned to run, but three more men blocked his path. He readied himself for a fight, wishing it were more like in the movies where the bad guys all stood back and came at the hero one at a time. No such luck. The six men rushed him at once, and for all of Dex's training, he was no match for six large men, and the state he was in didn't help matters. He struggled as they lifted him off his feet, carrying him back into the lab he'd come from.

"What the hell are you doing?" Dex pulled at his limbs, trying his hardest to free himself, but it was futile. They thrust him down harshly onto the chair and started restraining him. "Get the fuck off me!" The straps pulled tight against his ankles and wrists. His head was forced back, a large padded strap stretched across his forehead. They finished and retreated. Dex tugged against the restraints, pulling, and jerking his arms. Nothing. His heart pounded fiercely, and he tamped down his panic. Isaac came to stand beside him.

"What are you going to do with me?" Dex demanded.

"I only want to talk."

Dex let out a derisive laugh. "Talk? Okay. Let's talk. What would you like to talk about? The Knicks? The state of the economy? You losing your fucking mind?"

Isaac pulled up a stool and perched beside Dex. "I'd like to talk about you."

"Me."

"Yes. I think it's time you reconsidered joining me."

Dex gaped at the guy. Was he serious? Had he really lost his mind? "Why in the hell would you think I'd join you?"

"Dex, despite what you may believe, I'm trying to save you."

"Save me?" The concern and gentleness in Isaac's voice as he spoke to Dex confused him. Something had most certainly snapped in the guy's head. And what was this obsession he had with saving Dex? He decided he needed some answers. "Save me from what?"

"From those animals," Isaac replied with a sneer. "I couldn't save my brother, but I can save you."

That's what this was about, what it had always been about. Gabe. "Do you think saving me is going to absolve you for what you did to him?"

Isaac jumped from the stool so quickly, it clattered to the floor. His hazel eyes blazed with fury, saliva shooting from his mouth as he spat the words out. "I didn't kill Gabe! Those animals did! Sloane Brodie killed my brother, and he's going to burn in hell for it."

"You confessed. You killed Gabe. It might have been an accident, but you killed him, Isaac. You can't blame Sloane for that. Your brother's death is on your hands."

Isaac shook his head fervently as he started to pace. Dex continued to struggle against his restraints, hoping to loosen something. Did Isaac truly believe if he "saved" Dex, everything that had happened with Gabe would vanish? "What is it you're expecting to happen, Isaac? That I'll flip some switch in my head, and suddenly I'll see things your way? That I'll start hurting innocent Therians, planting bombs in youth centers?"

"Not at first," Isaac said calmly.

Shit, the guy really had lost it. Dex watched as Isaac adjusted the straps on his bulletproof vest, put his stool on its feet, and resumed his seat as if nothing had happened.

"You'll be restricted to the Order's main facility for a while. You understand how the mind works, Dex. Humans can be conditioned if exposed to certain environments long enough. With time, you'll come around to our way of thinking."

"You mean like Stockholm Syndrome?"

Isaac's grin sent icy shivers up Dex's spine. "See, you're getting it already."

"You might as well kill me," Dex replied through his teeth. He'd rather die than end up Isaac's personal puppet.

With a resigned sigh, Isaac stood to look down at Dex. "You remind me so much of Gabe. He was so spirited. Stubborn as hell too." Isaac's fingers touched Dex's cheek, and Dex stiffened, his stomach reeling, and his skin crawling. "He was special, like you." Fingers trailed down Dex's jaw and over his lips. "Beautiful."

Dex's eyes widened, and for the first time, he felt true fear. "Isaac…." Dex's voice broke, and he closed his eyes for a moment. "Please."

"I'm sorry, Dex." Isaac reached down and unzipped Dex's pocket containing the tablet. "I believe you have something that belongs to me." He removed the case and moved onto his other pocket to remove the drive. "One of my guys has been working on getting me network access and should come through any moment now. A slight setback, but that's okay. I prepared for it." He shook his head sadly. "I knew you would refuse. I'd hoped you wouldn't, but I knew you would." Isaac walked off, and Dex fought as hard as he could against the straps, letting out a frustrated cry when nothing happened. Oh God, what was Isaac doing? Dex could hear the man tinkering behind him.

"What are you going to do?"

"What I set out to do. Make your lover suffer and destroy the THIRDS. And you're going to help me do it."

"I'll never help you," Dex spat out.

Isaac approached the chair, a syringe containing a tiny amount of clear liquid in his hand. "Oh, but you will, Dex. You just won't know it."

The needle plunged into Dex's neck, and he arched his back, letting out a violent cry, both in anguish and from the physical pain. He didn't know what Isaac was pumping him full of, but he was scared, scared of what he might do, of hurting Sloane. As his vision blurred and his body seized, the air rushed out of his lungs as his muscles went taut. The last thing he felt was a tear roll down his cheek. Then he felt nothing at all.

CHAPTER 13

"SLOANE, WE'VE got a problem."

Sloane tapped his earpiece, hearing a surge of gunfire and shouting in the background. "Cael? What's going on?"

"We've got company. As soon as our teams went in, Isaac's followers started jumping ship, but when they fled the building, someone started shooting at them. It's that Therian group from the news. I don't know how they knew we were here, but they knew. It's a mess. Lieutenant Sparks is sending backup."

"Shit." Just what they needed. "Okay, keep me posted. It's quiet up here, but I doubt it'll stay that way."

"Copy that. And Sloane?"

"Yeah?"

"Get my brother out of there."

"Affirmative." Sloane turned to his team. "We're going to have to split up. We've got unwanted visitors downstairs making a bigger mess of things. If anyone finds Dex, Shultzon, or Isaac, you call for backup immediately. I want you checking in every ten minutes. Go." The team broke off, each heading in a different direction.

Sloane wasn't familiar with this part of the facility. He'd spent years here, undergoing all kinds of tests and treatments, a good deal of which he thankfully couldn't remember. He and Ash had never been permitted to leave their floor. In between their sessions with doctors, psychologists, and scientists, they'd spent most of their time in the room they shared or in the classrooms. He turned a corner, walking cautiously through a set of double doors with high windows and froze. It was a long white corridor, the lights almost too bright, and at the end, a set of white double doors, exactly like in his nightmare.

For the briefest moment, he thought he might be at home, or in Dex's bed, having a bad dream, but he wasn't. At least this time he had his weapon. He edged toward the doors when he heard a familiar voice.

"Sloane, help me please."

This time it wasn't Gabe, it was Dex.

Rifle in hand, Sloane hurried toward the doors, unsure of what he was going to find on the other side. An image of Dex lying in a pool of blood flashed through his mind, and he quickly pushed it away. This was not a dream. Dex needed him. Sloane ducked to one side of the large doors and carefully peered in through the glass, hearing a voice he knew well, one he wanted to shut up for good.

"Come in, Sloane. Let's chat."

Isaac Pearce.

Sloane tapped his earpiece, speaking quietly. "Guys, I found Isaac, and he's got Dex. He says he wants to talk. I'm on the eighth floor, Wing C. Calvin, you know what to do." Taking a deep breath, he pushed open one of the doors and walked in, his teeth gritted. The expansive gray room looked as it did in his nightmare—empty, except for the man who'd killed his lover, shed innocent blood, caused chaos, and now kidnapped Dex, standing in the center in a bulletproof vest, a side arm strapped to his leg, and a grin that Sloane wanted to punch off his face.

"Where are they?" Sloane asked, keeping his rifle aimed at Isaac.

"How does it feel to be home again?" Isaac asked pleasantly, motioning to the drab room in serious need of paint. The gray walls were chipped, scratched, and filled with questionable stains. The floor was concrete. It contained no windows, only a solid steel door off to his right. "It's a bit clinical for my taste, but it has its appeal."

Sloane refused to be baited. He repeated through his teeth. "Where. Are. They."

"I should feel relieved, having everything I believed to be true about you confirmed," he patted the pocket of his tac pants containing something rectangular, "but instead, I'm disappointed. I'll be the first to hold up my hands and say, we—the Human race—only has itself to blame. The virus, the vaccine, the result," Isaac said, motioning to Sloane, "was all our doing. But instead of correcting our mistakes, we make them worse. We created mutations, and not only do we treat them as Human, but we start giving them rights. We allow them into our government. We hire *murderers* to enforce the law."

Sloane's jaw clenched. He wouldn't allow Isaac to distract him. Isaac had a plan, and Sloane had to make certain he didn't fall victim to it.

With a grin, Isaac called out. "Dexter, come out here please. And bring the good doctor."

Sloane watched, stunned, as the door on his right opened, and Dex walked through, dragging a bound up Dr. Shultzon with him. His partner's face was bruised, faint blood stains under his nose and across his cheek, but other than that, he looked perfectly healthy.

"Put him over there, will you. Place him on his knees."

"Sure." Dex did as Isaac asked, dragging the gagged doctor over to where Isaac pointed, lifting him, and pushing him onto his knees. Then he stood idly by. He'd been stripped of his tac vest, weapons, and uniform shirt. Sloane couldn't understand it.

"Dex?" Sloane received a smile from Dex, and his heart felt about ready to stop beating. It looked like Dex, talked like him, acted like him, but something was wrong. "What did you do to him?"

"Nothing your organization hasn't done to its own. I gave him a little concoction the THIRDS created containing scopolamine. The US government tried to use it as a truth serum back in the sixties, but unfortunately, along with the truth, they got a bunch of crazy ass hallucinations. Looks like the THIRDS found a better use for their new and improved drug—controlling their agents. The power of suggestion can be a wonderful thing. For example, I suggested to Dex that we're good friends. Isn't that right, Dex?"

Dex nodded. "We're good friends."

"You sick son of a bitch." Sloane took a step forward, only to have Dex step in front of Isaac. "Dex, get the hell out of the way,"

Sloane snarled, his glare on Isaac. He was going to tear the guy apart for what he'd done to his partner.

"Easy there, Sloane. Dex is protecting me because that's what friends do. They protect each other. You shoot me, and your partner will take the bullet, and he's not wearing any protection."

"What do you want, Isaac?" Where the hell was his team?

A loud bang echoed from somewhere behind him, and Isaac laughed. "Those doors are fortified. They locked after you came through. Both sets of doors. This facility was created to withstand feral Therians. Your team won't get through. And if they somehow manage, there's still the set of doors behind you. This will all be over by then. Dex, take this." Isaac handed Dex his gun.

"Calvin?" Sweat dripped down Sloane's face, and he ran through the variables in his head. Whatever Isaac's plan, the end result would be for him to get away with the files.

"In position," Calvin confirmed.

Sloane slipped his finger over the trigger.

"Dex," Isaac said, his gaze on Sloane. "Kill the doctor then kill yourself."

With those few words, Sloane felt the pain Isaac had intended. The bastard knew THIRDS protocol. Preserve civilian life. Sloane's duty would be to save Dr. Shultzon, no matter the cost. Dex took a step forward, and the rest happened in a blur. Sloane pulled the trigger, hitting Dex who fell to the floor, Sloane following his lead as he shouted the signal into his earpiece. "TARE!" A familiar 'pop' echoed through the air, and Sloane lifted his head from his position on the floor, his eyes meeting Isaac's lifeless stare.

Isaac had been counting on separating Sloane from his team, thinking Sloane would choose to handle the situation alone, and therefore fall into Isaac's trap, forced to make a choice: his partner or the doctor. He had been counting on Sloane's anger, on his hatred for him, believing Sloane would attempt to seek justice on his own. That's where Isaac had made his mistake. Sloane's anger and thirst for Isaac's blood hadn't clouded his judgment as it had Isaac's. Instead, Sloane drew on the strength of his team, of his family, and the man who'd come to mean more to him than he cared to admit, to gain clarity.

Sloane wasn't alone, and he hadn't needed his team to get through the doors. He only needed his best sniper to get through the glass.

Scrambling to his feet, Sloane ran over to Dex's side. To his horror, his partner was still reaching for Isaac's gun. His leg was bleeding where Sloane had shot him, but it was as if Dex didn't feel it.

Sloane wrestled the gun from Dex, and Dex fought against him. A blast exploded through the hall, filling it with smoke, and soon his team was blasting through the second set of doors, while Sloane did his damn best to restrain his drugged partner.

"Dex, stop it!"

"I have to kill the doctor then myself," Dex said, pushing and writhing to get free.

Sloane gritted his teeth, his full weight on Dex as he crossed Dex's arms over his chest and held them down.

"Sloane!" Ash came running, emerging from the smoke filled corridor with the rest of his team. "What the hell's going on?"

"I have to kill the doctor then myself," Dex answered, his face contorted with pain and frustration at not being able to carry out Isaac's request. Sloane had heard of the drug, had seen videos of victims sharing stories of how criminals had used it to rob them blind, simply by asking them for their belongings, by suggesting the victim take them to their homes. It was mostly used in foreign territories, often used to rob tourists. One whiff of the stuff, and the person was gone, though you'd never know from looking at them. And the most fucked up part? The victims never remembered anything.

Sloane shook his head, and turned his gaze to his startled teammates. "He's been drugged with something containing scopolamine. Isaac suggested he kill the doctor then himself, and now he's trying to do it. We need to knock him out, or he'll keep trying." Because that's what the drug did. Dex wanted to please his "friend." Thank God it would soon wear off.

"Shit? Scopolamine?" Rosa knelt beside Sloane, and took out her medical kit from her backpack. "That shit will fuck you up. He doesn't know what he's doing. I'll give him an anesthetic. When he wakes up, he won't remember what happened, so you'll have to explain the stitches in his leg."

"Better stitches than dead," Sloane replied, "Calvin, the files are in Isaac's pocket. Get them to Lieutenant Sparks." He looked up to find Dr. Shultzon standing before him, smiling warmly.

Sloane swallowed hard and gave him a nod. "Abraham." Words and emotions bubbled up from somewhere deep inside, but Sloane forced them back down. This was neither the time nor the place. He'd been sixteen the last time he'd seen the man who'd changed his life in so many ways.

There was a commotion down the hall as backup arrived, including Maddock who ran over to Sloane's side and dropped to his knees beside Dex. "What happened? Is he okay?"

Dex shook his head groggily, his lids growing heavy. "I need to kill the doctor…." He groaned, his head lolling to one side before he was out. Sloane debriefed quickly, though he would be filing a full report of the incident as soon as he got back to headquarters. The medics arrived, and Sloane stood, reluctant to leave Dex's side as they readied him for transport. Hudson and Nina gave Sloane grave nods as they walked past him to Isaac. Sloane couldn't help but note the way Isaac had fallen, the position he was in as he lay in a pool of his own blood, as Dex had in Sloane's nightmare. At least the real nightmare was over. Isaac Pearce was dead. Unable to help himself, he crouched down beside him, staring into his eyes, and speaking quietly.

"I hope you rot in hell, you son of a bitch." Maybe that made him a bad person, maybe he should be more forgiving, but fuck that. The bastard had killed Gabe, had kidnapped Sloane, and tortured him. He'd set off a bomb in a youth center, and then taken Dex with the intention of having Sloane kill his lover. No, there was no forgiveness in Sloane's heart for Isaac Pearce. Men like Isaac deserved what they got in the end, and if that meant Sloane was as fucked up as the rest of them, so be it. That wouldn't stop him from going after guys like Isaac. It was up to them whether they ended up walking out, or wheeled out.

Sloane stood, his sight down the hall where the EMTs were wheeling Dex away.

"Go ahead," Maddock said. "We'll clean up. Lieutenant Sparks is on her way. She wants to see for herself what's going on here. Someone's not been completely honest with her, and you know how pissed she gets when they keep her in the dark about these things."

Thanking Maddock, Sloane rushed off, hoping to make it to the ambulance before it drove off with his partner. The worst was over, but it wasn't completely over. He doubted the Order was going to simply disappear because Isaac Pearce was dead.

As Sloane rushed down the stairs, he thought about how close he had come to losing Dex. He had a lot to think about, and although he knew it would end up changing what was between them, Sloane knew what he had to do.

SLOANE PLACED a frothy cappuccino dusted with chocolate powder on the coffee table beside the couch, hoping it might help get Dex out of his funk. His partner had been given some time off for his leg, though the stitches would fall off soon. The wound hadn't been deep, and although Dex had sulked for a few days after Sloane had told him what happened, he understood why Sloane had done what he did. Dex was more pissed off over not being able to remember anything since he'd been injected. He'd started to feel guilty, but Sloane put a quick stop to that. He couldn't let his partner drive himself crazy with what-ifs. Isaac was dead, Shultzon was safe, and Dex was alive. That's all that mattered.

Isaac's men had been rounded up, but the Therians who'd attacked the Order's followers had all escaped, retreating when THIRDS backup arrived. Calvin had handed the files over to Lieutenant Sparks, who'd been mighty pissed when she was shown the lab Dex had been drugged in. They'd been informed the facility was closed for good, and an investigation was underway for who was using the lab, and why, though Sloane wasn't buying any of it. It was undoubtedly more cloak-and-dagger shit from their organization. Dr. Shultzon asked Sloane if he'd like to meet up for coffee, and Sloane said he would consider it. He'd taken Shultzon's number. Once Dex had been released from the hospital, Sloane had stayed with his partner to take care of him, growing more worried by the day at Dex's stillness.

"I can't keep doing this."

Sloane stopped on the way to the kitchen and turned around. "What?"

"Pretending it doesn't hurt every time you push me away. Pretending I'm okay with the way things are. I said I would wait for you, and I would, that I would take things as they came, okay. I understand you needing time. I do, but this getting close only to run in the other direction kills me. We've been through a lot of shit together, and every time, you act like it's no big deal. After what happened in the facility, I realized… I want more."

"You're right." Sloane couldn't put it off any longer. "I don't know how you can look at me the way you do, now that you know."

Dex looked down at his fingers with a frown. "I didn't read the file."

"What?" Sloane came around the couch to look at Dex. "But… you had it in your hands. Everything about me was in there."

Closing his eyes, Dex drew in a deep breath. When he opened his eyes, he met Sloane's gaze head on, and Sloane was taken aback by the intensity he saw there. "I want to get to know you, Sloane, the real you, not through clinical accounts from some shrink. I want to hear it from you. I want you to trust me. When you're ready to do that, I'll be here to listen."

Sloane could see Dex's heartache, and he hated being the cause of it. Dex was right. They couldn't keep going the way they were. "I was fourteen when I tried to kill myself." Sloane took a seat on the coffee table across from Dex, his hands clasped between his knees. "Dr. Shultzon found me and put me back together, physically and mentally. By then I was with the THIRDS. He was convinced I was a viable asset, that I wasn't the soulless animal I'd been convinced I was. But I was so messed up, I couldn't do it. I was so scared.

"The first time I almost died, I was eleven years old and living in a padded cell, waiting for the day I'd either go as crazy as they said I was, or find a way to end it all. I was never supposed to have gotten out of there. Somehow, Shultzon found me, fought to get custody. Well technically I was property of the U.S. government." Sloane frowned at the memory. "He was nice to me. That's all it took for me to agree to anything he told me."

"That night you, you mentioned a 'her.' Who was she?"

"My mother." Sloane took a deep breath and let it out slowly, the ache in his heart a familiar deep throbbing he knew would remain there for the rest of his life. "I killed her, Dex. I killed my mother." He braced himself for a gasp, for the horror—or worse, pity, in Dex's eyes, but it never came, only a gentle touch to Sloane's hand as Dex leaned forward, his voice gentle.

"What happened?"

"You've met me and Ash. Any other First Gens you meet will be as fucked up or more, depending how well they've learned to cope. When our first shift happened, there were no classes, no First Shift Response Kits, or Therian Youth Centers. I didn't know what the hell was happening to me. No one knew what was happening. When we were born, all our parents had been told was that we were different, our DNA was different. They wanted to study us, find out what was wrong with us. My father blamed himself. He'd fought in Vietnam, came back infected like so many of the others with the Melanoe Virus. He was one of the lucky ones to survive, even after the Eppione.8 vaccine was administered.

"He was just another Human unaware of how it was changing his blood, how it would change my mother's, how the mutation would solidify itself in their unborn son. I was born healthy, looking like any other Human baby, except for my eyes." Sloane let out a humorless laugh. "They thought the mutation was in my eyes. They had no idea. The first time I shifted, I was terrified. The pain was excruciating, and I thought I was going to die. It was like I was trapped inside this animal, looking out at my parents, with no control over my own body. I wanted what any frightened child wanted, his mother." Sloane swiped at a tear rolling down his cheek, his bottom lip quivering as he attempted to continue, his voice breaking. "I grabbed hold of her, and my claws...." He looked down at his hands and shook his head. He could still see the blood. "I didn't know. I couldn't understand what was happening until my father threw me into the wall. I saw her, lying there so still, blood everywhere. When I tried to go to her, my father kicked me. He lost it. If the police hadn't arrived, he would have killed me. The names he called me...."

Dex rubbed his hand soothingly over Sloane's head, brushing his hair tenderly away from his face. Sloane leaned into the touch, his eyes closed as he continued.

"The police arrested him. And me? You know who came for me? Animal Control. The most fucked up part? I'd shifted back by then.

Here I was, this scrawny little kid, naked, covered in blood, and I was dragged away by Animal Control. I was institutionalized. My father killed himself shortly after. It was all in that file. What happened with my parents, the institution I was in, the hell that came after, all the way up until I was recruited, how Dr. Shultzon was the one who decided to give us a second chance at life, who understood, but it came with a price. They would turn us into agents for their new organization, but they had to study us first, understand us. Every day there were tests and more tests, poking, prodding, shifting under predefined conditions." He straightened and wiped his eyes. "You should know those meetings you think I go to every month aren't meetings, at least not work related. They're psych evals."

"Aren't those quarterly?" Dex asked, puzzled.

"These aren't the standard ones. They're to make sure I don't have a relapse. When Gabe died, I was sent to a rehabilitation center just in case. Although they didn't know about our relationship, they knew we were really close. They were afraid I might go off the rails. It wouldn't be the first time it's happened to a First Gen agent. The THIRDS is good with keeping that sort of thing quiet. Ash is the only one who knows all this, because he was there with me. If it hadn't been for him, I wouldn't have made it this far." He let out a heavy sigh, his chest feeling somewhat less constricted now that he'd confessed everything. He was afraid to look up, afraid at what he might see. Dex was a sweet, compassionate man, but that was it. He was a man, a Human. He couldn't ever truly understand what it meant to be… different.

"Hey."

Dex's soft voice forced Sloane to look up, and he drew in a sharp breath, speechless by the loving smile on Dex's face, his eyes filled with warmth and concern.

"What happened wasn't your fault. Thank you for your honesty, but I have to tell you that now that I know…."

Sloane braced himself, his heart in his throat.

"I think you're even more amazing. Everything you've been through, everything you've suffered, and look at you. You go out there, and you risk your life for this city and the citizens in it. No matter how much shit they throw your way, what they call you, how they see you,

you get up every morning, and you do what you gotta do. I know I gave you shit about you being *the* Sloane Brodie, but the truth is, you are, and everyone respects you for it. I respect you."

Sloane opened his mouth, but nothing came out. He didn't know what to say to that. Dex smiled at him, and Sloane dropped to his knees in front of Dex. He threw his arms around him and drew him close, his face pressed to Dex's chest. "Thank you," Sloane managed to whisper, squeezing Dex tight. He closed his eyes as Dex ran his fingers through Sloane's hair. He didn't know how long they stayed like that, but after a while, Sloane stood and took a seat beside Dex, summoning up the courage Dex so adamantly believed he possessed.

"Dex?"

"Yeah?"

"I'm going to ask you something. Feel free to say no. Are you.... Are you busy Friday night?"

Dex blinked at him. "Not for you. Why?"

Deep breath. "I thought maybe we could go to Jersey, and uh, go on a date. Something other than the usual burgers and beers. There's this restaurant, and—"

"You want to take me to a restaurant?" Dex's jaw hung open.

"Yeah." Sloane shrugged, the butterflies in his stomach fluttering madly. He couldn't keep himself from smiling. "That's what boyfriends do. Take each other out. Date."

Dex's grin was the most beautiful thing Sloane had ever seen. "You said 'boyfriend' without losing consciousness."

Sloane chuckled. "I did." Dex bit his bottom lip, and Sloane could tell he was bursting with excitement. He'd done that. He'd put that smile on his lover's face, that sparkle of mischief and affection in his eyes. As much as his head told him to run, his heart fought him to stay.

"I'd love to go out on a date."

Sloane drew Dex into his arms, mindful of his leg and kissed him. The thought of being in a relationship again scared the hell out of him, but it wasn't nearly as frightening as the thought of having almost lost Dex. He knew their job was dangerous, and they never knew which day might be their last, but shouldn't he then try to make the most of his time with those he cared about? He cared about Dex, wanted to be with him. Loved holding him, kissing him, touching him. Loved his jokes, and his strange taste in music. His obsession with cheese snacks, and love of gummy bears. Sloane was still uncertain about so much, about their future, but he wanted to try.

Dex kissed him passionately, his arms around Sloane's neck. They took things slow, exploring, tasting, breathing in each other. Sloane leaned into Dex when his cell phone went off.

"Fuck's sake." He snatched it up off the coffee table and groaned.

"What is it?"

"Your dad. I swear, if I didn't know any better, I'd think he knew, because he has one hell of a way of ruining the mood." Sloane answered the call and held the phone to his ear. "Sarge, what can I do for you?"

"You with Dex?"

"Yeah."

"Put me on speaker."

Sloane put his phone on speaker and placed it back on the coffee table.

"Please, don't say it," Dex groaned at his dad.

"We've got a big problem."

With a frustrated grunt, Dex fell back onto the couch in a slump. "I told you not to say it. One day. Would it be too much to ask for the nut jobs to take one fucking day off?"

"Crazy doesn't take vacation, son. We've identified the Therian group attacking the Order. They call themselves the Ikelos Coalition, and unlike the Order that's made up of mostly civilian extremists, these guys have training. The violence is escalating. Isaac's death has left the Order without a leader, and it's turning into a feeding frenzy. We might have stopped the Order from waging war against us, but now they're at war with the Coalition, and innocent civilians are getting in the way."

"So now we've got two levels of fucked up to deal with," Dex muttered. "Great."

"Actually, three."

Dex and Sloane looked at each other before Sloane addressed their sergeant. "What's the third?"

"We have reason to believe someone inside the THIRDS is feeding information to the Coalition."

"Shit."

"Exactly. It wasn't a coincidence the Coalition knew where the research facility was. They didn't figure it out. Someone told them. There's a traitor in our midst, boys, and we need to find them. I expect to see you both back at the office tomorrow bright and early. Hobbs will be back on duty. There will be cake." Maddock hung up and Sloane tapped "end" on his smartphone's screen. They sat quietly for a moment, mulling over what they'd been told, when Dex spoke up.

"What kind of cake do you think it is?"

Sloane stared at his partner, whose expression was dead serious. He couldn't help it, he burst into laughter.

"What? I'm serious. It better be ice cream, or chocolate. None of that marzipan shit. I hate that stuff."

With a laugh, Sloane drew Dex into his arms and kissed the top of his head. Dex settled against him with a soft sigh, and Sloane told himself to remember this moment. Things were going to get tougher, and their jobs more dangerous, especially with the new Therian threat. He'd have to push Dex harder in his training, and Sloane would have to do the same for himself. His thoughts strayed to Maddock's words. They had a traitor in their midst. Someone had given out the location of the facility to the Coalition. Whoever they were, they'd better be prepared for a fight, because as soon as Sloane got his hands on them, that's what they were going to get.

"Hey."

Dex's voice snapped him out of his somber thoughts, the smile on his face filling Sloane with more warmth and hope than he'd felt in a long time.

"For tonight, let's leave the crazy outside. Just you and me in here."

Sloane liked the sound of that. "Just you and me." He bent his head, touched his lips to Dex's and allowed himself to get lost in this amazing man's kiss. The world might go to shit tomorrow, but tonight, while he had Dex in his arms, everything was as it should be. Dex was right; they had been through a lot. In the end whether that would hurt their relationship or strengthen it, who knew, but at least they were in this together. From here on out, Sloane knew whatever happened, his partner had his trust, his back, and more importantly, his heart.

CHARLIE COCHET is an author by day and artist by night. Always quick to succumb to the whispers of her wayward muse, no star is out of reach when following her passion. From historical to fantasy, contemporary to science fiction, there's bound to be plenty of mischief for her heroes to find themselves in, and plenty of romance, too!

Currently residing in South Florida, Charlie looks forward to migrating to a land where the weather includes seasons other than hot, hotter, and, boy, it's hot! When she isn't writing, she can usually be found reading, drawing, or watching movies. She runs on coffee, thrives on music, and loves to hear from readers.

Website: http://www.charliecochet.com

Blog: http://www.charliecochet.com/blog

E-mail: charlie@charliecochet.com

Facebook: https://www.facebook.com/charliecochet

Twitter: @charliecochet

THIRDS from DREAMSPINNER PRESS

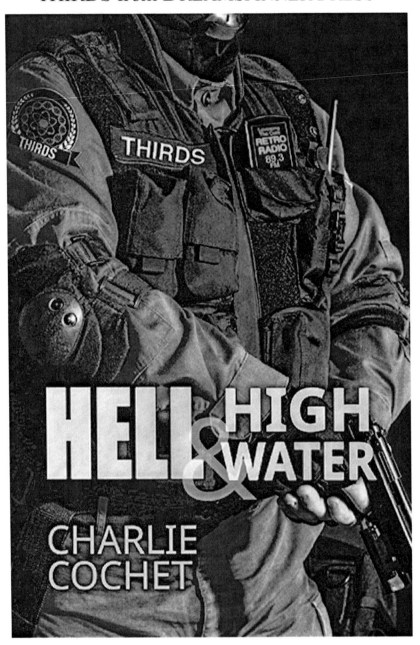

http://www.dreamspinnerpress.com

Auspicious Troubles of Love from
DREAMSPINNER PRESS

http://www.dreamspinnerpress.com

Auspicious Troubles of Love from
DREAMSPINNER PRESS

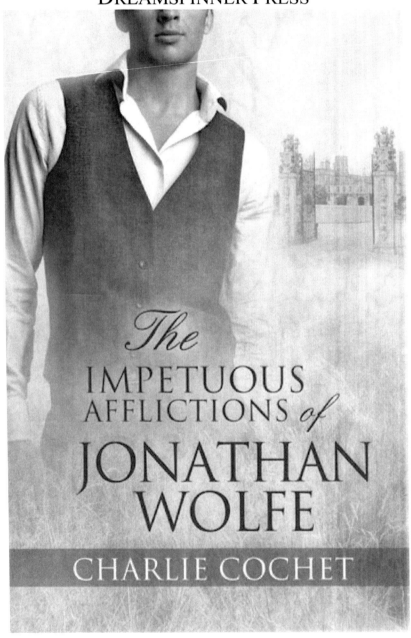

http://www.dreamspinnerpress.com

North Pole City Tales from DREAMSPINNER PRESS

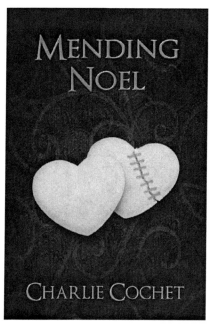

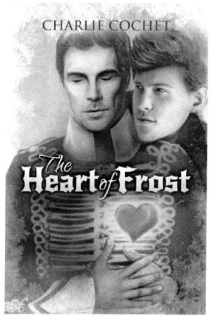

http://www.dreamspinnerpress.com

CPSIA information can be obtained at www.ICGtesting.com
Printed in the USA
LVOW08s2352290914

406423LV00011B/288/P